I0566413

The Blood Hounds

Ron Schwab

Uplands Press

OMAHA, NEBRASKA

Copyright © 2020 by Ron Schwab

All rights reserved. No part of this publication may be reproduced, distributed or transmitted in any form or by any means, including photocopying, recording, or other electronic or mechanical methods, without the prior written permission of the publisher, except in the case of brief quotations embodied in critical reviews and certain other noncommercial uses permitted by copyright law. For permission requests, write to the publisher, addressed "Attention: Permissions Coordinator," at the address below.

Uplands Press
1401 S 64th Avenue
Omaha, NE 68106
www.uplandspress.com

Publisher's Note: This is a work of fiction. Names, characters, places, and incidents are a product of the author's imagination. Locales and public names are sometimes used for atmospheric purposes. Any resemblance to actual people, living or dead, or to businesses, companies, events, institutions, or locales is completely coincidental.

Ordering Information:
Quantity sales. Special discounts are available on quantity purchases by corporations, associations, and others. For details, contact the "Special Sales Department" at the address above.

Uplands Press / Ron Schwab -- 1st ed.

ISBN 978-1-943421-45-9

The Blood Hounds

Chapter 1

TRACE CROCKETT KNEW it was not going to be a good day when he woke up in his hotel room, rolled over, and reached for the compliant body that had shared his bed the night before. But her side of the bed was empty and cold. It did not appear she had just gotten up for a quick pee in the chamber pot. He sat up and cast his eyes about the dusky room that was just beginning to lighten from a new sunrise sifting through the curtained window. He pushed back the sheet and light blanket and swung his legs over the side of the bed. He started to stand but plopped back on the bed when the effort sent his head spinning.

He tried again, this time pressing his palm against the wall for support. He stood there, naked, waiting for equilibrium to arrive, thinking about the lithe, raven-haired beauty he had met in the hotel dining room the night before. The eating area had been crowded to over-flowing when the woman came up and asked if she might join him at the table. Her dark eyes and flawless, lightly bronzed skin suggested a tad of Indian or Spanish in her lineage. She was a petite thing with regal bearing. How could a man have said anything but "I'd be delighted" to such a ravishing creature?

And she had been an engaging and enjoyable dining companion, obviously an educated woman of breeding, but now, as he thought about the exchange, Trace realized he had learned next to nothing about her. She had deftly steered the conversation in his direction. He thought her name was Audra-something. He was not a serious drinker, but he remembered having a few glasses of chardonnay—tasted terrible—because that was the lady's preference. They both had eaten steak dinners. What else would one eat in Kansas City? She was a toucher, repeatedly pressing her fingers to his arm and laughing when he told an anecdote she found funny or clever. Several times she had taken his hand and allowed her grasp to linger.

He, of course, had insisted on paying for the meals, and Audra had suggested they take a stroll before retiring to their rooms. It so happened she was lodging at the Cattlemen's Inn as well. They got up from the table, and his mind was blank from that point, except for erotic images that stuck with him now of the romp in his room later, Audra's perfect body entwined with his in about every way imaginable. Her energy and enthusiasm had left him sated and exhausted. He was not a man without experience, but it occurred to him this morning that he might have been a novice compared to his night's companion. The recollection was bringing new life to his loins.

But she was no whore. Audra had class. She had not asked for money. It had just been one of those magical nights when strangers meet and are magnetically drawn to each other. Otherwise, he would not have presumed to attempt to seduce a lady of such culture at their first meeting—the second, perhaps, but not the first. And then it struck him. He had not drunk enough spirits to be hung over like this. Surely she had not doctored his wine, had she? And if he was not seducer, had the woman been seductress?

His head was starting to clear some now. He snatched his undershorts and trousers from the floor and pulled them on, thinking that such sloppiness was not his style. He was a bit obsessive when it came to neatness and order, and it was almost unthinkable for him not to have hung up his suit pants properly. He conceded, though, that the brain between his thighs had been known to override good judgment and ingrained habits on occasion. He found his white shirt tangled with the bedsheets and slipped it on, and with a sense of trepidation, he stepped over to the straight-back chair where he had draped his coat. Trace slipped his fingers into the inner coat pocket where he habitually kept his wallet. Empty. Then, scanning the room, he saw the missing wallet lying on top of the chest of drawers. He gave a sigh of relief. In his fog or urgency or whatever had blotted out part of his night, he must have tossed it there.

He went to the chest and found the wallet neatly folded, but resting on top was his silver Pinkerton's National Detective Agency badge, which he usually kept pinned to a flap inside the leather wallet. He brushed the badge aside and picked up the wallet and opened it, certain of what would be missing from the contents. Yes. The money was gone, except for a dollar bill. The other sixty dollars in twenties had departed with Audra. She had left him more than enough for a decent breakfast in the hotel dining room, but his appetite had disappeared with the money.

Thankfully, he still had ten gold eagles—a hundred dollars—secreted in a compartment of his cowhide-covered valise. Or did he? He rushed to the valise sitting where he had left it, upright in a corner of the room. It did not appear to have been moved. He pulled it away from the wall, laid it out flat and opened it. His extra shirts and undergarments were neatly folded, and his .44 short-barreled Smith & Wesson holstered and attached to its shoulder harness seemed undisturbed. He slipped his hand beneath the contents, fingers probing for the tiny latch that released the cover of the valise's false bottom. He pressed the button, and the cover raised a few inches, allowing admittance to the hidden space. The little cotton bag that held the coins was there. The gold eagles were not. The bitch had left him broke.

Even worse, this was not a story he could share with his friends or report to the law. A Pinkerton agent robbed by a pretty lady? The other agents would never let him forget it. Some damned cop would probably leak it to the newspapers.

He got up and pulled his watch from the watch pocket of his trousers. Almost seven o'clock. He had an appointment with the Kansas City office manager at nine o'clock. He had hoped to go to the bathing room near the back on the main floor and have a nice hot bath to start his day, but that would take all of his dollar and leave nothing to tip the boy who fetched the hot water for the tub. There was a pitcher of water and ceramic bowl on the chest and small mirror attached to the wall above, so he guessed he could get out his straight-edged razor and shave.

Before cleaning up, he checked the closet. His extra suit was hanging there, and the canvas sling-bag that held his Army Colt and disassembled Henry rifle had not been raided. He decided to wear the fresh suit and try to find an establishment that could clean and press the rumpled one and take care of his laundry before he departed for wherever Carl Chirnside, the Pinkerton manager, was sending him. And he was going to have a good breakfast with his dollar. He did not have the money to pay the five dollars for his hotel room anyway. He chided himself for going first class, which was an admitted bad habit. He could have found a decent room for a dollar somewhere in town, and he would never have met up with that damned woman.

He was glad to find Audra had not used the chamber pot, leaving it fresh for his use. That told Trace she had likely not stayed long after putting him to sleep for the night. He shaved and dressed in his fresh blue, western-cut suit and buffed his black cowboy boots to a near mirror-shine. Looking in the mirror to tie his red, string bowtie and comb his coarse black hair, he thought he could use a haircut. He liked his hair crawling down his neck just a mite, but he did not want a cut that remotely took on a girlie look. He was confident Carl would negotiate with him for expense money, and perhaps he could visit a barber while he waited for his clothes to be washed and cleaned. He would find a barber shop that offered baths out back. A hot bath would improve his disposition.

While Trace enjoyed a breakfast of coffee, eggs, bacon, and hotcakes, the latter topped with hot maple syrup, he figured out a strategy for escaping the hotel. He would claim he had lost his wallet but offer up his slingbag of weapons for hostage until he returned with the money a few hours later. He would show his Pinkerton badge as evidence of his credibility, although there was a calculated risk here since some folks hated the Pinkertons for their union-busting work.

After breakfast, he brought his bags to the lobby and walked up with faux confidence to the clerk's counter. A skinny young clerk with peach-fuzzed cheeks and wearing a white shirt with black sleeve garters got up from his chair at the desk behind the counter, offered a forced smile and said, "May I help you, sir?"

"Yes, I'm J.T. Crockett, room twenty. I need to speak with you about checking out."

The young man rubbed his chin thoughtfully and turned to the pigeon-holed box on the wall behind him, reached into a port numbered twenty, plucked out a sheet of paper and handed it to Trace. "Here you are, sir. Your receipt. Paid in full."

"Paid?"

"Yes, sir. Your sister paid the bill last night, right after I came on duty." He pointed to the receipt. "See. Paid by Audra Crockett. Charming young lady. I must say I can see the family resemblance."

Trace grimaced. "Yes, I suppose. Well, it's just like her to take care of the bill early. May I ask, has she checked out, too? I thought I might try to meet up with her soon." He was gambling she had rented a room, as she had told him when she joined him in the dining room.

"Yes, she left when she paid your bill. I thought you would know she had a train to catch."

"She doesn't tell me much about what she's up to. She'll probably send a telegram to tell me where she ends up. Sometimes she uses a false name. Did she register under her own name?"

"Oh, yes. Audra Crockett, room eighteen, next to yours, as you no doubt know."

Chapter 2

TRACE WALKED THE mile to the Pinkerton office at the opposite end of town since he did not have the fare to pay for the carriage transportation available outside the hotel, which was only a few blocks from the railroad depot. He carried the valise in one hand, and the sling bag with his guns was tossed over his shoulder and anchored by the other. He had been assigned by the Kansas City office on at least a half dozen occasions, so he was familiar with the location.

It was a nice morning for a stroll, the sun's rays almost blinding, and he tugged the brim of his low-crowned hat down on his forehead to ward off the glare. It had rained the previous night, which was normal along the Missouri River in early June, but the humidity was more tolerable than it would be a month from now when the July stickiness seriously set in. It did annoy him, though, when he unsuccessfully tried to negotiate the muddy streets, most of which had been awarded only a token scattering of crushed stones and gravel for the roadbed. Fortunately, the buildings were lined with boardwalks and, in a few instances, rough concrete.

The Pinkerton office was hard for a passer-by to miss. Located in a small frame, clapboard-sided structure with a large window on each side of the front door, the building would not have been notable but for the sign. Above the door was a large spherical-shaped sign emblazoned with the Pinkerton logo, an enormous all-seeing eye, including lashes and a black eyebrow above it. Just below the eye were the words "WE NEVER SLEEP." The logo was framed with the firm name "Pinkerton's National" above the logo and "Detective Agency" below. Trace noticed that the building had been whitewashed since his last visit, and the sign had been recently painted.

He opened the door and entered the building, dropping his cargo on the oak floor. Carl Chirnside looked up from the single desk in the largely vacant space, the only room in the building, serving as office, reception area, conference room or whatever need was to be served at the time.

"Morning, Carl," Trace said, walking over to the desk, pulling back a straight-back chair and sitting down.

Chirnside, a stocky man with a cherubic face and generous paunch, smiled broadly. He did not stand but said, "Trace, good to see you. Take a seat."

"I have."

"Always on time. I like that about you, Trace. Never been late on me."

"Spruced up the place outside. Looks good."

"You know Allan Pinkerton. He's a tight old Scotchman, but he wants the place looking uptown."

"There really is an Allan Pinkerton? I've been an agent since my Army discharge in 1877—that's five years now—and I've never seen the man."

"What do you care? You get a hundred dollars deposited in your Fort Smith bank account the first of every month, don't you? And that doesn't count bonuses."

"What bonuses?"

Chirnside got up and limped to one of the five wood filing cabinets lined up behind his desk. Trace knew the limp was caused by a gunshot wound that took a chunk out of the managing agent's knee when the Pinkertons cleaned out a den of potential assassins plotting to go after Lincoln during the Civil War. Unfortunately, by the time John Wilkes Booth came around, the government had taken over protection of the President and terminated the Pinkerton contract. Chirnside, in his mid-fifties now, had been with Pinkerton from the beginning, over thirty years. Pinkerton, to his credit, had found a place for his loyal agent, who could no longer handle fieldwork.

Trace respected Carl Chirnside. The gimpy knee did not affect his keen mind, and his ego was apparently unfazed by the fact that the manager title included all clerical and janitorial duties in the office. Chirnside returned to his chair with a file folder, which he opened, spreading the contents out on the desktop.

"Ever been to Manhattan, Kansas?"

"Yep. Mustered out of the Army at Fort Riley five years ago. Riley's just down the road from Manhattan. I was only there a few months. Before that I was at Fort Sill in the Indian Territory under Mackenzie's command."

"Knew you were Army. How long?"

"Four years. Almost all of my service was in Texas and the Indian Territory during the Red River War. Fort Concho was headquarters during the Comanche wars, and I spent some time at Fort Davis. When the fighting was over, I followed Mackenzie to Sill when he took command there. Then I oversaw food distribution to the Comanche and Kiowa on the Sill reservation. That's when I got my fill of the government bureaucrats and sick of the corruption and decided not to re-enlist."

"You were a first sergeant?"

"Yeah. And I saw I wasn't going much higher. No commission prospects. I make more now than an Army captain anyhow."

Trace was certain Chirnside knew he had been booted out of West Point his final year over an indiscretion with a professor's wife. Worse, from his viewpoint, was that he had loved Dara Hummel, who was only a few years older than himself and half the age of her pompous husband. To avoid embarrassment to the professor or his lady, the superintendent had permitted him to resign without a blemish on his record. Having no money and no other prospects, he had enlisted in the regular Army. His West Point background had helped to move him up in the non-commissioned ranks. He still wondered if Dara had loved him or whether he was simply an instrument to satisfy her carnal needs. The latter would not have made him less willing, but it got complicated when love intervened.

"Well, you're one of the boss's pets now. You've got a future with the agency if you don't mess it up. The new job comes straight from Pink. Sent me a special delivery letter from the Chicago office. Usually lets me pick somebody for the job. But this time he said I had to find you. He said he needs a couple of blood hounds for this one.

You said you would be at your brother's in Fort Smith until you got another assignment, so I sent the wire."

"Blood hounds? I guess, in our business, that's a compliment." He wondered what Chirnside would think about his blood hound if he knew about last night's escapade. "You said a 'couple of blood hounds.' There's another agent?"

"You're going to work with somebody out of the Denver office. An agent named Darby Maguire."

"Never heard of him. Sounds like an Irishman."

"Lots of agents you never heard of. We're a big outfit, you know. You'll meet Maguire at a law office in Manhattan. Three days from now, you've got an appointment at nine o'clock at Locke & Locke. You will be meeting with Myles Locke, the firm's senior partner."

"That suits me. I can hang around Kansas City another day, maybe two, depending on rail connection schedules. Manhattan's almost due east from here and not much more than a hundred twenty-five miles, I'd guess, in the north part of the Flint Hills. Cow country. If I was ever able to take up ranching, I'd look for a piece of land in east Kansas. Thousands of acres of tall grass prairie. Seems like you're in the middle of nowhere, but you're not all that far from markets and civilization."

"Still don't have ranching out of your head, do you?"

"Yeah, and sooner rather than later. A bit more than a year and I'll be hitting thirty. This is an interesting job, but I don't want to be doing it when I'm thirty-five. My paycheck goes to my brother Jim's bank at Fort Smith. He stashes fifty dollars a month for me and sends the rest where I tell him if I can't pick it up. I still live well enough with a little expense money from the agency." He figured it was time to start laying groundwork for expense money.

"Well, you might be interested to know, there's a handsome bonus for success on this job," Chirnside said.

That remark grabbed Trace's attention. "I've heard of the bonus jobs, but I've never seen one yet. How much?"

"A thousand dollars to be split between the two agents, if they're successful."

"And what's success?"

"You've got to find a young woman or prove she's dead. And it's a cold trail. That's why the boss man called for the blood hounds. You're looking for somebody who's been considered dead since April of 1867."

"Over fifteen years?"

"I'll let lawyer Locke give you the details. He's the law wrangler for our client. But it involves a little girl who was kidnapped for ransom when she was just short of two years old—she'd be seventeen now. Her grandfather came up with the ransom money, but he went to the law, and the local sheriff's people messed up the exchange. The kidnapper got spooked and left and ran. The kidnapper's note said the little girl would be killed if the ransom wasn't paid. The kidnapper didn't make another contact. They couldn't come up with any clues, and, after a year, they assumed the little girl was dead. Grandpa could never quite accept the outcome and pushed the law to follow up for years. He also hired another agency that came up with nothing."

"I hope this lawyer can give us more to go on than you have."

"I don't know. Pink said Grandpa's still alive and that the lawyer will arrange for you to meet him."

"That's something, I guess. What's his name?"

"You'll find out when you see the lawyer. The boss says this is top-drawer secret. He didn't even tell me, which pissed me off a mite."

"I'll need expense money."

"You know, the boss even mentioned that you're the top expense account agent. He thinks you live a bit high on the hog when you're on a case, padding your salary with the agency's expense money. Maybe you don't need to stay at the top hotels and eat at the most expensive restaurants."

"It's part of my cover. The bad guys don't look for a Pinkerton agent in comfortable accommodations," Trace insisted.

"Pink said to budget you a hundred fifty in gold eagles to start. Maguire will have twice that and has been instructed to share if you get short. You can wire for more funds if something unexpected comes up in the way of travel cost—a horse and tack, for instance."

The expense money was more than Trace had expected, but he bristled at the notion he was going to be at the mercy of some other agent's allowance. It was an insult, and he had half a mind to decline the assignment, which would likely end in his termination with the agency. He sighed and then replied, "I don't take kindly to the expense money limitation. You're not starting the agents out on an equal footing. Does that mean this Irishman is the agent in charge?"

"No," Chirnside said, "you're partners. You will have to work things out between you on the decision-making. If you can't get along, wire the home office, and the boss will designate one of you as agent in charge. I can guarantee he would not take kindly to being put in that position, though."

"We'll see how it goes. I can get along with most folks. It's the expense allocation that stinks."

"Maguire's just holding some of the money for you. The boss says things are getting tight at the agency. He's got to pay more attention to where the dollars are going."

"I'll bet Robert and William are hitting the old fart for more money." Robert and William Pinkerton were Allan's sons and held important positions in the agency. He knew his remark was petty. By all accounts they were competent agents and managers, and most employees were confident the agency would not skip a beat when Allan Pinkerton died or retired, the former being more likely than the latter. Trace was just rankled about the expense money business.

Carl Chirnside opened a desk drawer and removed a leather pouch with a drawstring closing its opening. He flipped the little sack across the desk. "I got your expense money at the bank yesterday. Remember, you'll have to keep track of what you spend it for and refund what you don't use. Don't recall ever getting money back from you, though." He grinned and chuckled.

Trace picked up the pouch of gold coins and stuffed it in his coat pocket. Now he could get that haircut and bath, and maybe a new suit, if the tailor could do a rush job. He slid the chair back and stood up. "I've got things to do, Carl. I'll let you know where I'm at. Hopefully, I can wrap up this job fast. I already don't like Maguire."

Chapter 3

TRACE STROLLED DOWN the sidewalk along Poyntz Avenue, Manhattan's main street, noting that the town of some 2,500 residents boasted at least two general stores, several inviting restaurants, liveries, shoemakers, blacksmiths, and about every service or retail provider a person might seek. Taverns were noticeably absent since Kansas had adopted prohibition several years earlier. He had been told that many towns ignored the law, and it would not surprise him to learn that alcohol, like bordellos, could be found off the main street, perhaps on the outskirts of town.

He had stayed the previous night at the Wheaton Inn, a new hotel not far from the depot that was as nice as any he had enjoyed during his travels. This morning, he had started the day with a nice bath and barber's shave in the facilities attached to the hotel and, afterward, had partaken of a nice breakfast of biscuits, fried eggs and bacon in the elegant Wheaton dining room. Now, attired in a gray tweed suit he had purchased before leaving Kansas City, he felt ready to meet the lawyer and the Irishman and see about earning that bonus. He chided himself only a bit for dipping too deeply into his expense allowance.

Trace approached a single-story limestone building wedged between two other commercial establishments. It seemed half the structures in the town were built of limestone, and he remembered now that this had been true of buildings at nearby Fort Riley. It made sense, he guessed. The tall grass prairie that blanketed the Flint Hills was rooted in the native rock. Building materials at some locations would be located in a man's back yard.

He read the simple sign on the wall adjacent to the office door: "Locke & Locke, Lawyers." Below were listed the names of Myles Locke and Cameron Locke. He entered the office and was greeted by an attractive middle-aged woman, who introduced herself as "Reva." She gave him a warm smile and said, "You must be Mister Crockett."

"Yes, ma'am. But 'Trace' will do fine."

"Your partner is with Myles. I'll show you to his office." She led him down a hallway and stopped at an open door. She stuck her head in the doorway. "Myles, Trace Crockett is here." Then she turned to Trace. "Just go on in."

Trace entered, and she closed the door behind him. He stopped when he got a glimpse of the occupant of a chair in front of the desk and at first did not notice the rail-thin man with silver hair stepping out from behind his desk.

"I'm Myles Locke," the man said in a mellifluous voice and extended his hand, offering Trace a firm grip. He stood about six feet tall, a few inches shorter than Trace, and wore a neatly pressed black, vested suit showing a bit of wear on the coat sleeves, certainly a garment Trace would have discarded by now. Trace guessed the age of the lawyer to be a bit on either side of seventy.

"My pleasure, Myles. I'm intrigued with the little I know about the case you've got for us."

"Oh, forgive me. I understand you haven't met your partner. Trace, this is Darby Maguire."

A woman dressed in a rust-brown skirt and matching jacket stood and offered her hand. He took the hand, surprised by her business-like grip, and found himself flustered by the knowledge he would be partnering with a female. She was tallish, perhaps five and a half feet without her high-top shoes. Slender, with wheat-blonde hair done up in a bun that he thought gave her a frumpy look. Wire-rimmed eyeglasses perched on her nose, but Trace could see dark, brown eyes appraising him from behind the lenses.

"I guess it's time we got acquainted," Trace said, "if we're going to be working together. I didn't know I was partnering with a woman. I mean, that's okay. Just took me by surprise. Do I call you 'Miss Maguire' or what?"

She smiled, and he got the impression she was enjoying his discomfiture. He wondered if that damned Chirnside knew all along that he was being sent to partner with a female. Probably.

"You may call me 'Darby,' and I'll call you 'Trace' in the absence of objection, although I know your full name is 'John Trace Crockett.' Trace was your mother's maiden name. Your father's name was John, so I suspect you took up your middle name to avoid confusion," she said with a voice that had a slight Irish lilt.

The snoopy woman was showing off her homework. This did not have the makings of a happy partnership.

He was rescued by the lawyer, whose twinkling eyes suggested he found the situation humorous. Locke said, "Why don't you both be seated, and we can get down to the business you're here for."

Darby said, "Excellent. Trace and I can discuss our rules of engagement later."

Trace assumed she was trying to make light of their conversation, but he thought it sounded like she was preparing for a war. Well, now that the element of surprise had been removed from the mix, he would consider his own strategy.

Darby sat, and Trace took the chair next to her, sliding it away from the woman to create some physical distance between them. He saw her pull a binder and pencil off the desk, opening it, and placing it in her lap. She evidently intended to take notes. She looked expectantly at Myles Locke. Trace surreptitiously studied Darby. His first impression had been that she was a mousy creature, but when his imagination let her hair down, removed the spectacles and put a smile on the pinched lips, she came out a more than handsome woman.

Locke yanked him back to his job. "Your client is Congrave Wheaton. I've been his lawyer for many years, and he has signed a waiver of attorney-client confidentiality to allow me to divulge whatever information about his affairs I think you might need. I take my obligations seriously, and I will be very stingy with facts that I don't think pertain to your goal. You will meet Con Wheaton later this morning, but he has asked that I be your contact during the investigation."

"Wheaton?" Trace asked. "I'm staying at the Wheaton Inn, and I heard that name when I was stationed at Fort Riley a few years back. Prominent businessman, as I recall. I assume he owns the hotel."

"Yes. Con has fingers in many pies. He got his start quarrying limestone for builders. From there he established kilns around Riley County to convert the stone to lime. After that, it was ranching. He has a manager running a first-rate ranch operation deep in the Flint Hills between here and Council Grove to the south. Besides owning the Wheaton Inn, he deals and invests in real estate. He had the foresight some years back to buy up land along the route he predicted a railroad would be forced to take from Kansas City. Very astute. Obviously very wealthy, but he has been very generous to the community, particularly with his contributions to Kansas State Agricultural College here. Riley County has been good to him, and he has been good to Riley County."

Darby said, "But he's got a problem, or we wouldn't be talking with you."

"I have some folders here with newspaper articles, notes from the sheriff's and U. S. Marshal's reports and everything Reva and I have been able to dig up on the history of the case. I think you will want to study these before you leave Manhattan. Time is not presently critical. Our conference room will be available for your use, if you wish."

He pushed some folders across the desktop, and Darby reached for them and then hesitated and looked at Trace. "I have a briefcase. Shall I put the papers in it for now?"

Of course, she would have a briefcase. Probably carried his extra expense allowance in the thing. "Yeah, that would be okay."

Locke continued. "I assume you've been given a thumbnail sketch of the project, but I'll try to fill you in enough that you can focus on questions you have of Con when we meet with him at his home. Con is about seventy-two years old, just a few years older than I am, but he hasn't been blessed with the best of health. The door can close on any of our lives at any time or age, but Con has reason to believe it's about to shut on him, and an important loose end has come up."

"The granddaughter," Darby said.

"Yes. I assume that you've been told that Miranda Wheaton was abducted over fifteen years ago."

"Yes," Trace said. "The Kansas City office manager said she was two years old. I wasn't told her name."

"Miranda Lee Wheaton, born April 20, 1865. Abducted April 1, 1867," Darby said, flipping a page of her notebook.

This woman was quickly becoming a pain in the ass, Trace thought. He intended to set a few things straight when they discussed her so-called "rules of engagement."

Locke said, "The girl was—or is—the daughter of Con's son, Henry Wheaton, who was a Union cavalry officer during the war. He was killed in action a few months before the war ended. Never saw his little girl. The mother, Lydia, and Miranda were living with Con at the time of the kidnapping. Six months after the little girl was taken, Lydia took her own life. Hanged herself from a support beam in the stable. She was a sweet lady, quite pretty. Auburn hair and on the petite side. But she'd always been fragile emotionally, and I guess the loss of her daughter was more than she could bear."

Darby said softly, "How sad. So, is Mister Wheaton's wife living?"

"No. His first wife, Henry's mother, died when their only child was no more than ten years old. A second marriage left Con a widower a second time five years later. He married a third time just before the Rebellion. Romy was twenty-five years younger than Con, and they had a rather turbulent marriage. It ended in a rather nasty divorce a few years after the war was over."

Trace noticed that Darby was writing feverishly in her notebook. He said, "Then the divorce must have been going on about the time of the kidnapping?"

"Let me think a moment." Locke paused and rubbed his chin thoughtfully, looking up at the ceiling as if seeing a calendar there. "Court decree was entered just before Christmas of '66. Technically, it wasn't final till six months later. I remember because it was the last divorce I handled. My son, Cameron, joined the practice soon after and took over that work, thank God."

Darby asked, "Could I see your file on that tomorrow here in the office? I think I'll check the court records, too. I might have more questions after that."

Locke said, "I don't see why not. Look, you are going to hear most of this story again when we meet with Con, and you'll find a chronological list of events as reconstructed in the folders I gave you, with names of people involved. You are obviously wondering why, after all these years, this ugly creature has raised its head again."

"Yeah," Trace said, "that's exactly what I've been trying to figure out."

"Well, Con never gave up. There is a standing reward of one thousand dollars for information leading to the arrest of the abductor, and there has been continuous advertising all these years. But the triggering event happens to coincide with a serious decline in Con's health. Understand that Con has no blood kin—unless Miranda is alive. The provisions of his will determine who takes his estate, regardless, but if Miranda is alive, he wants her to be the primary beneficiary of his estate, excluding any charitable and other personal bequests he has made. After recently receiving a letter, which I am going to tell you about, Con had me prepare a new will, which provides that the property will go to various beneficiaries, unless Miranda appears to make her claim within six months after Con's death. As executor, I am authorized to spend whatever funds necessary to make a search for Miranda's whereabouts. If she is proven dead, of course, the will's provision for her becomes irrelevant."

Trace asked, "But she's been assumed dead all these years, though her body was never found?"

"Yes, but this changed when the correspondence came a month ago. Enclosed was a gold oak-leaf pendant with the letters 'MLW' engraved on the back—he has the pendant. Con swears that it's the pendant he gave Miranda the Christmas before she was taken. She was also given a matching chain bracelet with an initialed oak-leaf attached. These items were both taken from her room the night of the abduction. The bracelet was returned with the ransom demand."

Darby asked, "Who sent the letter? I don't know why I ask. If you knew, you wouldn't need Pinkerton involved."

"We don't know, and that is one of several reasons Con employed the Pinkerton Agency. Foremost, was this, however." He took an envelope from the desktop and handed it to Trace. "Perhaps, for Darby's benefit you would read this aloud."

Trace looked at the envelope, noting that Wheaton's name and address were typed on it. No return address, but a Dodge City, Kansas postmark. He plucked a single sheet of paper from the envelope and unfolded it, his eyes scanning the page. Brief and typewritten. He read: "Wheaton. I know where your granddaughter is. Contact the Pinkertons. Have them send Trace Crockett to Dodge City with one hundred double eagles. I will find him." Trace looked up. "No signature, of course. Why me?"

"We were hopeful you might know," Locke said.

Trace shook his head in disbelief. "I don't know anybody in Dodge City. But I guess it's a passing-through sort of town. Ranchers, cowhands and that sort. Fort Dodge is nearby. There could be a soldier I knew stationed at the fort, I suppose. I've never been there."

"I have," Darby said. "I taught at a little one-room school near Dodge City for two years before I joined Pinkerton. That's been three years. I know some of the shopkeepers and farmers that should still be in Dodge or the vicinity. I suspect my past connection there had something to do with my assignment to the case."

Locke withdrew a pocket watch from his vest pocket and glanced at it. "A carriage should be in the front of the office now. It's time to visit Con Wheaton. I should warn you: Con's a blunt-spoken man. Very astute and intelligent, but he does not filter his thoughts before he speaks. These days he might wander from the topic a bit, and he's given to philosophic meanderings. Just be patient, and you will get your questions answered."

Chapter 4

DARBY WAS NOT surprised to find that Congrave Wheaton resided in a castle-like mansion constructed of limestone, enormous slabs of the rock rising from the earth for several rows to furnish a foundation. Two turrets jutted above each of the front corners to enhance the medieval look. Locke's single rap with a brass knocker on the mammoth oak door got an immediate response from a tall, exotically attractive woman, whose light mahogany skin suggested mixed African and white heritage. Her professional attire signaled she was not a housemaid or servant.

"Elisabeth, Con is expecting us, I believe," Locke said, leading the visitors into the high-ceilinged entryway. "My guests are Trace Crockett and Darby Maguire. Folks, this is Elisabeth Denney, Con's assistant and good right hand."

The woman smiled politely and nodded, "Mister Wheaton is waiting in the library, follow me." She turned and led them down a long hallway before stopping and gesturing that they should enter an open doorway.

Upon entering the expansive room, Darby's eyes were instantly drawn to walls of book-lined shelves, more volumes than she had seen in any public library, except Denver's. She knew that many wealthy folks acquired books for display, but she noticed that covers on some of the titles were well-worn.

Her attention turned to the wizened man sitting in a wood-framed wheelchair with cane-covered backing at a long table. He was studying the visitors with translucent blue eyes, and, as they approached, she saw a keen intelligence there that one should not underestimate, she thought. His thinning, white hair was shorn close to the skull, his eyebrows, thick and ragged. She guessed he might have been a tall man once, given the long, gangly arms stretched over the table, but hunched as he was, and swallowed in a thick, wool robe, it was hard to tell. A smoking, near-flattened cigarette dangled from his lips, ashes breaking off and falling in his lap. *God, don't let him burn up this magnificent library*, she thought.

Myles Locke made the perfunctory introductions, after which Elisabeth Denney gestured for Darby and

Trace to be seated at the table facing Wheaton. She took a chair next to her employer, and Locke found a place a few spaces from Darby, apparently positioning himself as a spectator for the moment. The parties sat in an awkward silence at the table, and Darby decided she would open the conversation. Trace Crockett had said nary a word since their departure from the Locke office, and it seemed unlikely he was going to take any initiative. Wheaton saved her the trouble.

He coughed and tossed the still smoldering cigarette in a pottery bowl with a mound of others. "Kids. Pinkerton sent a couple of kids," the old man croaked, his voice sounding like he was trying to kick splinters out of his throat. "Twenties, I'd say. Both of you. Boy's closing in on thirty. Girl's some years behind, but not a lot. When I was twenty, I knew everything. Had all the answers. My fifty-year-old pa was a senile old fool, as far as I was concerned. Then, I found I knew less for sure when I hit forty. Finally, when I came to sixty, I figured out we don't know anything. None of us—not about what matters. We're fooling ourselves if we think we do. So, what are you kids going to do for me?"

Darby was surprised when Trace replied, "Mister Wheaton, I'm starting to figure out I barely know enough to get along in this world, but that doesn't keep me from trying. Hard work doesn't scare me, and my dad always said I had more persistence than brains. I think I'm stubborn enough to get your answers, and Darby here will more than make up for my shortcomings in the brain department. I can't promise results, but, if we don't find your answers, it won't be for lack of trying."

The old man had another coughing fit. Then he looked at Trace with one squinted eye, and Darby saw that Trace was meeting Wheaton's gaze unflinchingly. Damned if the old buzzard wasn't liking what he heard and saw.

"Maybe you'll do, boy," Wheaton said. "Fire your guns. I'll try to answer your questions. Got to piss first, though." He wheeled his chair back, and, with some assistance from Elisabeth, went out the doorway.

Darby turned to Trace. "I don't believe it. I think he likes you."

"That happens occasionally."

Trace's sarcasm suggested her words were not well chosen. "I didn't mean there was any reason not to like you. He just changed his tone so quickly."

Trace did not comment.

Myles Locke intervened. "You will get along fine with Con. He's just testing you a bit. Don't hesitate to speak your minds. Don't give him an inch if he tries to put you on the defensive. He'll respect you for it."

They waited quietly for Wheaton's return, as Darby considered Trace's exchange with Wheaton. Her partner had been nothing but complimentary of her—and he hardly knew her. She was not unaware that she had been jockeying to establish authority at their initial meeting. Another female Pinkerton agent had warned Darby that she carried the proverbial chip on her shoulder when she dealt with male agents and had suggested that Darby pick her battles more carefully when it came to power struggles with her male counterparts. She resolved to back off and give Trace Crockett a chance, knowing herself well enough to admit there would be inevitable relapses.

Congrave Wheaton rolled his chair back into the room while Elisabeth Denney held the door open. The woman was an enigma to Darby, who had not yet figured out how she fit into Wheaton's life. She decided she would make it her business to find out. Miss Denney seemed a reserved sort, and her type often held a store of information they did not relinquish easily.

Wheaton took his place at the table. "Let's see what we can get done, folks. I'm paying good money for your time, but I can't say I won't interrupt again. I spend half my time dribbling bloody piss these days. Puke up most of what I eat. Doc says the Grim Reaper's closing in, so what do you need from me?"

Trace said, "I suppose some of the questions will be answered in the materials your lawyer gave us that we haven't had a chance to read yet, but I'd like to hear just how you believe Miranda was taken all those years ago. What happened?"

Wheaton coughed and spat a wad of green phlegm in his water glass. "It was during the night. There was some rain that evening, but not a rip-roaring thunderstorm like we tend to get in these parts. Gentle pitter-patter. Miranda had just moved into her own room a few months earlier. I'd pressed her mama—Lydia—to move the girl from Lydia's bedroom to the one across the hall. Lydia read to Miranda at bedtime like always. Girl went right to sleep. In the morning, she was gone. Just disappeared."

"Where was the bedroom located?" Trace asked.

"Upstairs. Like I said, across from Lydia's. Mine was at the end of the hall. Other bedroom was vacant."

"Did anyone stay in the house besides you and Lydia?"

"Cook came in, but we had a maid in the downstairs servants' quarters. Name was Charlotte. She died five years back. She was like another mother to Miranda. To Henry, too. She was a free colored woman and came with us when we moved to Kansas from Illinois. Same time as Myles here did. We were Free Staters. We came to help with the vote to keep Kansas an anti-slavery state when it joined the union. Myles was a judge back in Illinois, and I started and sold businesses—fancy word, I guess, is entrepreneur. We both found niches in Kansas and stayed on."

Wheaton was digressing, and Darby had little patience for it. "And Charlotte was in the house that night?"

Wheaton had another coughing fit, and his voice rattled when he replied, "Yes, ma'am, and none of us heard anything."

"So what did you do when you discovered Miranda was missing?"

"I ran out to the stable and sent the stableman to fetch the sheriff. That was my big mistake."

"Stableman. You didn't mention him. Did he live on the grounds?"

"Yes, ma'am. Had two rooms at the rear of the stable."

"Why did you say it was a mistake to send for the sheriff?" Darby asked.

"Because he was—and is—a buffoon. He was here when the postmaster showed up with the message and Miranda's bracelet from the kidnapper an hour later. No way we could keep the law out of it by that time. On top of that, he took the bracelet 'for evidence,' he said, and lost the damn thing."

Trace said, "The postmaster? The letter couldn't have been mailed and delivered in that length of time."

"No. No, of course not. Hubie Jones—the postmaster—said it was dropped in the night box. Envelope said, 'Life or death. To Con Wheaton now.' Well, Hubie closed up the office, grabbed his horse and headed for our place."

Locke said, "This is all written down in my file notes. Postmaster's still Hubert Jones, if you need to talk to him."

"What about the stableman?" Trace asked.

Wheaton replied, "Said he didn't hear or see anything, either."

"Where is he now?"

"Don't know. Left about six months after they took Miranda. Just disappeared one day. Didn't give notice. Got his monthly pay the day before. Thought it was strange. I liked the young man."

Trace said, "So he worked for you another six months after the abduction. How long before that?"

"Maybe three or four months. Not much more than a kid when I took him on."

"Local boy?"

"No. Came from Louisiana. Said he was orphaned by the war. Like thousands of others. My other man had just died. Kid showed up at a good time."

Trace turned to Locke. "His name in your files?"

"Yes. Robert Longtree. We don't know much about him, frankly."

Trace asked, "What was your prior stableman's name? How did he die?"

Wheaton said, "Orval Hollaway. Went fishing in the Big Blue east of town, just north of where it joins up with the Kansas River. Fell in and drowned. Orv had been a river rat all his life but never learned to swim. Just forty-two years old. Didn't have a wife or kids. That was a good thing."

"Did anybody see him fall in the river?"

"Can't say."

"Who found him?" Trace asked, half to himself.

"Sheriff might know," Locke volunteered. "Sheriff Rudy Tisdale. I suspect you'll want to chat with him anyway."

"Miss Denney, I wonder if I might ask you some questions?" Darby said.

The woman looked at Wheaton. "Go ahead, Elisabeth. No secrets. Tell 'em anything they want to know. I got to piss again. Maybe Myles can help me to the water closet."

Locke got up and left the room with Wheaton. Darby noted that Miss Denney was tapping nervously on the table with the fingers of her left hand. She had previously seemed very composed, almost detached, during Wheaton's questioning. Darby asked, "Miss Denney, how long have you been working for Con Wheaton?"

"I started a few years after the war, so it's been nearly fifteen years, I guess. About the time Miranda was taken."

"What have been your job duties during that time?"

"I've been his personal secretary almost from the beginning. I took over my father's job when he died. I was only eighteen years old at the time, but I had spent a good deal of time in the office with my father before that. I was an only child, and my mother had died when I was ten. Con is a kind and generous man, and he encouraged my father to bring me to work when I wasn't in school. I ran errands and did filing and the like when I wasn't reading one of the books from this library. He was like a second father to me and very dedicated to seeing that I read all the classics."

"Your father was Mister Wheaton's secretary?"

"Yes. George Denney. I'm sure you look at me and think I must have been born a slave. Well, I was not. I come from a long line of free Negroes. I was educated in schools with white classmates in Illinois when my father worked for Con there and continued after we came to Manhattan with the Free State people."

Elisabeth Denney made the statement with obvious pride and a bit of defensiveness, and Darby knew that she must step carefully if she did not want to trigger the woman's hostility. She also noted the use of Wheaton's first name, suggesting the relationship between employer and employee was an informal one, not unusual given the duration. "I gather, then, that you were acquainted with the ex-wife, Romy, and the daughter-in-law, Lydia?"

"Yes, and I saw the little girl, Miranda, many times. She was a beautiful red-haired imp and had the run of the place. You see, Con always maintained his business office here in the home. He employed trusted managers for his enterprises and stayed out of their hair unless the numbers from the reports told him something was amiss. Only then would he visit the operation to evaluate the problems."

"I see," Darby said, "so there would have been a fair number of people who entered and departed the house during a week's time?"

Miss Denney seemed to ponder the question. "Yes, I suppose. Ten or twelve, perhaps. Mostly managers. Often schemers with business ideas for Con to invest in.

Occasionally he would find one worth his attention. He has a nose for sniffing out a project with potential."

"You said you knew Romy. What can you tell me about her?"

Miss Denney again hesitated before she spoke. "Beautiful. Ruthless. Gold digger. A conniving bitch."

Miss Denney did not like the former Missus Wheaton. Darby had almost forgotten about Trace Crockett's presence and turned to him. "Questions?"

"No," Trace said, "continue."

Darby shrugged. "Myles Locke intimated the divorce wasn't amicably settled. If you can tell us about it, perhaps we can spare Mister Wheaton from that topic. I assume money was a major issue?"

"Money and grounds. Con filed for the divorce. Grounds were adultery."

"I see. And who was the lover?"

"There were several, but the one named in the divorce filings was Jerome Goddard."

"And does Mister Goddard still reside in the area?"

"Oh, yes. He is President of the Flint Hills State Bank. At the time, he was a vice-president, but his family owned the bank, and he recently succeeded his father. We do business with him. Con doesn't hold grudges, and he was very aware of Romy's wiles, having succumbed himself at a vulnerable time. Jerome is married and has a family now, a model citizen by all appearances."

"And Romy, did she do well financially in the divorce settlement?"

"Not from her viewpoint. Con and Romy had signed a prenuptial agreement. She was to receive ten thousand dollars in case of divorce. Con gave her twenty thousand. The sum did not stress him, but it would be a fortune for most people. She received more than she deserved."

"Where is Romy now?"

"I have no idea. She left town after the divorce."

"We've been told Lydia and Romy didn't get along. Realizing Miranda was very young, how did Romy take to her?"

"She disliked children generally and had nothing to do with Miranda, ignored her when the two were in the same room. She sometimes referred to Miranda as 'the heiress.'"

"A rival for the fortune Romy sought?"

"My opinion."

"I gather you and Mister Wheaton are quite close. Do you remember anything about the night that Miranda was abducted?"

Anger flashed in Miss Denney's eyes. "I wasn't here. And I don't take kindly to your snooping. I lived in my mother's small home a few blocks from here and walked to work every day as my father had. My mother died a few years after Miranda was taken, and Con suggested I sell the house and take an apartment here. I have two rooms on the second floor with my own water, bath and sanitary facilities. It's very convenient for work, and only a few homes in Manhattan enjoy such conveniences. Few people of my race—or any race, for that matter—have had the opportunities I've been given by Wheaton Enterprises."

Miss Denney had turned a bit defensive, and Darby did not want to alienate her. The conversation had been helpful, and she decided not to press her luck for the moment.

Chapter 5

WHEATON SETTLED IN at the library table, and, with Elisabeth Denney's help, rolled and lit another cigarette. Trace noticed how attentive the woman was to her employer's needs. Her devotion seemed genuine and reflexive, but she had been obviously touchy about the subject of her precise relationship with Wheaton when Darby probed the issue with her questioning. Did it matter? Probably not.

Wheaton took a puff on his cigarette and appeared to savor the tobacco's warmth before expelling the smoke through his nostrils and having a brief coughing episode. "Where were we?" Wheaton asked.

Trace said, "Mister Wheaton, I would like to take a look at the pendant that came with the letter from Dodge City."

"Elisabeth has it."

Miss Denney reached into a thin, leather briefcase that had been lying on the table near her chair and plucked out a gold chain with an attached pendant shaped like an oak leaf. Trace guessed that the pendant was an inch long, half that in width. The secretary handed the object to him, and he gave it a quick perusal and passed the object to Darby, who appeared to be examining it closely.

Darby said, "Mister Wheaton, I hope you don't have your hopes set too high. This contact could be a hoax. You're certain the pendant was your granddaughter's?"

"If not, it's an exact duplicate. Seems unlikely given the little dent in the gold just above the initial 'W.' I think it came that way. I remember noticing the flaw after she opened her Christmas package. It was on the backside, so it didn't matter."

Trace said, "Let's say we turn up somebody who claims to be your granddaughter. How do we know whether that person is her or a fraud?"

"Two things. She had a tannish birthmark, almost a half moon, with a little imagination, on her right butt cheek. It wasn't more than a half inch long when she was a little thing. Doc Ryan said it would likely be somewhat larger now—not a lot, but the mark would have grown with her."

Myles Locke interrupted. "I have included a sketch of the birthmark that Lydia made after Miranda disappeared with the folders I gave you. I don't know how accurate it is, but that should give you an idea."

Trace addressed Wheaton, "You said there were two things."

Wheaten coughed again and Trace noticed his voice growing weaker and more rasping. "Smallpox vaccination. Large scar on upper left arm, like she had two vaccinations. For some reason, hers got more corrupted than most and she got damn sick from it."

Trace said, "That probably wouldn't be unique, but the two together would make identity mighty conclusive. Of course, we can't walk around like we're looking for Cinderella, asking young women to disrobe so we can find a match. But it's something."

Darby said, "Tell us what she looked like as a little girl."

Locke said, "You'll find a few daguerreotypes in the folder."

"But they won't tell us about coloring, that sort of thing."

"Flame-red hair, sprinkling of freckles across the bridge of her nose and spreading out onto her upper cheekbones," Elisabeth Denney said. "Fair complexion."

"How tall were her parents?" Darby asked.

Wheaton replied, "Henry was a tall young man. I'd guess about your height, Trace, a few inches over six feet and lean and hungry looking like yourself, too. But Lydia was a little mite, probably wouldn't make a hundred pounds soaking wet. Starved down to almost nothing after we lost Miranda."

Trace could see the old man was about done in. "I think Darby and I need to go through the information in the folders. One of us will probably want to speak with you again, Mister Wheaton, maybe tomorrow. Myles, I'd like to speak with Darby after we leave here, if you could drop us at a good eating place. We'll probably take you up on the offer to headquarter in your conference space while we're in town. That will give us a chance to talk with you some more." He looked at Darby. "Does that sound like a plan, ma'am?"

"Yes, I'm fine with that."

Chapter 6

MYLES LOCKE HAD steered them to the perfect restaurant, Trace thought. Charlie's Chuck Wagon served his kind of food. Nothing fancy. Roast beef, fried potatoes, beans, and Dutch oven-cooked apple cobbler. Grub like he used to eat as a kid on his father's Tennessee ranch before the Rebellion, until the Yankees marched through and slaughtered most of the cow herd and burned down the house and outbuildings. He noticed Darby Maguire was working on her plate like a starving cowhand.

Myles Locke had politely declined Trace's invitation to join them for the noon dinner, which he had likely guessed was tendered out of courtesy. The lawyer had probably figured it was time for the two agents to get acquainted. He had kindly entered the small building and introduced them to the owner, who sat them in a corner for privacy.

They had been eating mostly in silence, exchanging only a few comments about the good food and prompt service, and Trace decided it was time to talk business. Darby did not give him a chance to start the conversation. She reached into her briefcase, stuffed with the lawyer's folders, and pulled out a small leather bag. She spread the drawstring and began plucking gold coins from the contents, pushing the coins to his side of the table.

"Seventy-five dollars," she said. "An eagle, three doubles and a five-dollar gold piece. The extra expense money you're entitled to. It doesn't get us off to a very good start if I'm holding your money. I don't know what it's about, and I don't care. I'm embarrassed about it."

"Somebody aiming a message my direction that I draw too generously on my expense funds. Probably some clerk working out of a closet in the Chicago office."

"Well, that's no longer my concern. We've got work to do. You really didn't know you were going to be working with a woman, did you?"

"Kansas City office manager didn't say, and I just assumed I was meeting up with an Irishman. I guess 'Darby' can fit man or woman."

"Yes. My father figured on another boy—he already had four—and wouldn't change the name. Mom got Kathleen for my middle name, but the first stuck. Do you have trouble working with a female?"

"Don't know. Never tried it. Usually on solo assignments, but if I've had a partner, it's been a man. I know Pinkerton hires a fair number of female agents. The first, Kate Warne, is a legend."

"I read all about her when I was a girl in Boston. My father was a cop there, but the city didn't hire women for police work . . . and Boston turned out not to be my destiny," she said, somewhat wistfully, Trace thought. "I came west to teach school, but while I was in Dodge, I saw an advertisement in an old Denver newspaper that announced Pinkerton was looking for female agents. As soon as the school term was finished, I headed for Denver."

"I don't care what your sex is, so long as you carry your share of the weight. I just got caught by surprise. We'll have trouble if you're a bossy sort, though."

"I've been told that I am. Rein me in if I'm out of line. Hopefully, you can put up with me for this one job. After this, we go our separate ways. I just want my split of the bonus we're going to earn."

Trace looked up when a man and woman entered the café. A middle-aged man dressed in business attire and a young, raven-haired beauty who had her hand locked on her escort's elbow and was laughing and smiling and acting as if she were hanging on every word the man spoke. He studied the couple as they took seats near the front of the dining area. The woman had not looked his way, but he knew her—or who she claimed to be: Audra Crockett.

"Have I lost you?" Darby asked.

Trace slid back his chair and stood up. "Excuse me."

He walked over to the table, moving in behind Audra's chair. The man looked up at him. "Sir?"

"I would like to speak to Audra . . . privately." The woman did not even turn her head at his voice.

"You must be mistaken, sir. My guest is Lady Sally Wordsworth."

He stepped around to the side of Audra's chair and looked down at her with angry, smoldering eyes. She looked up at him with an innocent expression that betrayed not a hint of recognition. "Hello. Should I know you?" Audra said with a perfect British accent.

"Audra Crockett. Yes, we've met. And I wish to speak with you. Now."

"I am very sorry, sir. I do not know you and have never seen you before. I must ask you to leave. Reggie and I are simply here to enjoy a pleasant dining experience."

"After we talk."

"Must I send for the law?" Reggie asked. "Or ask the manager to remove you from the premises?"

Darby had moved in beside him now, her hand tugging on his arm. "Trace, the last thing we need is trouble."

He took a deep breath and followed her back to their table. "We are going to trade places," Darby said, "so you have your back to the lady. I don't want any more distractions. What was that all about anyway?"

"Personal business. She owes me money. A significant amount."

"She didn't seem to recognize you, but I heard you say her last name was Crockett. Do you think she's a relative of yours?"

"She knew me. She's a con artist."

"Now, this does sound interesting."

Darby Kathleen Maguire had heard all she was ever going to hear about Audra Crockett. "I've said all I'm going to say. Let's talk about the case." She smiled mischievously, and he could tell she was enjoying his discomfort.

"I spoke with Elisabeth briefly as we were leaving the Wheaton mansion. She will meet us at the Kansas State

Bank tomorrow noon to arrange for the two thousand dollars in gold eagles we will take with us to purchase the information from your friend in Dodge City."

"No friend of mine, but I'm anxious to see who he is. Or she."

"I thought we would spend the remainder of today and all of tomorrow morning completing our investigation and interviews here. A train leaves Manhattan tomorrow afternoon that will take us to the connections for Dodge City. With stops and transfers, we would arrive in Dodge midmorning the next day. I've got tickets and have sent two wires for separate reservations for two at the Dodge House. I don't think we want anyone to be aware we're together until we get the lay of the land."

"We don't?"

"Your contact might get spooked if he—or she—sees us together. Don't worry, I'll have your back. Sleeping cars were too expensive, but I did get us a compartment with bench seats on each side that will give us some private space to talk while we travel and a bit of room to stretch out to sleep."

"You seem to have everything all planned out."

"Am I being bossy? I'm sorry. Did you have something else in mind?"

"No. I think your plan should fit." Truth was, he was glad to have somebody looking after the details, but it would have been nice to have been consulted first. And her idea of not appearing in Dodge City as an obvious pair made sense.

Darby said, "I thought we made a good team at Mister Wheaton's house."

They had worked well together, he conceded to himself. "Yeah, we did okay."

"Would you like to talk to the sheriff? I suspect a man would have more success with him. Most lawmen I've encountered are wary of a woman's questions."

"I could do that. I want to stop by my hotel room first and then I'll head for the sheriff's office."

"Where are you staying?"

"The Wheaton Inn."

Darby slid her eyeglasses down the bridge of her nose and peered over the rims. "Oh. I've heard it's a fabulous place. Too pricey for me, though. I'm at the Manhattan Hotel just down the street from here."

Damn her. He could tell she was judging him, and not favorably. It was none of her concern if he chose to live a little high on the hog sometimes. He wondered what kind of dump the Dodge House would be. He tossed a look over his shoulder. His friend, Audra Crockett, was still seated at the table with Reggie. She seemed unperturbed by their encounter. Perhaps, if he kept his eyes open, he could intercept the thief later. The woman had cleaned him out and doped him up, so he was left with nothing but memories of their erotic interlude. Then it occurred to him that his recollection of their time in bed was so fuzzy, he could not even claim an enjoyable image of their time together.

Darby slid a Morgan silver dollar across the table. "My half of the meal and a tip. I thought you might want to pay the bill. It would give you an opportunity to pass by your lady friend's table. I'll meet you at the Locke conference room after you talk to the sheriff. I'll start shuffling through the folders."

Chapter 7

TRACE WAITED IN an alleyway across the street from Charlie's Chuck Wagon, hoping that the woman he knew as Audra Crockett might come out and split off from her escort, giving him a chance to confront her. He finally abandoned his post, figuring she and Reggie were working out the details of a later rendezvous. Trace was not unmindful that Darby Maguire would be interested in a report of his progress, or lack of it, and decided it was time to start earning his pay.

Sheriff Rudy Tisdale had his booted feet propped up on his desktop and was leaning back in his swivel chair, his Stetson tugged down low on his forehead when Trace stepped through the doorway. He lifted his hat and eyed Trace but did not alter his position. The sheriff was a big, bear-like man with a brushy, white moustache drooping over his upper lip and a sizable belly that lopped over his belt.

"Sheriff Tisdale?" Trace asked.

"Who's askin'?"

"My name's Trace Crockett." He pulled back his coat, revealing the Pinkerton badge pinned to the lining. "Pinkerton National Detective Agency." The badge impressed some lawmen and triggered instant cooperation. Others turned hostile and suspicious. Tisdale appeared to be among the latter.

"What's your business here?"

"An old case. The Wheaton kidnapping. May I sit down?"

That got the old sheriff's attention, and he hoisted his feet off the desk. "Yeah, go ahead. What about the Wheaton case?"

Myles Locke had warned Trace that the sheriff suffered from runny mouth disease and had not been made aware of the recent developments. Trace's instincts told him this was a man better left out of the loop. Besides, at the commencement of an investigation, it was Trace's practice to trust no one.

"Con Wheaton has employed the Pinkerton Agency to review the circumstances surrounding the girl's abduction and determine if there's a possibility anything was overlooked."

"Why in the hell would he do that? The girl's long dead. Damn, I'd guess it's been twenty years."

"Fifteen, to be exact. He just feels a need at this time in his life to learn if there was something that might shed more light on what went wrong the night of the botched exchange or a missed clue that might help complete the story of what happened to the girl."

"I could take offense at that."

"Mister Wheaton has not even suggested that you might have missed something. He has the highest regard for you. He said you were the man to talk to if we wanted some insight," Trace lied. "Perhaps you would have some files I could look at that would help me get a handle on what happened."

"Ain't got any files."

"No record at all of the case?"

"Don't like paper, and whatever we had that far back is long burned up by now."

"Maybe I can pick your memory." Trace thought it was likely going to be slim pickings. "What do you remember about a stableman that used to work for Mister Wheaton—Orval Hollaway?"

"I knew Orv. Drank some beer with him."

"Mister Wheaton said he drowned."

"Yep. That's what we ruled it."

"That's what you ruled it? What do you mean by that?"

"Well, a boy found the body washed up on a sandbar. Big lump on the side of Orv's head. That could've kilt him or knocked him out. Likely hit his noggin on a rock when he fell in. Lot of rocks in the river where the Blue meets up with the Kaw—that's what we call the Kansas River hereabouts."

"If he was found on a sandbar, how do you know he was ever in the river?"

"Clothes was soaked yet when I got there. Hadn't been dead all that long. Boy came right to me when he came across the corpse."

"Did the county coroner examine the body? Maybe that office would have some records."

"Ain't no coroner records. Find one of the docs if we need one. I decide if we need somebody. Orv was dead as a can of corned beef. Didn't need no doctor to tell me that."

Trace decided he was not going to learn any more from this line of questioning, so he shifted to the night of the abduction. "You were at the Wheaton house shortly after Con Wheaton received the note from the kidnapper, isn't that right?"

Tisdale straightened in his chair and puffed his chest out like a Tom turkey. "I was there and took charge of the situation right away."

Given the failure of the mission, Trace could not imagine the man's pride of command. "So what was the plan that night?"

"Exchange was to be on the Big Blue River bridge. Con was to wait on the west side of the bridge with the money right after sundown the next night. When the kidnapper saw Con, he would bring the kid to the middle of the bridge, and they would make the trade."

"Makes some sense, I guess. They'd both be out in the open. On the other hand, they would each be vulnerable to a sniper. How were you involved?"

"Con told me to stay clear out of it till he had the girl back. I didn't say nothing, but it was a matter for the law, and I couldn't let some outlaw get away with the money. So unbeknownst to Con, me and two deputies crossed the Blue upriver with the idea of slipping in behind the kidnapper when he got on the bridge. I had a deputy who was a sharpshooter during the war, and he had orders to take the bastard down as soon as the girl was free. But the kidnapper never showed. Con was pissed as hell when he found out what we done—hardly spoke to me since. But I think the guy just got cold feet and killed the little gal. Likely buried her out in the hills someplace."

"Who knew you were going to try to ambush the abductor?"

Tisdale rubbed his chin, pondering the question. "Boys at the livery. That'd be about it. I didn't even tell my wife, and the deputies was hardly more than kids and didn't have women."

"Could you write down the names of the deputies for me?"

"Don Raymond's dead. He was my sharpshooter. Took a bullet in the back a month later. Max Pierce left not more than six months later. Don't know where the hell he is these days. Could be dead for all I know."

"Who killed Raymond?"

"Don't know. Happened one night when he was on foot patrol downtown."

"Family here?"

"Nope. No local roots."

"How long had Max worked for you before the kidnapping?"

"Oh, I'd say almost two years. What're you getting at?"

"Just looking for possibilities. Would he have known Robert Longtree, Wheaton's stableman?"

"Oh yeah, Robbie used to hang around here some, and him and Max drank beer and chased women together. Usually went west to Junction City. I didn't want my deputy sewing wild oats in my county. Things ain't so prim and proper west of Fort Riley as they are here on the east side. Even got a few whorehouses for the soldier boys and anybody else with a dollar."

"I recall that. I was stationed at Fort Riley before I mustered out." The sheriff was apparently unaware of the more discreet, refined prostitutes within his own bailiwick, or chose to turn his head. Trace generally avoided such places for fear of disease, but he did fondly remember Manhattan's Alice. He thought of her occasionally and hoped life had carried her to something better by now.

Tisdale said, "I thought you looked like you had some soldier boy in you."

Trace found himself tired of this man, who may have singlehandedly cost a little girl's life. He stood to leave, "I have to move on, Sheriff Tisdale. I thank you for your time. I might stop back if I have further questions."

Chapter 8

DARBY WAS ANXIOUS for Trace to return to the Locke office. She had scanned the material in the lawyer's files and folders, impressed with the thoroughness of the reports. When she told Myles Locke as much, the lawyer had credited his secretary, Reva, with collecting and organizing the materials. "Reva makes things work around here," Locke had said.

The lawyer and his secretary-assistant had an obvious affection and respect for each other, Darby had noticed. Nothing illicit or improper. It was one of those relationships born of complementing skills and personalities that formed an efficient, comfortable unit, nurtured by mutual caring. She wondered if there was any chance that she and Trace Crockett might eventually form such an effective team. That verdict was far from in.

When Trace entered the conference room and took a chair on the other side of the table, Darby sensed he was stewing about something. His interview with the sheriff apparently had not gone well. "Something's troubling you," she said.

"That obvious, huh?"

"Yes."

"The sheriff. I just confirmed what Con Wheaton said. The man's a buffoon. It seems likely that little girl died or disappeared because of his incompetence. Or, at least, he bungled the best chance of getting her back."

"Tell me what you found out."

Trace related the gist of his conversation with Sheriff Rudy Tisdale. "There are a lot of coincidences that should be investigated if the abduction was fifteen days ago, instead of fifteen years. But our job is to find Miranda or confirm what happened to her, not to solve the crime."

"I agree, but there is the question of whether we can find her without identifying the kidnapper."

"We won't know that till we make contact with the mystery man in Dodge City—if this isn't a hoax."

"I've worried about a dead end there. But that's why I think we need to put as many pieces together as we can," Darby said.

"Well, my first three pieces are Romy Wheaton, or whatever her name is now, Robert Longtree, the stableman, and Deputy Max Pierce. I just don't know if they fit together."

"Myles Locke's notes have a lot of information on Romy, very little on Longtree and nothing about the deputy."

"What should I know about Romy?" Trace asked.

Darby pressed her fingers into one off the folders and plucked out three daguerreotypes, reaching across the table and spreading them in front of Trace. One was an image of Romy Wheaton attired in a lady's riding britches and boots, astride a white gelding. One displayed only face and shoulders, and the other presented her dressed in a ball gown, displaying an immodest amount of impressive cleavage, which she was confident her partner was examining with interest. "This is the ex-wife," she said.

"Attractive lady."

"Black hair, blue eyes, about my height—five feet, six inches tall. Charming personality when she chooses, but otherwise, quick-tempered and shrewish. Smart in a manipulative, conniving way. Had a slight French accent. Maiden name was Coquet. Father was a trader. She had roots in St. Louis. Con Wheaton met her there when he was on a business trip. Encountered her at her father's home, as a matter of fact. I have five or six typewritten pages on her and some of the divorce papers if you want to do some reading."

He pushed the daguerreotypes back. "Not necessary. You can tell me if I need to know something."

Darby was learning that Trace Crockett did not want to be burdened with details. That suited her fine. She was obsessive about documentation and paper research, sometimes to the extent of bypassing her instincts. "I wonder if someone should talk to Jerome Goddard?"

"Why don't you just say it? You would like me to talk to Mister Goddard."

Caught. She smiled sheepishly. "He would probably be more comfortable talking with a man about an affair with another man's wife. And, he might have some information about Romy that would be useful." Trace looked at her as if annoyed at her remark, and she wondered if he had taken offense at her words. She could not imagine why.

"I'll try to get in to see him tomorrow morning. Bankers are good information sources. Most I've run into keep up with the local gossip. I'll talk to the postmaster, too. I don't expect much there, but the small towners seem to know everybody's business."

Darby said, "I want to talk to Elisabeth Denney again. I think she knows more than she's said. I'll do that in the morning, and Elisabeth and I will meet you at the Kansas State Bank at noon." She picked up one of the folders and handed it to Trace. "Newspaper clippings. I thought you might want to scan these to get a feel for the public side of the kidnapping at the time. I don't think we need to take much of this with us. I will take a few more notes to refer to, but I prefer to travel light. Jot down anything you want to remember."

"I'm not much on notes. My guess is you've got plenty for both of us."

Sarcasm? She couldn't tell for sure. It didn't matter. She found herself feeling comfortable enough with him, even liking the man. And, as a bonus, he was quite pleasant to look at.

Chapter 9

TRACE WAITED IN the cramped lobby of the Flint Hills Bank. It was a small, single-story structure on Poyntz Avenue, just a few blocks east of the Locke law offices. The bank president evidently occupied the only private office. There were three teller stations, two occupied by male tellers and the other by a petite, young woman. A middle-aged man sat at a desk just outside the president's office, probably a vice-president or other officer.

Trace had shown his Pinkerton badge to the young lady when he entered the bank, offered his name and requested a private word with Jerome Goddard. She had returned a pleasant smile and quickly disappeared into the president's office. She was returning now, followed by a fit-looking man with salt and pepper hair, who Trace guessed to be in his early forties. The man stepped out into the reception area with an extended hand, and Trace stood and accepted a firm grip.

"Mister Crockett, I'm Jer Goddard. Peggy says you would like a private word. Come on into my office."

"I appreciate your taking the time for me. I shouldn't be long."

When they were seated in the office, Trace cast his eyes about the single-windowed room. Tidy but unpretentious with the usual plaques and certificates on the wall, and a framed photograph of Goddard, an attractive woman and three children on a shelf behind the desk. The family, Trace assumed. "Mister Goddard—"

"Please, make it 'Jer.' What can I help you with?"

"Jer, I would like to speak with you about Romy Wheaton."

The banker's face blanched noticeably, and his congenial expression turned grim. "She was a long time ago."

"More than fifteen years," Trace said. "Please understand, I'm not here to dredge up an old scandal. Anything we discuss will not go beyond my partner and myself, and I promise you we are very discreet."

Goddard sighed. "Well, my wife knows. Romy was in my life before I met and married Kate, so it doesn't concern her. The public record of the Wheaton divorce is buried in the courthouse vaults, and I don't think anyone searches those out anymore. But tongues will still wag after I'm planted in the cemetery. Small town ghosts. Live with them or run. And I love this town, so I'm not running. What do you want to know about Romy?"

"The Pinkerton Agency has been employed by Con Wheaton to look into some questions about Miranda's kidnapping. Mister Wheaton's health is not good, as you probably know, and he would like to find out what really happened."

"There is no better man than Con Wheaton. I'm ashamed and embarrassed about my part in disrupting his life, and it makes me sick thinking of what happened to that little girl. It really hit home when I had children of my own. Terrible thing."

"Do you know where Romy is now?"

"No. She disappeared after the divorce. We had broken off our . . . uh . . . relationship not quite a year before that. I should say Romy broke it off. When Con found out, she dumped me like so much garbage. She wanted to save her marriage—or, I should say, her fortune."

"Her marriage was all about money then?"

"Yes. I was totally in love with her—or I thought so. She was incredibly beautiful and had this way of making you think you were a god. Maybe you've known such women."

"Oh, yes. I understand." And he did, of course, having had his own adventure with a married woman and paid a price for it. Jerome Goddard had no idea how much empathy his visitor had for the banker's seamy dilemma.

"Anyway, for about six months my brain wasn't in my head. I would have done almost anything Romy asked. Fortunately, bedding her was all she demanded. And, I will give her this: I professed my love for her again and again, but she never reciprocated, never said she loved me or hinted she might leave Wheaton and marry me. I guess I was just a toy, a willing one at that."

"Did she express any guilt about her affair with you?"

"No. Never. I doubt she had any. Some of us carry guilt even when there's nothing to feel truly guilty about. Not Romy. You know, I think there are some people in this world who aren't troubled by conscience. They pursue what they want ruthlessly without a thought to those who stand in their way. She wanted Con Wheaton's fortune, and, looking back, I think she would have done whatever it took to get it. She always complained about having signed an agreement not to claim his estate in case of death or divorce but seemed convinced she would talk him into cancelling it soon."

"Did she say how she would do this?"

"No. But she had made it her business to know everything about her husband's financial affairs. From my connection with the bank, I knew a great deal, but she was much better informed. Romy was smart as hell."

Trace asked, "Would she have been capable of abducting Miranda?"

"I'd never thought about that." He hesitated only a moment before continuing. "I suppose with Romy anything would be possible. But it still seems rather farfetched."

"Did Romy ever say where she might go if she left Manhattan?"

"Not precisely. She hated it here. Said the people here were too provincial. She used that word a lot. She found us too engrossed with work and morality. Boring. She even chided me for it, when we rendezvoused for purposes that were immoral by the standards I was raised by. If she had somehow got hold of Con's money, she would have headed west. She talked about that all the time. The future was in the West."

"Any particular place in the West?"

"No. But someplace warm. She hated the cold."

"Did she have any friends here that she might have stayed in touch with?"

"No women friends that I know of. There was mutual contempt between her and most of the ladies in their social circle. There was one man she saw a lot of, but he left not many months after she did."

"Who was that?"

"Young deputy sheriff, Max Pierce. She would meet up with him sometimes and go horseback riding in the Flint Hills. Made me jealous as hell. She claimed they were just friends from St. Louis days. I guess they would have been about the same age. I just know I hated the son-of-a-bitch. I realized later that her horse wasn't the only thing she was probably riding. After it was over between us, I wondered about something."

"What was that?"

"She mentioned more than once that if she could produce an heir for Con Wheaton, that would change everything when it came to his money. She could make a whole new deal with him. She wasn't having any luck with Con. I wondered if Romy was using Pierce and me for stud service."

Chapter 10

THE TRAIN HAD been an hour late pulling out of Manhattan. The delay had seemed to make Trace fidgety, but Darby had seen it as an opportunity to talk about their respective morning interviews. Trace had related his conversation with Jerome Goddard, which had added to the accumulation of coincidences, but Romy Wheaton's role in any abduction still seemed highly speculative and probably irrelevant to their task. Trace's postmaster interview had yielded nothing and had accomplished nothing but to provoke the old man's curiosity.

They occupied a private compartment with pull-down blinds on large windows and a flimsy door. The detectives sat on wooden bench-seats facing each other, Trace scooting off to one side of his seat to make room for his long legs. With the barely muffled clickity-clack of wheels against rail, they had to speak loudly to communicate.

Darby said, "Before I went to the Wheaton mansion to talk with Elisabeth Denney, I stopped by the Locke offices to visit Myles again. There was something that had been bothering me."

"What's that?" Trace asked with little enthusiasm in his voice.

"I was reluctant to pry but decided that's what we're paid to do. Myles said Con Wheaton had waived lawyer-client privilege regarding all of his legal matters as far the Pinkerton Agency was concerned."

"Yes. Why don't you just cut to the chase?"

He was starting to annoy her again. "We were told that Miranda Wheaton is the major beneficiary of Con's will if she makes a claim within six months of her grandfather's death."

"Yeah. Go on."

"But who gets the estate if she is confirmed dead or doesn't make the claim?"

"Is this a game?"

"The cash and non-business assets making up about twenty percent of the estate will go to charities in Riley County, no matter what happens."

"The suspense is putting me to sleep," Trace mumbled.

The man had an irritating tendency to sarcasm, Darby thought. "What Myles calls the residue of the estate, including Wheaton Limestone Products, a six thousand-acre Flint Hills ranch known as the Bar W, as well as other assorted business enterprises, all go to Elisabeth Denney."

That announcement grabbed Trace's attention. "You're serious."

"Absolutely."

"Did you ask her about this?"

"I couldn't. Myles said he was telling me in confidence because of Wheaton's waiver. I was not to disclose the information to anyone but you. He thinks Elisabeth may be aware of the arrangements, but he's not certain what Wheaton's told her."

"The woman doesn't have much incentive to help us locate Miranda Wheaton."

"Regardless, she will receive a fourth interest in the businesses, and, if Miranda turns up, she is to be trustee over the other three-fourths until the granddaughter reaches the age of thirty-five. If she's a successful manager, her own share could grow considerably over that time. She will be a wealthy woman no matter what happens."

"Some folks never have enough."

"I know. And I'm a natural skeptic. I don't trust anybody until I get to know them."

"I suspect that includes me."

"That includes you."

Trace just shrugged and seemed unperturbed by her comment. "So, what do you think of Miss Denney? Learn anything new?"

Darby said. "We had a pleasant conversation over coffee and sweet rolls in the Wheaton parlor."

"Your morning already sounds better than mine."

"She didn't specifically say so, but I'm quite certain Elisabeth and Wheaton were lovers. I think she loves the man."

"It's hard to picture that. She'd be thirty or thirty-five years younger than the old boy."

"But fifteen to twenty years back that gap would not have seemed so great as it does now, given the state of his health. And there are some folks on this earth who measure love as something more than mere physical attraction."

"Really? Is money a factor?"

"You have a rather warped outlook on humankind."

"I'm just not ready to take her off the suspect list."

Darby said, "I'm not removing anyone from a suspect list. Our focus is very narrow. Find Miranda or confirm her death. Suspects are relevant only if they help us find out what became of Miranda."

"But the quickest way to do that would be to nab the abductor or killer."

"I don't disagree, but we're on our way to meet up with a mystery person who might make it unnecessary." Darby paused, pondering how to frame her next remark. "But I didn't finish telling you about my conversation with Elisabeth."

"I'm listening."

"She's disturbed about the letter writer's request for you to meet him in Dodge City. She's suspicious that you're a part of some scheme to wring money out of Con Wheaton. And she's skeptical about the pendant being Miranda's. She says after fifteen years, it wouldn't have been that difficult for someone with knowledge about the engraving to come up with a rough replica. Con can't see well, and his memory isn't so perfect for him to identify the pendant with a hundred percent certainty. He is seeing what he wants to see. That's what she thinks."

Darby had expected an angry reaction from Trace but got none. "And what do you think?" Trace asked.

"She could be right about the pendant."

"And about me?"

"She's wrong. Whatever happens in Dodge City will prove it."

"Thank you. Now, I'm going to take a nap." He leaned back against the passenger car's wall and tossed one leg upon the bench, tugging his hat down over his forehead.

"But we need to talk."

"We have the remainder of the afternoon and all night to talk. I'm tired."

She decided she wasn't in a mood to talk to this man anymore anyway. She pulled out her notebook and started to review her entries. A few minutes later, her eyelids closed, and her head drooped forward, chin resting on her chest. The notebook fell from her hands and slid down her lap and onto the floor.

Chapter 11

TRACE STARED OUT the window as the train rolled down the tracks, watching the panorama of the vast, starlit Kansas prairie pass by. He had declined the conductor's offer to light the small kerosene lamp mounted by the entrance to the compartment. Darby was sleeping on her bench seat, curled up in a fetal position with her head resting on her bulging carpetbag. She had tucked her eyeglasses into a small leather pouch and dropped it into the bag that evidently carried her female grooming things, and probably a pistol and her Pinkerton badge and credentials, in addition to the other mysterious stuff women carried in such bags. After positioning the bag, she had closed her eyes and dropped instantly to sleep.

Trace found himself gazing at her face, peaceful and lovely in the soft moonglow that illuminated it. She had looked the stern, old maid schoolmarm when he first encountered her at the lawyer's office, but now, as he studied the gently carved features of her face, he recognized the subtle beauty there. She opened her eyes a moment, apparently sensing his perusal, her eyes meeting his questioningly, and, embarrassed, he turned his head away.

He was still dubious about the woman as a detective partner, but he was stuck with her and determined to make the best of it. She had not been a hinderance to this point, and he had to admit she had been damned efficient at attending to the detail side of the investigation.

The conductor had mentioned earlier that the train would arrive in Dodge City at about eight o'clock in the morning, a few hours earlier than the detectives had expected. He plucked the watch from his vest pocket. Fifteen minutes after five o'clock. They would need to talk before arrival. As Darby had suggested, he did not think it wise for the two to make an appearance as a couple, certainly not until they scouted the lay of the place. He decided he would wake Darby in another hour to discuss a strategy.

Fifteen minutes later, Darby awakened, sat up, and yawned. "That was nice, but the bed was a little hard. A room at the Dodge House will be welcome tonight."

"I hope so," Trace replied, still not trusting his partner's selection of sleeping accommodations.

She stood up and stretched. "We need to talk, but I have to go pee first." She left with her carpetbag for what passed for a toilet on the train, a closet-like room with a few wash bowls and a single wooden commode that delivered the waste down a chute and emptied it onto the track bed below. The same facility was used by males and females, and foot or hand pressed against the door served as the only lock. From his own visit during the night, he knew the odor of the place was not improving with the miles and that men with poor aim were making spots on the floor a bit slippery and the toilet seat a bit damp. Of course, the jostling by the train did not help. He assumed that during a Dodge City layover, someone would scrub-out the facility with lye water. Or they might not.

A half hour later, Trace was wondering what was taking Darby so long. He pondered checking on her but discarded the idea. He did not know her that well, and she might not take kindly to his rapping on the toilet door. He supposed ladies had chores to tend to that he would rather not know about. He rubbed his stubbled cheeks, remembering he needed a shave. Well, he wasn't going to do it in the train's waste dump. He would find a bath and change into a fresh suit after he checked into the hotel.

The door opened, and an old lady with a cane started to enter. He got up from his seat. "Ma'am, I'm sorry. You have the wrong compartment."

"Sonny," she said, her voice quivering and shrill. "I know where I'm at and where I'm going."

"Ma'am. You're mistaken . . . " He stopped, recognizing the gray dress. "Darby?"

Darby lifted the veil that draped over her eyes from the little felt hat perched on her gray hair and grinned mischievously. "I guess it works."

She leaned her cane against the wall and sat down. Trace took his place on the facing seat. "I wouldn't have ever recognized you but for the dress." He shook his head in disbelief. "The cane. Where did that come from?"

"The latest in aluminum. A telescoping cane that fits in the carpetbag."

"And why the disguise?"

"I don't think we should be paired up by anybody when we get off the train in Dodge, do you?"

"No. I was going to talk to you about that. If we get off the passenger car separately, I don't think anyone will match us up."

"I thought I would leave first and check in at the Dodge House. I requested second floor rooms. I'll leave my door ajar so you'll know which room I'm in. Tap on the door and give me your room number so I can find you. I think we should each notify the other when one of us leaves, but we shouldn't know each other outside the hotel for now. Any ideas on how to be found by your friend?"

"After I get a bath and shave and maybe a bite of breakfast, I thought I'd start with the saloons."

"Makes sense. I need to clean up, too. Maybe we could agree that you will venture out about one o'clock. I'll start checking out the town shortly after."

"I'm okay with that. If we don't make a connection before, we'll return to our rooms at five and talk then," Trace said.

"Agreed."

When the train pulled into Dodge City, Darby departed first with her suitcase and carpetbag. The conductor, obviously confused by the presence of an elderly passenger he did not remember, assisted her with the suitcase, assuring her there would be a carriage and someone to assist her with transporting the baggage to the hotel.

Trace gave Darby a twenty-minute lead and then grabbed up his suitcase, gun sling, and the canvas-draped hanger carrying his extra suit and headed for the exit. He stepped onto the boarding platform that joined the little clapboard depot building and surveyed the surroundings. He shook off an offer of assistance from a young man with a carriage but gave him a dollar for directions to the Dodge House and recommendations for the best restaurants and taverns, as much as the ride and baggage assistance would have cost. The hotel was only a few blocks from the depot, and he thought the walk would give him an opportunity to scout the town.

As Trace strolled down the dusty streets, he found no surprises. He had landed in a growing, dirty cow town, like several he had visited during his Army days in Texas. The town appeared to be a collection of hastily constructed clapboard buildings thrusting upward from the prairie, most lining Front Street, the town's main commercial street, it appeared. The Dodge House was a two-story structure and looked somewhat more substantial, but its exterior siding needed painting. A three-story hotel with a stone front, obviously a recent addition to the town, faced the Dodge House from the opposite side of the street and looked more inviting to Trace. He supposed Darby had saved fifty cents a day in room costs by setting up in the Dodge House. Giving his partner the benefit of the doubt, he guessed their lodging at the

Dodge House would attract less public attention, if that really mattered.

Dodge seemed prosperous enough, occupied by a variety of commercial establishments, including a large general store and a blacksmith's shop with adjacent livery, as well as at least three saloons, two of which had second floors that likely functioned as bordellos. He caught a glimpse of a furniture store that also offered undertaking services. Further down the street he could make out buildings that appeared to house offices, probably a few lawyers and a doctor or two. He would take a walk down Front Street later and take inventory in case he required merchandise or service before he left the town. Right now, Trace didn't know if he was visiting Dodge City for a day or a month. His immediate concern was a decent room and a place for a bath and shave.

Chapter 12

EARLY ARRIVAL HAD allowed Trace to find his room, grab a hot bath and shave at a barber shop attached to the hotel, and eat a burnt steak in the hotel's dining room. The boy at the depot had warned him about the hotel cuisine, but Trace had opted for convenience, as had Darby, doubtless going for cheap, sitting at a table on the far side of the room. The room arrangements had turned out to be opportune. At check-in, a young clerk with unflattering chin whiskers had informed Trace that he should enjoy a quiet stay since he was located at the far end of the hall and the occupant of the room opposite his was "a little old lady."

After eating, Trace returned to his room and waited for Darby to return to hers. When he heard her door shut, he went across the hallway, tapped twice and entered.

"Is your room satisfactory?" Darby asked.

"It's okay. Not luxurious, but I didn't see any rats or cockroaches."

"They're very clean rooms," Darby admonished. "And we won't be spending much time there. I assume you won't be entertaining so anything extravagant would be a waste of good money."

"I don't know about entertainment opportunities yet, but I'll make the best of it."

She shot him a disgusted look. "Not funny. We're working for Pinkerton. Forget about your social life."

Darby was a little short on sense of humor, Trace thought. "Well, I'm going to start detective business now and head for the first tavern. I'll be here at five o'clock unless something comes up before. Where do I find you if I need to?"

"Don't worry. I'll find you. Take off your hat if you need to talk with me."

"You're planning to follow me, aren't you?"

"I hope you don't object?"

"I guess not. Just seems strange. You do carry a gun?"

"Smith & Wesson. Strapped to my thigh under my dress."

"I'll take your word for it."

"Damn right you will. I can see you've got a shoulder harness outfit inside your coat. Most gunfighters would notice."

"I don't care. A warning not to push their luck with me."

"I'll talk to you back here later. I hope you strike gold out there."

He gathered he had been dismissed so he turned away and opened the door a crack to confirm the hallway was vacant and then stepped out. He had already decided his first stop would be The Long Branch, which was the largest of the saloons he had seen and was freshly painted and had almost an elegant look by cow town standards. It occurred to him that Dodge City appeared blissfully unaware of Kansas prohibition laws.

This early in the afternoon probably was not the best time to lure his contact, Trace supposed. The saloon was a rather sleepy place, a few cowboys at the bar and several tables of card players to the far side. A bored-looking prostitute leaned against the railing at the foot of the stairway leading to the rooms on the second floor. She would feign enthusiasm if approached, but she did not seem to be hustling business. A closer look revealed a woman with ample bosom and a face that would have once been pretty but now sagged with too many years of the whoring life. She looked fifty, but Trace suspected she was ten to fifteen years younger. She had chosen a rough existence, or, more likely, circumstances had forced it upon her.

He strolled up to the bar and instantly took notice of the polished, walnut bar top, a diamond on the dusty plains that would likely be unappreciated by most. A husky bartender with a brushy, but neatly trimmed, moustache took his order for a beer and returned with a mug of the brew that was surprisingly cool. Trace flipped a half dollar on the counter and told the man to keep the change, buying some time in the saloon since he wouldn't be drinking much.

The bartender eyed him with curiosity, Trace guessing that his suit and shined boots were not usual attire in the establishment. "Looking for somebody?" the bartender asked.

"Not exactly." Trace replied. "Somebody's looking for me, I hope."

The bartender's brow furrowed with confusion before he shrugged and turned away. Trace took his beer and claimed a chair facing the entryway at a table near the bar. He sat down and sipped at his drink. He had tasted worse beer someplace but could not recall where. The single beer was enough, and he made it last the better part of an hour, before he decided to move down the street and test another establishment, reminding himself he might be playing this game for several days. What did they do if the note writer didn't show? The detectives had no other clues. He started to get up when he saw the prostitute meandering his direction in a nonchalant manner. There was no one else nearby so Trace knew he was the target. He remained seated and waited, not interested in the woman's wares but curious about her move.

He stood as she approached. "Ma'am?"

"Name's Sadie, nowadays. Can I sit?" she asked, with a voice that sounded like it came from a throatful of gravel.

"Sure." He pulled back a chair, and Sadie dropped into the proffered seat. "My name's Trace."

"I thought so. He said to keep a look-out for a duded-up stranger—tall, darker man with soft, green eyes that make a female melt." She looked at him and winked. "You fit the bill."

Trace flushed. "I'll take that as a compliment."

"It is. Man like you don't need to pay for what I usually offer, but I got somethin' else."

"I'm listening."

"A message. For a price, of course."

"An eagle do?" He reached in his pocket and plucked out a coin, flipping a gold eagle onto the table.

Sadie scooped up the coin. "More than do. I like you."

She should, he thought. Sadie had no doubt been paid by the sender, as well, probably half as much, maybe less.

She bent over, half hidden by the tabletop, and appeared to be searching beneath her skirt for something. In mere seconds, she straightened and handed him a small folded sheet of paper. "Cain Abel sent this. He said you'd remember him." She slid her chair back and stood, reaching over and gently patting his cheek, and sighed. "Ten years back, you and me would've had an afternoon to remember. See you around, love."

Trace unfolded the message and read: *Sunset. Back door. Jubal's Livery. Bring money. Cain.*

Sergeant Cain Abel. He could forget neither the man nor his name. He always thought Cain's parents must have had a sense of humor, tagging their newborn son with that moniker. Abel and Trace had both served under Mackenzie during the Comanche wars. He had considered Abel a competent noncom, but they had not been close friends. The man had lied quickly to save his own skin and never hesitated to put the blame for missteps on others. Somehow it did not surprise him that Abel might have stumbled into something nefarious.

Trace got up and left the saloon, deciding to take a tour of the commercial blocks before returning to the hotel. He specifically wanted to get the lay of Jubal's Livery before he made the evening visit. The business was not the same one as the livery he had passed on his walk from the depot to the Dodge House.

He located the livery at the opposite end of town, set off a short distance from the town proper, not far from the stockyards that lined the railroad tracks. A large pen of horses indicated the owner might be in the business of selling and renting horses. The place was clearly set up to serve the ranchers and drovers that came to town with the vast herds of cattle that had built Dodge. Unfortunately for the town, the rails spreading like a spider's web throughout the southwest were starting to open new cattle markets for the ranchers, and the flood of cattle traffic flowing toward Dodge City would eventually dwindle to a trickle. Stockyards at Fort Worth, Texas were already pulling away herds from south Texas and making a dent in the panhandle market. A fledgling town of Amarillo was an imminent threat.

Trace walked over to the stables and stopped at the double-doored entry for horses. From there, he could see an identical opening at the opposite end, which he took to be Cain's "back door." Huge barn. Several dozen stalls with pens for overflow. Most of the stalls were empty, but this would be slow season for the cattle business.

"Howdy, friend."

Trace turned to the sound of the deep voice behind him and saw a barrel-chested man with a white, trimmed beard and twinkling blue eyes. He was only a few inches shorter than Trace, probably in his late fifties or early sixties. Trace extended his hand and received a bone-crunching grip. "I'm Trace Crockett. I was looking over your facilities. Nice."

"I'm Jubal Snyder, proprietor of these nice facilities. You got a horse to put up?"

"Nope. I came in by rail, but I love horses."

"Cavalry, I'd guess."

"You guessed right. And ranch-raised."

"Looking for an investment?"

Trace supposed his attire hinted at money. "No. I'm just a traveling salesman."

"What are you selling?"

"Uh." He hesitated. He should have anticipated the question. "Medical supplies. I see you've got two doctor's offices in town. I thought I'd lay over a day and see if I might do some business."

"I think you're selling bullshit, but it ain't my concern, and it ain't none of my business. You don't seem like a bad feller. And I was cavalry, too, during the War of the Rebellion, and before that, the Mexican War. Noncom. Sergeant Major at discharge. I'm guessing you was commissioned, maybe a captain."

"Wrong. You outrank me. I mustered out a First Sergeant. Red River War."

"Fought Comanches, huh. I got a part-time man. Works mostly nights. Says he fought in that war. I wonder if you know him. Name's Cain Abel, believe it or not. Claims he was a cavalry sergeant, and he does know horses."

Trace said, "There were thousands of soldiers in that conflict strung all over west Texas. I'd have no reason to question his claim." He hoped he had weaseled his reply carefully enough. He did not like lying to this man.

Snyder said, "I was only half kidding about the investment. I'd get out if I got the chance. Kansas legislature killed Abilene, Wichita, and other cow towns with the Quarantine Line. No Texas Longhorns allowed east of the line. Farmers in the east part of the state don't want Longhorns up here because they got ticks that spread Texas Fever to other critters. Now they're talking of putting in a law that covers the whole damned state. Town's got two or three years before the cattle markets dry up anyhow. The railroad that made us is breaking us now.

And there's rumors Fort Dodge is going to be closed-up come fall. That'll kill the soldier business that made the town before the cattle drives came along."

The two men told war stories for the better part of an hour, before Trace said he needed to move on. He thought he had made a friend, and a man never knew when a friend might come in handy in a strange town.

Chapter 13

"YOU SEEMED TO enjoy your visit with the man at the livery," Darby said. Trace sat on the only chair in her room, and Darby was perched on the edge of her bed, where she had tossed her wig and cane.

"An important person works there: our letter writer."

"Seriously? So you know who it is?"

"I do. Cain Abel."

She cocked her head and squinted her eyes. "Who is it really? It must be someone you know."

"He is someone I know, and his name is Cain Abel. Army acquaintance." Trace told her about his encounter with Sadie at The Long Branch and handed her the note bearing Abel's message.

She looked at the note and shook her head disbelievingly. "And you're meeting him at the stable tonight. I can't believe our good luck."

"Skill, ma'am. Don't underestimate my detective skills."

She ignored his remark. "Do you think there's any danger in your meeting up with this man?"

"Not much. I'm handing him money for information. A simple exchange."

"A lot of money. Enough to make him a wealthy man by some standards. I worry that this is all a fraud."

"Con Wheaton knows that. He was willing to take the risk."

"I'll follow to back you up just in case."

He already knew her well enough to conclude argument would be hopeless. "What would a little old lady be doing out on the street after dark?"

"I won't be a little old lady."

"I'll tap on the door before I leave."

Back in his room, Trace changed into a pair of faded blue denims and a pull-over buckskin shirt. He hitched his cartridge belt with the holstered Army Colt above his hips, and then slipped the revolver from its holster and loaded cartridges into the cylinder chambers. He squeezed the pistol grip, reacquainting himself with the weapon he had not fired for several months. He placed his hat atop his head, thinking that it matched his current wardrobe better than the suits he wore. But this was his lucky hat, and it was impractical to travel with a hat for each occasion. A physician friend had told him that his obsession with his wardrobe went beyond idiosyncratic, and Trace conceded he probably overdid it. He blamed West Point.

He wished he had a good book to read because sitting in the hotel room staring at the wall while waiting for nightfall was testing his patience. He got up and went across the hall and rapped on the door to Darby's room. She opened the door just a crack, signaling that she was not going to admit him to the room.

"I'm going to find a place to eat," he said. "You'd be welcome to join me."

"Thanks. But I don't think we should be seen together yet. Go ahead. We'll talk after your meeting with Mister Abel." She pushed the door shut, so it appeared the discussion was ended. Sometimes the woman did not seem very sociable. Most times, for that matter.

Trace had spotted a ramshackle restaurant on a side street earlier in the afternoon, and that was where he headed. It was at first glance uninviting with a warped, unpainted board front and a window so covered with dust and bird poop, a man couldn't see through. The printed sign in barely legible letters designating the establishment as "The Wrangler" had even been nailed on lopsided. But the flow of traffic in and out of the eating place told Trace the restaurant was one of those that sold food, not atmosphere.

The interior of the restaurant was no more elegant than the outside, but his culinary judgment proved accurate. He enjoyed an excellent meal of beef ribs, beans and fried potatoes, topped off with a huge slice of apple pie. The restaurant's capacity was no more than fifteen people, forcing him to share a table with several strangers, but nobody came to the place for conversation. Customers ate quickly, and the dishes were cleared as the last forkful hit the diner's mouth, signaling it was time to move on to make room for the next patron.

When Trace stepped out of the restaurant, only a sliver of sunlight lingered on the western horizon. He returned to Front Street and strolled with feigned leisure along the boardwalk toward Jubal's Livery at the opposite end of town, furtively scrutinizing the other occupants. He was always uneasy about a rendezvous—and he had more than his share during his tour with Pinkerton. A clandestine meeting usually promised information, but on a few occasions, he had run into ambush.

He caught a glimpse of one man, hat pulled low on his forehead and head sunk into his shirt like a turtle, leaning against a storefront on the opposite side of the street. He had a holstered pistol slung low on his hip, telling Trace he was a gunfighter or wannabe. He walked past a scrawny mustachioed cowboy, wearing a hip length cowhide jacket, leaning against a hitching post and lighting up a cigarette. The man appeared unarmed and, barely looking up, gave a friendly nod, and Trace returned a "howdy."

When he reached the livery, he took note of the shadowy forms of two men standing near the horse corrals, to all appearances checking out the dozen or so occupants. He could not tell if they were armed or not now that the sun had all but disappeared. He made a sharp turn and walked along the side of the stable to the rear, pausing before reaching the corner and touching his fingers to the grip of his Colt before stepping out into the open.

There was no one waiting outside the entrance, so he warily crept into the stable. "Good evening, Trace. Been awhile."

Trace turned to the sound of the voice and saw the lean form of former sergeant Cain Abel slip out from behind a stack of prairie hay. A man of average height, Cain, like himself, had maintained his Army weight. The sallow-faced man with black hair had added a tuft of chin whiskers to his thin moustache. Trace could not remember seeing Abel out of uniform, and it was strange, somehow, seeing him in cowhand garb: leather vest, ragged denims and the like. The last time Trace had seen him was at Fort Sill, however. "Hello, Cain. I couldn't figure out who'd invited me here till I got the message from your Long Branch friend."

"Sadie? Yeah, she's my friend. We trade favors now and then—although she prefers cash. Bet she squeezed you for some, too."

Trace shrugged. "We got business. Let's get to it." He moved deeper into the stable, away from the open entryway, not liking his exposure to the moonlight there.

"We got business if you got money."

Trace patted the looped pouch attached to his belt. "You can count it when you tell me enough to convince me you know something my client's interested in."

"Don't trust me?"

"No more than you trust me. We're not soldiers on a battlefield anymore."

"No, we ain't that. But sometimes fighting redskins is a party compared to battles we get into out in the civilian world."

"Tell me about your battle and why you baited Con Wheaton. Is his granddaughter alive or not?"

Abel stepped to within a yard of Trace and leaned in and spoke, his voice not more than a whisper. "I think she's alive, but I can't swear to it."

"Think? That's not worth two thousand dollars."

"I'll give you a taste of the information I got. If it ain't enough to whet your appetite, you can walk away."

"Spit it out."

"The gal I'm talking about had her seventeenth birthday in April. She's a red head with eyes blue as the sky. A looker. A real looker. Like the woman that claims to be her ma."

"But what makes you think she's Miranda Wheaton? What you've told me doesn't prove a thing."

"I'm not trying to prove. That's your job. I'm offering a lead."

"I haven't seen it yet."

"I had a spy in the house. The gal's mom has a book full of newspaper stories about the Wheaton girl's kidnapping stashed in a little chest with a tiny kid's clothes and pictures of the girl, three of them showing her naked at different ages. I didn't see them myself, but it sounded sick. That's where the pendant was—in the chest. My spy took the pendant. Left everything else there, just the way it was. Take my word, this woman—the so-called mother—was planning to make some money off this red-headed gal. Big money."

"How do you know this?"

"Like I said. Have to take my word for it. I know. I worked for these folks for five years."

"I want names and places."

"I want my money."

A gunshot cracked, echoing through the stables, and Abel's head jerked back, spattering blood on Trace's face before he toppled over. Trace crouched and backed against a stall gate, reaching for his Colt, as his eyes searched for the source of the gunfire. He saw the assailant's silhouette against the moonlight in the open back entryway and ducked when another shot was fired, striking the wood panel and driving splinters into the side of his neck. A third shot from outside the building turned the gunman around, just before another bullet struck the man, who screamed and crumpled to his knees and then fell forward.

The horses were whinnying and stomping in their stalls, not panicked, but agitated and spooked by the racket. Trace moved out of the shadows and knelt next to Abel, whose body was still as a stone. A check of the man's pulse confirmed that their interview had concluded. He started to get up when another burst of gunfire came from the other end of the stable and a piece of lead dug into the packed earth a few feet from his knee. Trace got off two wild shots at a shadowy figure moving away from the stable. He heard the bark of two more rapid gunshots and a moan before the other man went down.

"Trace, are you okay?" It was Darby's voice.

He stepped out into the runway and saw the skinny cowboy walking his way from the front of the stable—or the person he had thought was a cowboy. "Darby? You were the cause of all that commotion?"

"Two for two," she said matter-of-factly, as she approached. "Sorry I was late. I saw two men headed this way, and they split, one going toward the front and the other angling off to the back. I couldn't be certain they were up to no good. I figured to take out the back one and warn you about the other. But he got off his shots first, so I took him down and ran for the front."

"What's going on here?"

Trace recognized the deep baritone of Jubal Snyder's voice calling from the front entrance. He stepped forward with arms raised. "Jubal, it's Trace Crockett. My partner's with me. Come on back and I'll explain."

There was silence, and then an oil lamp lit up the far end of the building and started moving their way. When Jubal reached the detectives, he saw the prone body with the bloodied head of Cain Abel stretched out on the stable floor. "Oh, shit. What in the hell happened? I was coming in to talk to Cain about work I needed done tomorrow, and I find a dead man out front. Now this."

"You'll find another at the back of the building. You're entitled to an explanation. My partner and I are detectives with the Pinkerton Agency. I had a meeting here with Cain tonight. Somebody didn't want us to have that meeting and followed me here—or was waiting. I don't how they knew. But Darby had my back and likely saved my life. Unfortunately, the gunman got to Cain first."

"What's so important somebody'd go after Cain?"

"He said he had information that was going to solve a fifteen-year-old abduction case involving a little girl." Trace gave Jubal a nutshell rundown of the Wheaton case.

"Never heard of it, but I was finishing out my Army enlistment back then. Did Cain help any?"

"Not much. He started to give me the important low-down when gunfire broke out. I'm not sure where we go from here."

Darby had remained quiet and stepped back into the light's fringe. Jubal turned to her. "You're the one what shot the gunmen?"

"Yes, sir. I was backing up Trace."

Jubal cocked his head and eyed Darby suspiciously. "I'll be damned. You're a lady, ain't you?"

"I try to be."

"Never seen a woman with a moustache. Never seen one do that kind of shootin', for that matter." He turned back to Trace. "Now, how do we explain this to the city marshal?"

Trace said, "I'm surprised somebody didn't come running when they heard gunfire."

"Nah. Goes on all the time around here. Marshal Carper don't come unless asked. His knees shake when trouble brews. He'd rather we just wrapped this up in a package for him. Give him a reason to overlook it."

"We'd rather not get mixed up with the law on this investigation—unless you recommend Carper as somebody who might help us."

"No. We had Bat Masterson or Wyatt Earp in Dodge during the late seventies. Those guys would've jumped right in. This feller jumps out. If he knows something, he'd be afraid to tell you."

"So," Trace said, "two dead men outside the stable. We don't want to cause trouble for you. This is your call."

Darby interrupted. "Jubal turns off his lantern and goes home. Trace and I go back to our rooms at the Dodge House. Jubal comes in late because he thinks Mister Abel is working. Somebody else finds the bodies and goes after the marshal. Or, if they don't, Jubal reports it. We're all dumb about what happened here. Jubal can't figure it out."

Trace asked, "What do you think, Jubal? Are you okay playing dumb?"

"Dumb's my middle name. Jubal Dumb Snyder." The stable went black.

Chapter 14

DARBY ASKED TRACE to distract the desk clerk while she sneaked in the back entrance to the hotel and raced up to her room. As it turned out, subterfuge was unnecessary, because the clerk was in the dining room apparently trying to charm a young woman who looked desperate to escape. If he did not already have an appointment, Trace thought he might have come to her rescue.

After Darby disappeared up the stairway, Trace followed her. Darby's door had been left ajar for him, and he knocked twice, opened the door, and walked in.

"Sit down," she said. Darby sat on the edge of her bed and was peeling off her fake moustache, looking a bit ridiculous as the tip of her tongue licked the flesh above her lips. She smiled sheepishly, "Honey. Got a dab from the kitchen. Works as good as glue and easy to clean off. I used glue once and ended up with a scab moustache."

"You make a habit of wearing fur on your face?"

"As a child, I wanted to be an actress, and I earned small parts, and even a major role or two, for amateur stage productions in Boston and did make-up for other actresses and actors. No prima donnas in small theatres. You do a bit of everything. I decided not to starve for my art and took up teaching. But I've found acting quite useful in my detective work."

"You had me fooled when I walked past you on the street. I'm glad you were there tonight. You saved my life, possibly twice. Thanks."

"You're quite welcome. I wasn't about to let my bonus slip away."

She tossed her hat on the bed beside her and shook her hair loose. This was the first time he had seen the beautiful gold mane that flowed to her shoulders. He watched as she gathered it and tied it into a ponytail with a little cord. Hair down, eyeglasses abandoned and a smile on her face, she was every bit the stunning woman he had suspected she was hiding. "That was darn good shooting at the stable. Are your spectacles fake, too?"

"No. I am what they call farsighted. I can see distances, but I have a difficult time reading without my specs.

But, so much for my disguises, what about the late Cain Abel? Did you learn anything? I assume you held onto the money."

"Yeah, I've got the double eagles in my money bag." He tapped the pouch clinging to his belt. "But I didn't learn much before the gunmen turned up. It appears Cain worked for a man and woman, who may have been holding the Wheaton girl all these years—if she is, in fact, Miranda Wheaton. However, I didn't learn any names, and I have no idea where they are to be found."

Darby said, "They must not be far from Dodge if Abel wanted to meet you here. It's fair to assume the gunfighters showed up because of concern about what Cain knew. It seems unlikely their boss would have been many miles away."

"Tomorrow, we start with what little we have. One of us should talk to a photographer, if the town has one. Cain says daguerreotypes and photographs—naked ones . . . or nearly so—have been collected of the girl over the years and kept in a chest with the pendant and little girls' clothes."

"I brought one of the girl's photographs. If we could compare that to one taken not many years later . . . ."

"It could be serious evidence to identify the young woman."

Darby said, "There is a photographer in Dodge. I saw a sign off Front Street. Of course, any photographs might not have been taken here, and the photographer may not have a copy or any records. The odds of the same photographer being here over a fifteen-year period wouldn't be all that great."

"I'd like to have the photographer take a photograph of Cain and the other two dead men before they're buried on Boot Hill. Somebody might know where they worked if it was a place nearby," Trace said.

"Let me take the photographer," Darby said. "Maybe you can check the saloon gossip tomorrow and talk to Sadie again. From what you said, she and Cain were more than casual acquaintances. We both need to think about this. We could meet for breakfast if you're okay dropping the charade now."

"I'm fine with that. No point at this stage, and it might be wise for us to stick a little closer in case there are any more guns looking for us out there."

"Breakfast at eight? I'll meet you in the dining room."

Trace took that as his dismissal and stood up. "Yeah, I'll be there."

Chapter 15

TRACE WAS SURPRISED to find the door to his hotel room unlocked. He had no concern that he had left it unlocked when he departed earlier in the evening. This was someone else's undoing. He eased the Colt from its holster and readied it to fire. He pushed the door open but stayed in the hallway, stepping off to one side, waiting for a gun blast to drive a bullet through the empty doorway. Silence.

He waited. Then lamplight appeared from within his room delivering at first a dim, hazy illumination and then rising enough for visibility. Still gripping his Colt, he inched around the door frame and peered in. He could not believe it. She was lying on his bed, shoes off, but otherwise clothed, although the skirt of her dress was pulled indecently above her knees. He holstered his gun and stepped in, closing the door behind him.

"Good evening, Audra," Trace said. "If that's your current name."

She scooted up in the bed, pushing a pillow against the headboard and resting her back against it. She also positioned her skirt to cover her tawny, shapely legs, which Trace deemed unnecessary.

"Audra is my 'always name.'"

"But Crockett is not."

She giggled. "A name of convenience. My last name is Scott. As in 'Sir Walter.' I don't use it often, however."

"How did you get in here?"

"The desk clerk. He's desperate to be deflowered. No, I did not oblige him. I told him I wanted to surprise my brother."

"You've got a lot of nerve coming here after stealing my money. You owe me a hundred sixty dollars."

"Less than that. I did pay for your room."

"Your generosity overwhelms me. What the hell are you doing here?"

"Business. Why don't you take a seat? We'll have a civilized discussion."

Trace sat down, wondering how this woman had ended up presiding over his hotel room. He did not need two women running his life.

"I'm seated. Tell me about the business."

"My partner was killed tonight. I'm forced to negotiate a new arrangement."

"Your partner?"

"Cain Abel. We had a business deal."

"Cain? You were in on his scheme? Do you know what he was going to tell me?"

"For the two thousand dollars, I do."

Audra Scott had certainly grabbed his attention. "Tell me about your connection with Cain. Convince me you know something."

"I met Cain at an establishment where I worked. He was employed as foreman for a big cow outfit not far from the town."

"What town? What kind of work did you do?"

"We'll get to that when we talk about the money. Just hear me out."

"I'm listening."

"This cow outfit grew its herds by rustling cattle from the herds that traveled north to Dodge. I don't know a lot about cattle, but it seems Cain's outfit peeled off just enough head from each herd that passed by that either nobody noticed or didn't think it was worth the time and trouble to track the thieves down. The catch was not to get too greedy."

"You're saying Cain was more cattle thief than fore-man."

"I suppose you could say that. But he made the mis-take of striking out on his own and cutting off some of his boss's beef to market on his own. He had a few cow-hands helping that kept Cain's cattle in a canyon and drove them off to market when they collected enough to make it worthwhile. He took half the money and the oth-ers split half. Somebody tipped off the boss. Cain's part-ners ended up dead, and Cain barely hightailed it with his life. I went with him to Dodge."

"I don't understand what this has to do with Miranda Wheaton and her pendant."

"I earned my living as a *fille de joie*."

"Sounds like something to eat."

"Only occasionally. I was a prostitute, a whore, if you will, but I detest those words and won't take kindly to such terms tossed my way. I was associated with a bor-dello, but my room there was only for sleeping. I was very selective about my clients and often provided hotel ser-vices or home visits for those who preferred discretion and could afford me. For a fee, Cain often acted as an agent for customers who required secrecy and did not wish to contact me through the bordello. That's how I learned about the girl we believed to be Miranda Wheaton."

"Cain was your pimp?"

"Don't be uncouth. Agent. He was my agent." She winked and offered a seductive smile that made him want to drop the conversation and join her on the bed.

Trace said, "Let's quit wasting time. You give me names and places, and you earn the money, but I'm not giving you a nickel without the information up front. If you don't want to talk, get the hell out of my bed and out of my room."

"I won't leave. My life is in danger, and it's your fault."

"My fault?"

"I saw the killings at Jubal's before I headed for the hotel. The men that murdered Cain were from the Lazy P. That's where Cain worked. I recognized a third one hiding in the shadows across the street from the livery, and I know he saw me. Robbie Longtree. You can bet he's still in town."

"Longtree? He's been with the Lazy P a long time?"

"Okay. I guess I'm forced to trust you. He was there when I showed up in Stone Creek—that's the town. It's down in No Man's Land south of here. Just across the east border from the Indian Territory and north of the Texas panhandle."

Trace knew about No Man's Land from his studies at West Point. Congress had designated the area the "Public Land Strip," a strip of land thirty-five to forty miles wide cut off from Texas upon the state's admission to the union to comply with the Slave State-Free State balance mandated by the Missouri Compromise. Anything north of the cut-off line was required to be slave-free, but that left a strip over one-hundred sixty miles east and west not attached to any organized body. As he recalled, the borders touched Kansas and Colorado to the north, New Mexico on the west and Indian Territory to the east. It was a bizarre result. The area had no official government or law, and unsavory sorts were reported to congregate in the unofficial settlements there.

Trace asked, "Just out of curiosity, how'd you end up in No Man's Land?"

"My pa and I were in a small wagon train headed west on the Santa Fe Trail seven years back when I was fifteen. Ma had died of cholera, along with my two brothers, a year earlier. Pa caught me naked with one of the boys, beat me with his horse whip and dumped me off in Dodge. See, my mother was half Cherokee, and Pa always called us kids the 'breed's brood.' He'd been looking for an excuse to get me out of his way."

"Can't figure some folks. I've got a streak of Cherokee blood in me—lots of Tennesseans do. Always been proud of it."

"Not my pa. I guess he wanted Ma for his carnal pleasures, but he was embarrassed by her, too, and the kids she birthed. Anyway, I wandered the streets of Dodge for two days, and a couple of stinking cowboys took me for free one night and beat me up afterward. I didn't have a dime—that boy Pa was so upset about got his poke without paying the quarter. I got lucky, and a lady from the China Doll bordello saw me wandering on the street and took me in. I got fed and my whip cuts were cared for."

"That's terrible. I can't believe any father would do that."

She shrugged. "I guess he wanted to start over with a clean slate. He said he wasn't sure I was his anyhow. Ma wasn't like that, but she was a handsome woman, and Pa was always jealous when a man looked at her a second too long. Claimed she was flirting. He hit her more than once for no more than a smile at a friendly man. I never missed Pa for a minute after he dropped me here. But I was scared to death."

"I'm sorry," Trace said, thinking this was one tough woman.

"Short of it is, I learned the business right here in Dodge. Then six months after I showed up, my friend, Estelle—she was the one who found me—told me about Stone Creek. No services for miles around. She wanted to start up her own place there and asked me to go with her. She was like a mother to me. An educated woman. Taught me how to behave for the high-paying customers. Helped clean up my grammar. Some men will pay a big premium if they think they're getting class. That's when I came up with the idea of being a special kind of *fille de joie*—one who performs services selectively and discreetly outside the bordello."

"And you're still in the business?"

"Retired mostly. I have some money and now have the luxury of choosing customers carefully."

"And you're a thief on the side."

"Treasure hunter. My profession led me to the little treasure at the Lazy P Ranch. And your two thousand dollars will let me close up shop for good."

"You saw the girl?"

"No. Nothing like that. She is known as Sarah Pierce, by the way. Last fall, the girl and her mother took a trip back East to look for properties, I think. Cain said the wife was tired of living her life on the godforsaken prairie and wanted to return to people and conveniences, no nearer to Stone Creek than St. Louis. They expected big money soon, and she was looking for a change. They were to be gone a month and the Mexican servant was going with them. They have a cook, and there was not that much for a servant to do in the absence of the ladies. I had pleasured Max Pierce on a few occasions at the hotel in Stone Creek, and he asked Cain to employ me as a servant during Romy's travels. I was to be paid for every night at the nice ranch home whether he required my services or not. Suffice it to say that I earned my fees. He was not a repulsive man, however, and bathed often. He treated me like a queen, never any rough stuff like I'd heard he'd done with other girls at Estelle's place."

Trace's heart started racing when she mentioned Romy. The mention of Max Pierce had told him they were on a hot trail. "Romy? Have you ever met her?"

"No, but I saw a framed photograph of her on Max's bedroom wall of all places. She is quite beautiful. But Max claimed Romy was a cold fish who usually rejected his advances. Of course, that's what all the married men say. Most are probably liars."

"But Cain said he had a spy find a chest. You were the spy?"

"I never thought of it that way. We were making money off my work there, but I always keep an eye out for bonuses."

"Like what you find in a man's wallet or hidden in his bag?"

"Well, yes, sometimes. In this case, I added a dash of chloral hydrate to Max's drink one night—almost overdosed him. He slept till almost ten o'clock the next morning. I had all the time I needed to search the house. That's when I came across the chest stashed in Romy's closet. They did have separate bedrooms, so Max might have been telling the truth when he said he had to beg for a poke."

"Chloral hydrate. That's what you put in my drink?"

She shrugged. "It's easy enough to come by if you know the right doctor. I started using it for clients who showed signs of wanting to get rough. I figured it was better than having to shoot a randy bastard with no manners. No man hits me anymore. One that did is dead."

Audra's eyes told him that she had squeezed the trigger without remorse. "So, you found the chest?"

"Yes, the chest was what got this started. It was a small thing, maybe a foot wide and tall, a few feet long. You could shove it under a bed. Padlocked, but I'm good with locks."

Trace said, "That doesn't surprise me."

Audra evidently either did not catch his sarcasm or chose to disregard it. She continued. "I read the old newspapers. Saw the little girl's nightgown. And there was a dress and shoes that must have been taken with her. The pendant was in a little box, so I thought it might mean something, and it was gold, so I took it."

"Did you see some daguerreotypes or photographs?"

"Three . . . of a naked girl. The same girl at different ages, maybe five, ten, and fourteen or so. No face or bosoms. Right side view from waist to knees. Photographer was focusing on her hip and bum. I suppose he was trying to catch the half-moon there. But I thought it was extremely weird."

"Birthmark?"

"Seems likely. Is that significant?"

"Could be. Did you learn anything else about the girl while you were there?"

"I started asking Max questions about her, just casual at first. He made a point of saying the girl was no blood relation. Repeated that every time I brought the subject up. He called her his stepdaughter. He raved about her red hair and beauty, her long legs and perfect ass and other female parts. One evening, I put just a drop of chloral hydrate in his drink, enough to loosen his tongue, and then I gave him a serious grilling. Sometimes Max was so confused he didn't make sense, but he's obsessed with Sarah—and not in a platonic way. I'm sure he's been humping that girl, probably for a long time. I don't think Romy's absence is why he required my services."

Trace was stunned. A new complication to work out. He was nearly convinced Sarah Pierce was the abducted Miranda Wheaton, but he wasn't certain the young woman was waiting to be rescued. On the contrary, she might have been near, with the coaching of her so-called foster parents, to making her appearance without the Pinkerton search, if Cain and Audra had not intervened.

Trace asked, "Pierce never specifically mentioned the kidnapping or how Sarah came to be with the couple?"

"No, and after he dropped off to sleep that night, I packed my bags and found Cain at the foreman's cabin and demanded he hitch up a buggy and get me back to Stone Creek. I told him about what I'd found in the chest, and that's when we started planning. We were going to wait a spell before we made a move, and might have waited for the coming cattle drives, but somebody at the Lazy P snitched on his sideline business and he had to make tracks earlier than we planned. A month or so back we rode out together for Dodge."

"How did you come to meet up with me in Kansas City?"

"Cain knew you were a Pinkerton agent and thought it would be safest if someone he'd recognize made the connection for the money and information exchange. That way, he would only show himself when he was certain it was safe. He sent me to follow you there. You weren't that hard to find. He said he was certain you were attached to the Kansas City Pinkerton branch, so I kept an eye on the Pinkerton office during the day. He said you liked to live high on the hog, so I looked for my brother at the two best hotels nearest the railroad station—told the clerks I wanted to surprise you."

"You did. But I don't know why you went through all that trouble."

"Cain worried about the law getting involved, or a bunch of agents showing up to trap the letter sender. I kept track of you in Kansas City and knew you'd be headed to Manhattan, so I got a ticket on the same train. I saw you get on the train in Kansas City, so I hopped on another car. That's when I met Reggie. Kind of a stuffy sort, but he speculates in land and carried a good amount of cash."

"He probably had a lot less when he left Manhattan."

She ignored his remark. "Most of it he deposited in a local bank for purchases, so he still had most of his money when I took the train to Dodge. If I could have stayed another day, it would have been nice."

"I hope you would have paid for his room and breakfast."

"That's not kind. I was perplexed, though. I didn't see you board the train in Manhattan, but I found out you bought a ticket for a private compartment."

"Of course, you did."

"I got off the train before you did, but I didn't see the lady you were with in Manhattan. She had to be a Pinkerton. Somebody came with you, though, or you'd have been a dead man at Jubal's. I was watching when those gunslingers moved in, and then I saw the cowboy sneaking up behind the one at the rear entrance. Just a minute late for poor Cain, though. The cowboy was Pinkerton?"

"The cowboy was Pinkerton, but the cowboy was also a she."

"The lady I saw in Manhattan?"

"Yeah, she likes to dress up some."

"I had a client like that once. Asked to wear my panties and underthings. He said it helped him get the old pole up. I said okay, but he had to pay me double. He gladly paid, and it sure as hell worked. Hard as a rail spike. Didn't matter to me. Believe me, I've seen stranger things in my line of work."

"I didn't mean it that way."

Audra giggled. "You're sure serious tonight. You weren't that way when I first met you."

"I don't want to talk about it, unless you're ready to talk about the money you stole."

She acted again as if she didn't hear him. "Do I get my two thousand dollars now?"

"We will need to talk to my partner first. She may have questions. I need her approval to release the funds. We'll need specific directions to Stone Creek and the Lazy P Ranch. You can go back to your room, and we'll get together in the morning. Hotel dining room at eight o'clock sharp."

"I'm staying here tonight."

"You mean, my room?"

"That's here."

"You can't."

"It's okay. I've seen you naked. You've seen me. We've been intimate, if you prefer the refined description of our past relationship."

"Why can't you go to your room?"

She pointed to the corner of the room, and Trace saw two suitcases. "I moved my stuff in here after the clerk let me in your room. I'm not taking chances."

"What chances?"

"I'm keeping an eye on my money till I'm paid. And, if somebody wanted Cain, that same somebody might be looking for me. I'm putting myself in your custody."

"I'm not a lawman."

"You've got two pistols and a rifle here, and the weird gunfighter across the hall. Besides, you're not the kind to throw a lady to the wolves. You can't help what you are."

"I'll talk to Darby. You can stay with her."

"Do you really want to go through all this again tonight. She's probably sleeping by now."

"There's only one bed."

"Yes, I can see that. There's room for two. We can make this a memorable occasion."

"I'll sleep on the floor—in front of the door. I can barely recall our last memorable occasion. But I do remember the financial outcome." He stepped over to the bed, plucked a pillow off the vacant side and tossed it by the door. "You won't lock the door if I step out to use the privy, I trust?"

"Of course not. You're my gallant knight protector. But we can share the chamber pot, if you like."

After relieving himself, Trace returned to the room and dug out an extra blanket from the closet. He slipped out of his boots and stretched out on the floor, blocking the doorway. He tried halfheartedly not to watch as Audra Scott disrobed teasingly and crawled naked between her covers. His feeble effort was mostly unsuccessful, and it took all his willpower not to listen to the begging from the guy in his britches. She turned off the lamp that had been flickering on the bedside table, plummeting the room into blackness.

"You know where to find me," she said, her voice soft and husky.

He expected to spend a sleepless night on the hard, oak floor, but he buried his head in the pillow and found that the day's events had sucked out the last of his energy, launching him quickly into deep uninterrupted slumber. He did not open his eyes until he felt the cold steel pressed against his temple.

Chapter 16

WHEN HIS EYES opened, Trace saw Audra Scott's face a few feet above his own, her dark eyes cold as ice as she knelt next to him. She had slipped into a flimsy nightgown, but her ample breasts were on the verge of breaking free. Ordinarily, he would have enjoyed the view, but the derringer thrust against his head was a distraction.

"Good morning to you, too," he said. "I'm sorry I overslept. Your gun really wasn't necessary." He felt the pressure against his flesh ease.

"I wanted you to know I could have killed you and taken my money, if I chose. I still could."

"You've made your point very well." She pulled the derringer back a few inches, and like a cat snatching a mouse, his hand sprung up, and his fingers latched on her wrist, twisting it sharply.

She dropped the weapon, lost her balance, and toppled over onto the floor beside him. Shrieking with pain while Trace maintained his vicelike grip on her wrist, she rolled toward him and with her free hand dug her fingernails into his cheek. He dodged away and clambered up, refusing to release his hold.

"You little bitch," he yelled. He dragged her across the room, grabbed her ankle with his other hand and heaved her onto the bed like a sack of grain. He slipped his Colt from his holster and pointed it at Audra, as she lay almost spread-eagled on the bed, wide-eyed, her nightgown pulled up nearly to her waist and one breast emancipated from its shield.

"Listen," she said, her voice weak now, "I wouldn't have shot you. I'm not a killer."

"Next time you'd better kill me. Anybody points a gun at me, I shoot back. No second chances. Man or woman. Got that?"

She nodded her head vigorously, rubbing her bruised wrist now. "Y . . . y . . . yes."

Before he could continue with his rant, he was interrupted by frantic hammering on the door. "Trace. Trace. Open the door."

Crap. Darby. The morning was starting beautifully. How was he going to explain this? He walked to the door and unlatched it, opening it no more than a foot. "Yeah. What do you want?"

"You don't need your Colt. I'm on your side, remember? I heard a commotion in here—and a woman's voice. Now, let me in."

He holstered his Colt, and before he could respond, Darby threw her shoulder against the door, yanking it from his grasp, and pushed it open and stepped in. When she saw the nearly naked woman on the bed, she froze, and her mouth opened and eyes widened in astonishment. "What in the hell is going on here?"

"It's not what it looks like. I can explain."

She wheeled and faced Trace, fury written on her face. "I saw this woman. In Manhattan at the restaurant. You said she owed you money. Are you taking it out in trade? This is totally unprofessional. You're on assignment. I've a mind to wire the agency for a replacement."

"You've got this all wrong. This is Audra Scott. She knows all about our case."

"I'll bet she does."

"No, no. She's the source of the information we're after. She was Cain Abel's partner."

Darby frowned and turned back to Audra who now was sitting on the edge of the bed, having tugged the gown over her hips and errant breast. "Is he making this up?"

Audra seemed intimidated by Darby. "No, ma'am. We've been discussing your search for the girl."

Darby was silent for a time as she studied the woman. "I suggest you both get dressed. It's almost eight o'clock, and I'm hungry. I will meet you both downstairs for breakfast. Get yourselves decent and don't keep me waiting." Without another word, she headed for the door.

When she was gone, Trace looked at Audra and shook his head with disbelief. "I think we'd best get dressed and get downstairs. Your reward and my job are at stake."

"I need a bath."

"Me, too. And a shave. Later."

"She's like a damned old grizzly."

"I wouldn't disagree. And while we get dressed, we've got to get our stories straight."

"I told you the truth. From beginning to end."

"I'm talking about how we came to know each other before Dodge. I don't want her to know I slept with you in Kansas City—or that you made off with my money."

"That's probably best left unsaid."

"I'm glad we agree on that. But how do we explain our knowing each other?"

"We hardly did. But that damn grizzly would sniff out a lie. I say we tell her nothing."

"But she will try to get it out of us," Trace said.

"I'm not telling her anything. It's not relevant, so it's none of her business. Keeping your mouth shut was always part of the stock in trade in my occupation. She won't get anything out of me as far as the two of us are concerned. You say whatever suits you."

Trace decided that Audra Scott was a smart lady, and, now that she had regrouped some, she might hold her own with Darby.

Chapter 17

D ARBY SAT AT a corner table in the small hotel dining room, facing the entryway, as she waited for Trace and the young woman to appear for breakfast. There were only a few other patrons in the dining area, most hotel occupants likely having departed to catch a train or start a workday. She had told the waiter she would wait and order after her guests arrived, but he had offered a cup of fresh coffee, which she gladly accepted. While she sipped tentatively at her cup, she thought about the recent development.

She hoped Trace had been telling her the truth about the new contact. After Cain Abel's death, they needed a break in the case, or the detectives might run in place for days. She tried to make sense of Trace's hosting the woman in his room this morning. Audra was a stunning creature, probably age twenty-two or twenty-three, a few years younger than herself, Darby guessed. Voluptuous for such a tiny thing. She supposed most men would be willing to bed the woman, given the opportunity. And she had no illusions that Trace Crockett would be immune to such charms. Handsome devil that he was, though, he likely did not lack for female volunteers.

Still, the atmosphere in the hotel room had yielded few clues. Trace, except for boots and coat, had been fully dressed, with gun belt on, and a pillow and blanket had been tossed on the floor near the door. The bed had been slept in, but the woman was attired more for lovemaking than sleeping. She told herself that Trace's off-duty time was none of her concern, and she had a few second thoughts about her angry outburst. Yet, on a Pinkerton assignment a detective was truly off-duty only at the risk of the destruction of the mission—or even his or her life and a partner's.

She looked up and saw Trace in his perfectly tailored suit enter the room with Audra Scott, her hand resting on his forearm. Audra, dwarfed by the tall, rangy Trace, walked with poise and was tastefully dressed in a high-necked, white blouse and gray skirt. Darby was eager to hear what Audra had to say.

Trace pulled out a chair for Audra and seated her before he sat down. Darby remembered he had done the same for her when they had dined together. It was obviously an instinctive thing, and she concluded that at his core, regardless of his occasional uncouth and unruly behavior, Trace was a gentleman. Not surprising, she supposed, given his wardrobe preferences and his West Point background.

"Good morning," Darby said when the newcomers were both seated. "First, I would like to apologize for my abruptness earlier. I suggest a fresh start." She extended her hand to Audra, who was seated to her right. "I'm sure Trace has told you, I'm Darby Maguire. I hope we can be friends."

Audra seemed surprised at the greeting but replied, "I would like that. I'm Audra Scott, also known as Audra Crockett." She quickly explained. "I told the desk clerk I was Trace's sister in order to obtain a key to his room. You should know that I was an uninvited guest in his room."

A skinny, tow-headed waiter, who appeared to be no more than a schoolboy, cleared his throat and placed coffee cups in front of Trace and Audra. "Coffee?"

Trace nodded. "Thanks."

Audra touched the waiter's arm and smiled, "Thank you, dear. What's your name?"

His cheeks blushed, and his shaky hand caused the pot to splash a dribble of coffee over the edge of her cup. "Taylor, ma'am. I'll get something to wipe up that spill."

"No need, dear." She dabbed at the little spill with her napkin.

She treated him with another smile, and Darby could see that Taylor was already in love. Some women could do that to men—young, old and in between. Darby admitted she was not one of those.

After Audra's little flirtation with the waiter, they placed their orders. While they waited, they made awkward small talk for several minutes before Trace directed the diners to business. "Audra knows we're Pinkerton operatives. She's been following me since before I checked in with the Kansas City office. She was Cain's partner and has all the information he was going to sell us. She's agreeable to making the exchange. I told her I had to discuss this with you, but she's told me things that make her credible."

Darby considered the possibility she might owe Trace an apology. Perhaps he had not been off-duty last night. She turned to Audra. "Why don't you just tell me what you told Trace? Then we can talk about this with us all starting from the same place."

Audra said, "Well, I first became involved in the story at Stone Creek in a place called No Man's Land. It began when I met Cain Abel."

She recited the story like a college lecture, Darby thought. Emotionless, matter of fact, speaking of her career as a prostitute without embarrassment or apology. Audra was obviously an intelligent woman. As a former schoolteacher, Darby could not help but notice Audra's near perfect grammar. She wondered how a woman like this could end up in a bordello, but then chastened herself for giving in to stereotyping. Who knew what private hells led a person to any place? She had tried to escape her own hell by heading west. Of course, the ghosts chased after her.

Darby decided to save her questions for later and allowed Audra to relate her story without interruption. They paused only when breakfasts were served: sausage and a stack of hotcakes with hot maple syrup for Trace, fried eggs, bacon and biscuits with jam for the women. Audra continued talking between bites and finished her tale soon after they had eaten. She then looked at Darby with expectant eyes, doubtless preparing for a barrage of questions.

Darby pondered what she had been told. She sensed that details were missing and had been glossed over. She assumed that Trace could fill in some of the blanks about his relationship with Audra. He probably would not. Oh, well. She knew about secrets, too.

"You've earned half the money," Darby said. "But we've got to know more. How do we find these people? Will you lead us there? We can't verify your story without locating the young woman."

"I want protection if I do that. Whoever killed Cain may be after me."

Darby asked, "Why would they even connect the two of you?"

"Max made the deal for me to stay at the house through Cain."

Trace spoke. "I've been thinking about this. Cain didn't get shot for cattle rustling. Too much coincidence they took him out when he was talking to me. They could have waited till later. Seems more likely they would have taken him back to the Lazy P so the boss could have seen him strung up."

Darby said, "That makes sense. So you're suggesting somebody knew what he was up to and decided to put a stop to it?"

"That's what I'm thinking."

"But how would they have known?"

Audra said, "Others knew I was at the ranch with Max. The cook. A few of the cowhands. Talk would've got around. Somebody who didn't like Max might have put a bug in Romy's ear when she got back."

Darby said, "That would have got Max in trouble, if she cared."

Audra said, "She cared. She didn't want him, but she didn't want anybody else to have him either. He was her property."

"Could she have known someone had been in the chest?"

"I suppose that's possible. If she checked the contents, she would have found out fast that the pendant was gone."

Trace said, "Everything you've said could have happened by now. Max might've spilled the beans about a guest in the house if Romy found the pendant was gone and confronted him about it. But none of this tells them that Cain had a plan to cash in on the Wheaton girl, or how or when."

"And you have it figured out?" Darby challenged.

"Not entirely, but somehow they must have learned that the Pinkerton Agency was looking into the abduction. If the gunmen were watching Cain to see if he made contact with an outsider, they tagged me as a possible

Pinkerton. Now that the three of us have been seen together here, it's safe to assume we're all targets. Those two didn't come here alone. There are at least one or two more. We're being watched. Count on it. Now, who sicced the dogs on us? Word had to come from Manhattan. Nothing else fits."

"But who?" Darby asked.

"I don't think we've got to answer that yet. But we'd better get to that gal fast. If she's Miranda Wheaton, and somebody in Manhattan doesn't want her found alive, her life is in danger. She might disappear real quick."

Darby gave Trace grudging credit. He had sorted out the possibilities and quickly taken them back to the start of their journey. He didn't name his suspect, but Elisabeth Denney was likely at the top of his list. Darby remembered vouching for Wheaton's assistant, and Trace was kindly not rubbing her nose in a possible misjudgment.

"Audra," she asked, "does Stone Creek have telegraph service?"

"Yes, it sits about twenty-five or thirty miles west of Fort Supply, and the wire comes out from there and dead ends at Stone Creek. Lazy P headquarters is five or six miles from town on twisted trails—on the fort side across the border in Indian Territory, but most of the

Lazy P's claimed land is in No Man's Land where Stone Creek sits."

"How far is Stone Creek from Dodge?"

"Hard to say. As the crow flies, eighty miles maybe, but Cain claimed it was a long two days at a fast lope with a spare horse to get to Dodge by horseback. Cain and I took the best part of three days last trip, but we didn't have extra horses. It took five days when Estelle and I first went there by buckboard, carrying all our belongings. There's lot of hill country between here and there. Some dead-end canyons to watch out for and a fair number of creeks to cross. Ground gets rugged as you work south. There are two big rivers. The Cimarron is near the Kansas and No Man's Land border, cuts on both sides, and not much further you hit the Beaver River. Some call it the North Canadian—it leads to Fort Supply eventually. They're no trouble to cross if there's no flooding, but this time of year rain can move in fast."

Darby said, "You need to set up a bank account here in Dodge, Audra. We'll deposit a thousand dollars in it now, the rest after we verify the information and locate the young lady who may or may not be Miranda Wheaton. Fair enough? We'd expect you to go south with us on our search." She looked at Trace. "That okay with you, Trace?"

He nodded approval.

Audra said. "I have an account set up. I brought all my money with me to Dodge because I knew I was finished with Stone Creek. Maybe one of you can go with me to the bank."

Darby said, "We're going to need a chunk of the balance of that cash and make a dent in our expense money in order to rent horses and get outfitted for the trip south. I'll wire the home office to make bank arrangements for more funds."

Trace said, "I think that's a good idea. A request from me might slow down the process some. I'll go talk with Jubal Snyder and deal for horses and tack. We'll need bedrolls and gear and whatever weapons you ladies are comfortable with. It will take today to get ready. I suggest we ride out before sunup tomorrow. Why don't you let me have the chat with the town's photographer? You can send the telegrams to anybody you think needs to be informed of anything. I suppose Pink should know our destination."

"I'm okay with that."

"The food's not so great here, but I like the logistics for keeping an eye out for would-be killers. I suggest we meet back here at noon, and we can talk about getting provisioned for the ride."

Darby said, "In the meantime, Audra can move her things into my room, if she wishes."

"It might be more proper," Audra said.

Trace rolled his eyes, "Yes, above all we must be proper. Can't sully the Pinkerton reputation."

Chapter 18

TRACE'S FIRST STOP was at Jubal's Livery. He was glad to see that the carnage from the previous night's gunfight had been removed. It appeared most of the horses had been turned out into the corral and that someone had tossed hay in a feed bunk that stretched along one side. He peered into the stable and caught sight of Jubal, pitchfork in hand, cleaning stalls at the back end, only a few paces from where Cain had gone down.

"Jubal," Trace called, walking down the runway.

The livery owner turned and waved, leaning his pitchfork against a post, then stepped toward Trace with a welcoming smile and hand extended.

As they shook hands, Trace asked, "Any problems with the law after last night's gun party? If there are questions, I can talk to the town marshal."

"I talked to him. Somebody found the body out front early morning and rousted out the old fart. He sent his deputy to fetch me, and, since I didn't know nothing about it, they called in the undertaker to cart off the corpses. I said I'd pay for plantin' poor Cain out on Boot Hill, but the others was up to the county. Old Silas—he's the undertaker—whined about that. Said they was on my property, and I should see them buried proper. County doesn't pay shit for burying, and I admit the poor devil gets more than his share of those. Anyhow, I don't think the marshal was going to look too hard to figure it all out unless somebody complained."

"My partner and I are going to be heading south to the Lazy P. Ever heard of it?"

"Yep. It's in the Indian Territory, at the east edge of the skinny panhandle that runs between Kansas and Texas. Took some horses down to Fort Supply a few times. Went by the place. Stopped once to see if I could pay to grain and hay my herd before I went on to the fort. Lady that claimed to own the place ran me and my boys off. She weren't hard to look at but mean as a cornered bobcat. She had some tough-looking gunslingers backing her, and I wasn't looking for trouble. Just beat the hell out. They was sure spooky about strangers, though. Don't expect a neighborly welcome."

"Can we rent some horses and a pack mule? I'll pay a dollar a day each above your usual rate for your best and leave cash security for their return."

"Well, I'd trust you for the return but given your line of business, the security would be welcome. Yeah, I got some good stock out in the corrals, and you being ex-cavalry, I'm betting you'd like to make the picks. How many do you need?"

"A pack horse and three mounts with some stamina. A good-sized horse for me. The other riders will be lightweight, so size is less important."

"Well, let's go take a look. I think I know which horse you'll be riding, but I'll keep my mouth shut."

Outside, Jubal pulled the gate open just enough for Trace to slip into the corral. He waited outside with three halters hanging from his hand, a booted foot propped on a fence board while he watched. Trace strolled several times around the corral's interior, selecting prospects before he eased in among the horses for a closer look, talking softly, touching and probing a few to check their spookiness. Not surprisingly, Jubal offered some quality animals. He walked over to the fence and reached between the boards, and Jubal placed a halter in his hand. He moved in among the herd and haltered a tall, thick-muscled, buckskin stallion and led him to the gate. Jubal opened it and took the horse.

"I guessed right," Jubal said, grinning as he handed Trace another halter.

Trace quickly retrieved a blood bay gelding and chestnut mare. They led the horses back into the stable and hitched them in stalls. "We head out in the morning. I'll want the other riders to come over with me this afternoon to get acquainted with their mounts. I saw you had another corral with pack animals. Choose one, would you?"

"Sure will. I got a mule I call 'Dynamite.' A bit on the ornery side—he'll nip you if you don't give him enough attention, but he can carry a good load, and he's tougher 'n a boot. That little mare you picked is fast as a cut cat. Handles good. Wouldn't carry a big rider so good, but I don't know your saddle partners."

"The mare's not going to be carrying much over a hundred pounds, I'd guess."

"You taking a kid down there?"

"A lady will be riding that horse."

"Let me guess. That little gal would be the one that come by to talk to Cain a few times."

"Yep. That's likely the one."

"Now there's a female that takes a man's breath away."

And his money, too, Trace thought. "You have an inventory of saddles and tack for rent, too, I assume."

"I do. If you're bringing the other riders back, you can all try them out and pick what suits you."

"We'll do that. I'll settle up with you when we come in later this afternoon."

Trace's next stop was the photographer. The sign above his studio door read, "Smiley Smith, Photographic Creations." Sounded fancy for a cow town, but since there was no evident competition, Trace supposed the name wouldn't matter much. He entered the narrow-fronted building and was greeted by a short, middle-aged man with orange-red hair done up in a bun like some women wore. He estimated the man would tip the scales at three-hundred pounds easy. The toothy smile told him the man was the owner of the establishment.

"I'm Smiley," the man said, reaching out with a fat paw.

Trace shook the photographer's hand. "Trace Crockett." He pulled his Pinkerton badge from his coat pocket and held it out.

"Pinkerton. I've heard about you folks. Frankly, I'd hoped you were a customer."

"I could be. I'm good for five dollars if you'll answer some questions, a gold eagle if I walk away with what I'm looking for."

Trace had not thought the smile could get any bigger, but it did.

"Have a seat." Smith gestured to one of the three chairs in the cubicle-like waiting area. He let himself down with a sigh, barely squeezing jiggling flesh between the arms of a wooden chair. "Not much chance we'll be interrupted here."

Trace took another chair half-facing the man. "How long have you had your place here?"

Smith rubbed clean-shaven, jowly cheeks thoughtfully. "Six, going on seven, years. Good money during the Earp and Masterson years. Sold a lot of stuff to newspapers back east. Corpses and stuff. Now the corpses I photograph are those of respectable, ordinary folks. Get some weddings and family things, but it hardly pays the bills. Thinking of pulling up stakes, but where do I go?"

"I'm looking for a photograph of a young woman, naked or at least half so."

Smith looked at him warily, and Trace realized the man was worried about a trap. He probably took a fair number of naked photographs, and some might mean trouble if discovered by the wrong people.

"I don't do nudes," Smith said, "with only rare exceptions. I'm a Methodist."

"The name 'Pierce' mean anything to you? Maybe three or four years ago?"

"Maybe."

"I'm looking for a photograph of a young woman, maybe fourteen or fifteen years old at the time. Worth two eagles if I walk away with one."

Smith's eyes bulged in disbelief. With a grunt, he unwedged himself from the chair and waddled away, slipping through a curtained door and into the dark. Trace guessed it was the studio area. He didn't know much about photography but surmised there might be a dark room for processing and a small office hidden in the depths of the building. Shortly, Smith emerged from the darkness with photographs in his hand. He walked over to Trace and handed him three photographs for examination, standing in front of him like a guard dog. "The girl's father asked for the poses. Told the girl to do it. She did what he told her. Nothing to me."

They were large, perhaps twelve by eight inches. The photographs had holes punched in the corners and had obviously been hanging on a wall someplace. Trace tried to erase the image of what Smiley Smith likely did as he stared at the images on a quiet afternoon in that back-room. Two were obscene, one with legs spread suggestively with muff in full view and the subject's fingers touching her nipples suggestively. The other showed her backside as she bent over, hands resting on a chair. He could not deny she was beautifully formed, but Sarah Pierce was just a girl, he thought, and he felt perverted just looking at the photographs.

Smith said, "You said 'one.' For two gold eagles. Make your choice."

Trace chose the third photograph, one with a side view, focusing on the right hip. He dug into his trouser pocket and pulled out the eagles and gave them to the photographer with the two remaining photographs. Smith nodded grimly and backed away. Trace got up, and, without a word, walked out of the place.

Chapter 19

AUDRA LAY IN bed, Darby next to her with a few feet between them. It was strange sharing another woman's bed after her professional trysts with seemingly countless men. Not that she was worried about any funny business. Before climbing into bed, Darby had donned a modest cotton nightgown, and Audra had been a bit embarrassed that her only nightwear was the skimpy gown she had worn in Trace's room the night before. Darby had not seemed to notice.

The kerosene lamp still burned low, providing a dusky light. She felt safe and secure here, glad she had come forth and gained protection from the Pinkertons, but she was still nervous about the mission she had signed on for.

"Audra," Darby said, "are you okay?"

"Yeah. A little scared, I guess. But excited, too, the idea of solving a mystery, perhaps helping a young woman. Sarah is Miranda, isn't she?"

"The photograph Trace turned over to me . . . the birthmark . . . the girl's got to be Miranda, beyond a reasonable doubt, as they say."

"And her grandfather died without knowing."

"Yes, it's sad. The telegram from Myles Locke was a shock. I didn't expect that news when I stopped by the telegraph office. I could see that the old man was in bad shape, but he seemed to have an incredible will. I expected him to live to see the results of our investigation. But the lawyer said that our instructions are unchanged."

Audra said, "Trace had everything all organized, didn't he—the horses and everything? Then he came up with the photograph. He figures things out. He's good at his job, isn't he?"

There was a silence, before Darby replied. "Yes, he seems to be. I've never worked with him before. I had my doubts at first."

"I didn't mean you aren't good, too. I'm like you, though. My first impression of him left me wondering."

"Something happened between you, didn't it? Before you and I met?"

"I can't talk about it."

Darby giggled. "I'll bet there's a good story there, but it will keep."

"I can't believe you and Trace haven't worked together before. You do your jobs like you each know where the other fits. Like a team of horses in tandem. And it's fascinating the way you plan things out. I love watching you work. And you are doing something important. I envy you."

"Well, you're a part of the team now, and I think you're going to fit in just fine. And now, we'd better get some sleep. We've got to move out early in the morning. Good night."

"Good night." Audra leaned over to the bedside table and turned the lamp switch till the last flicker of the flame died.

Darby seemed to drop off to sleep instantly. Audra supposed it was something a person learned to do in the detective business. Grab the shuteye when you can. You never know when the next chance will come. But it was only nine o'clock. The night would have just been getting started in Audra's previous life. And it *was* "previous." She was done with it. She would have a good stake when the search for the Wheaton girl was finished. She just had to decide what to do with it.

Darby had included her as a part of a team now. She really liked that thought. But she knew the real team was Trace and Darby, and they didn't seem to be aware of it. They were perfect together, and they were becoming more than detective partners to each other, but neither seemed to see that . . . yet. A pang of jealousy struck her, because for the first time she could remember, she was feeling—really feeling—something for a man. She had bedded Trace that first night because she was attracted to him. Slipping into her bad habits had been secondary.

And she would have welcomed him to her bed last night, finding herself disappointed when he did not join her. If you truly cared for someone and wanted something enduring, friendship and connections of another sort needed to come before carnal pleasures didn't it? She knew things about men that most women probably never learned. But she was close to illiterate in matters of love. She hoped her education awaited.

She tossed and turned a while longer, but soon sleep caught her by surprise.

Chapter 20

TRACE HAD NOT expected Jubal to show up at the stable this early, but the old sergeant-major was already saddling horses when the detectives and Audra arrived. The pack mule was tied not far from the storeroom where the party had stashed food supplies, bedrolls and other gear the night before. At Jubal's suggestion, they would leave their suitcases, carpet bags and excess clothing there for storage. He had promised his three cats would keep the mice and rats out of the stuff.

Trace saw a big, orange tabby cat sitting in the doorway watching the proceedings with interest. He looked like he could handle a good-sized rat easily enough, but Trace wondered if the critter was too well-fed to bother. He figured his suits would require a cleaning to get the barn smell and mouse turds out when he returned, but

Darby had insisted a hotel room was too expensive to rent just for storage.

The women backed off and let Trace command the packing of Dynamite, the mule, and enjoyed a good laugh when the creature bit Trace's shoulder. "Love bite," Darby had commented. When they had everything positioned and tied to a pack rack, he covered the food and gear with a canvas tarp and anchored it down with rope and his favored diamond-shaped hitches. He stepped back and examined the load with satisfaction.

"I'm glad we let you come along," Darby teased. "You may be useful after all."

He turned to the women, who were in remarkably good humor for the grim journey that faced them. They seemed to have formed a comfortable alliance now. He had never ridden a mission like this, military or civilian, with one woman, let alone two, and he was not sure what to expect. He hoped he wouldn't be mollycoddling a couple of powder puffs in the days ahead. It was one thing to fire a weapon, quite another to take on the furies of nature and long days in the saddle. He would find out soon enough, he guessed.

Darby and Audra could almost pass for cowhands, he decided, especially Darby, lean and small-bosomed and attired in denims and a blue cotton shirt. The golden ponytail dropping from beneath her low-crowned hat might betray her, but, from a distance, no one would notice. Audra might pass the distance test, too. Her long, black hair escaped the hat and flowed unbound over her shoulders. She was dark enough to pass for more than quarter-blood Indian. Up close, though, her chest would fool nobody. There was a woman hidden in those male garments.

When they were ready to depart, Jubal pulled Trace aside and spoke as softly as his deep voice allowed. "Didn't want to upset the women folks, but there's two jaspers been watching this place like hungry coyotes. My guess is they're going to be on your tail as soon as you ride out. They've likely been boarding their horses at Clem's at the other end of town, so I can't tell you what they'd be riding. Just watch your back."

"Did you get a close enough look to tell me what they look like?"

"One's tall and skinny as a scarecrow. Got a beard like mine, but it's black and could stand a trimming. The other's shorter, but no fat on his bones either. Dark. Might be part Mex. Thinks he's a gunfighter."

"How do you know?"

"Gun on each hip, slung low. Probably sees hisself as fast draw. Fool will learn the hard way he's not the fastest. Always somebody faster, sooner or later."

"Thanks, Jubal. You've been a friend. Hope to see you in a week or so. If at least one of us doesn't show up in two weeks, I'd appreciate it if you would wire the Pinkerton office in Kansas City. Go ahead and claim the horse rent deposit and sell the stuff in the storage room and keep the money for your trouble—won't amount to much."

"Don't like that kind of talk. I'm planning on getting my horses back."

Trace mounted his buckskin and rode out the stable entrance with the mule trailing on a lead rope behind him. Darby fell in beside him to his right, and Audra reined in next to Darby. He had been pleasantly surprised yesterday afternoon when they visited the selected mounts, and he learned that both women were competent riders and comfortable with horses. Audra, of course, had spent some time horseback on her journey from Stone Creek to Dodge City, but that must've been more than a month ago. He had no idea what riding experience a Bostonian might have, but he doubted Darby had ridden recently, and it had been months since he had been in the saddle for more than an hour or two. It was a good bet there would be three sets of miserable thighs and asses when they called it quits for the day.

They started at an easy walk as they moved onto the open prairie and crossed the wood-planked Arkansas River bridge outside Dodge City, giving horses and riders more time to get acquainted. Trace reined his buckskin nearer to Darby. "Jubal thinks we're going to be followed. He saw two suspicious-looking characters keeping an eye on the stable."

"That's what he was being so secretive about?"

"Yeah. He didn't want to worry the ladies. He's old school. Thinks women need protecting, that sort of thing."

"Yes, Allan Pinkerton's the only man I've met that doesn't think that way."

Trace shucked off what he tried to take as an unintended slight. "Anyway, tell Audra to keep a lookout. Let me know if you see anything. I don't want to bed down tonight worrying about whether somebody's going to jump us. If nothing happens before, I'm going to peel off late afternoon and backtrack some."

Chapter 21

EARLY AFTERNOON, AND Trace had still seen no sign of followers, but they would be hard to pick up in this country. The landscape south of Dodge City had changed from rolling shortgrass hills and fertile river bottomlands to steeper slopes, occasional canyons and rocky mesas as the riders' mounts loped southward. The trail snaked between hills that zigzagged in places and footing was sometimes tricky from washouts and gullies carved by spring rains. The gunmen could be trailing a hundred feet behind and safe from view.

They came to a clear stream that cut through the trail they had been following, and Trace called for a rest to water the horses. The riders dismounted, stretched and moved stiffly as they led their mounts to water. Dynamite did not wait to be led but nipped at the horses' flanks and hips and wedged his way between them to be first at the water source.

Trace looked skyward, worrying about what he was seeing there. They had commenced their journey with a radiant sun blooming from the east with a new dawn. But the azure blue sky had gradually turned to a dirty gray that blocked the sun's rays, and far to the southwest, he could see black and smoke-like clouds roiling, casting dark shadows over the distant landscape.

Audra said, "At most, we've got an hour before a gully-washer hits."

Darby, who had also lived in Kansas for a spell added, "Those clouds sometimes bring twisters. Never been in one, but I've seen the results. We need to be looking for someplace low or a cave to hole up in."

Trace said, "We've got to protect the horses. We can't get stuck out here without them. Ravines could fill up with water if the rain's heavy."

"I know a place," Audra said. "Cain and I came to Dodge this way. Can't be more than a half hour away before there is a little dead-end canyon that veers off to the west. I figured we'd bypass it today, but Cain and I stayed over there our last night before Dodge. No water course through there that I remember. Entrance from the trail isn't more than twenty feet wide, and the widest part of the canyon might be fifty feet at most. Part of the west wall leans in and juts over the canyon floor—gives three or four feet of cover if you're perched below."

"Let's move," Trace said. "Besides shelter from the storm, it might be just the trap I'm looking for."

"What do you mean?" Darby asked.

"If we're being followed like Jubal suspected, we need to put an end to it. I was planning to double back and set up an ambush. If we're having to stop anyway, I'll just wait for them at the canyon's mouth."

"We can both wait," Darby said.

"I'm not trying to cut you out of the action, but we've got to get shelter set up and the animals secured before we do anything else. I thought I'd help with that and then I'd find a spot near the entry to set up a watch post. These men may never show up. If you want to spell me later, you can. We can do shifts. Can you handle the Winchester as well as the Smith & Wesson on your belt?"

"Better."

Audra interjected, "Derringer's the best I can do with a handgun. But you can count on me with that new Winchester we picked up in Dodge. And that shotgun hanging in the loop on Dynamite would feel good in my hands."

"Let's move on," Trace said as he stepped into the stirrup and hoisted himself into the buckskin's saddle.

Audra's memory proved accurate. In less than a half hour, the riders reached the canyon's opening. Audra led the party to the shelter offered by the overhanging canyon wall. There was ample room to stake the horses near the wall and still have room to build a campfire and pitch two of the old Army pup tents they had brought beneath the natural canopy for added shelter.

The canyon floor was forested with oak and cedars and covered with fallen branches seasoned for burning. The hardwood oak had always been Trace's firewood preference, and he quickly harvested enough wood to see them through the night. Some was burning size. The rest would surrender to his axe later. By the time they had the two tents pitched and bedrolls tossed inside, a light rain started to splatter on the canvas. The crackling fire hissed at the assault, but he felt there was enough shelter that the coals would survive. If not, there was nothing he could do about it. He tugged his poncho over his head and pulled his Henry rifle from the scabbard near his saddle and readied to walk to the canyon's entry.

"I'm going to head back to the opening," Trace told his companions. He plucked his watch from his front trousers' pocket and opened the case. "It's three-thirty.

Darby, if you want to relieve me, come on down in three hours. One of you have a timepiece?"

"Always," Darby said, pointing to a leather pouch anchored next to the holstered Smith & Wesson on her belt. "I'll be there. We'll put together some supper."

"I'll cook tomorrow night."

"I'm counting on it. You're still sure you want the fire going? We're almost inviting them to come in."

"That's the idea. We are inviting them." He turned and headed toward the canyon entrance, which he estimated was a bit more than two hundred yards from their campsite. He had tried to keep an eye in that direction while they were setting up, worrying that visitors might show up early. He was confident Darby's guard shift would prove unnecessary. Either the stalkers would show up soon, or they would be forced to grab their own shelter for the night. And there was always the possibility they were a figment of imagination run wild.

When he reached the canyon opening, Trace climbed a protruding ledge of rock about five feet above the trail leading into the canyon. He had noted the spot when they entered, thinking it was high enough give him a decent view of the trail but low enough for him to escape quickly if need arose. Holding his rifle under his poncho, he leaned back against the stone wall and waited.

Chapter 22

THE CLOUDS WERE churning angrily above now, gray and midnight black mixed with sickly green. The rain had faded to drizzle, but Trace knew it was not ended. It was not yet five o'clock, but a dusky shroud had descended over the canyon and surrounding hills.

Trace heard a horse's whinny and a man's angry curse from the trail. Footing was probably tricky with wet stones and sticky clay underfoot. His bet was that the riders had taken the same trail to and from Dodge more than once before and knew about the canyon. Odds were that they would be seeking refuge from the impending storm here, but they would also be wary, knowing that their prey might have sought shelter in the canyon as well.

Trace flattened his back against the stone wall and considered the situation. He was not well hidden at his position once the riders entered the canyon. On the other hand, he would have the upper hand of surprise and reasonably easy targets. He decided to stay put. His first glimpse of the men confirmed Jubal's judgment: the scarecrow and the gunfighter. The scarecrow took the lead and rode into the canyon, followed by the gunfighter. He judged both men to be in their mid-thirties, not kids who didn't know the ropes. Although Trace was partially hidden by oak and cedar branches, the men likely would have caught sight of him if their eyes had not been focused further down the canyon, their attention likely captured by the odor of smoke wafting their way.

"We got 'em," Gunfighter said.

"Not yet," Scarecrow said.

Trace tugged his poncho back to clear his weapons and leveled the Henry in the direction of the intruders. "Freeze, gentlemen. My rifle's pointed right at you. One move for your guns, and I squeeze the trigger."

Both men turned their heads his way, eyes obviously searching for the speaker. But they made no move for their guns. Thunder roared, echoing through the canyon like a cannonade of artillery. Then a bolt of lightning flashed and cracked, and another, lighting up the sky and blinding Trace for just an instant. Gunfighter went for his Colt, getting off a quick shot, as Trace ducked away and fired the Henry twice, drilling lead into the man's gut. Scarecrow's mount, however, spooked by the lightning, had lunged ahead, crashing into the trees and was headed now in the direction of the camp.

Trace positioned himself on the ledge for another shot, taking aim at the hazy form half hidden by the tree limbs, as the rider broke through the trees and undergrowth. He aimed, but suddenly, the rock and earth beneath his feet, loosened by the rain, gave way and launched him into the air. The rifle slipped from his grip and he landed on the canyon floor on his back, his head flinging back and striking a shard of broken limestone. He lay unconscious on the ground when torrents of rains started pouring from the sky.

Chapter 23

"GUNFIRE," DARBY SAID before the downpour commenced. "I'm sure it was."

"I don't know," Audra said, "I thought it might have been breaking branches, or lightning snaps."

"Gunfire." She picked up her rifle, tossed her hat in the pup tent and pulled the poncho hood over her head. "I'm going to see if Trace needs help." She realized now that the devious bastard had put off her shift because he expected trouble early. She was pissed. And worried.

"You can't see anything out there. Wait till the rain lets up."

"And what if Trace needs help? What if he's pinned down someplace? Damn it. He's going to hear about this. Find cover and have your shotgun ready in case the wrong person comes this way."

Darby stepped into the torrent. The wind raged now, and she could only imagine what the force would have been if they had not found their canyon fortress. She moved snail-like away from their stone shelter, slipped once in the mud and dropped to one knee before regaining her balance and pushing ahead. Trees were swaying and bending in the wind now, branches snapping and falling about her. She had another enemy now: the storm.

She paused to listen but heard nothing except the hammering of rain and howling of wind bursting like a locomotive through the canyon. She trudged ahead, stumbling, sometimes falling, until she stopped at the sound of the angry voice. "Stop right there, bitch."

She obeyed, casting her head about to locate the speaker, readying her Winchester. She saw nothing but knew he had to be nearby, or she would not have heard him in the storm. She waited, taking care to keep her rifle hidden under the drenched poncho. Until the arm closed around her neck and began to squeeze. As she started to black out, she dropped the rifle and reached overhead with both hands, clawing frantically, finding flesh and digging fingernails deeply into his face and neck.

The assailant relaxed his grip, and Darby yanked her head free. She started to run but slipped in the mud and fell on her hip. She no sooner got up and recovered her footing than he was on her again, clutching her arm and pulling her to him, so close she could smell his rancid breath. A tall man, taller even than Trace. Skinny but strong. Water dripped off the brim of an already weather-beaten hat, and his face, where she had attacked him, bled faster than the rain could wash it away. She had done damage especially to a ripped eyelid, and his rabid eyes said she would pay.

She struggled to break free, but he held fast, and a fist drove like a sledge into her cheek and eye. She fumbled for her holstered pistol with her free hand, trying frantically to release the holster strap, but the effort was aborted when the fist smashed again into her nose with a sickening crack and she slumped to the ground. She heard the gun roar as she crawled in the mud, trying to clamber to her feet, dazed and on the edge of slipping into oblivion. Her first thought was that she would die now.

Then she felt hands tugging at her arm gently, a woman's voice coaxing her to move. Somehow, she ended up with her back resting against a tree trunk, suddenly alert now with the horrifying pain coming from her nose. Darby opened her eyes to find Audra kneeling beside her, head hovering above her and fingers pressing against her nose, sending shock waves through her entire skull.

"I cut up my kerchief, stuffed pieces in your nose to staunch the bleeding. Keep your head laid back. You're a mess. Got to get you back to the camp. Robbie's horse came right up to me, if we can get you on the critter."

"Robbie?"

"Robert Longtree. Worked for the Lazy P. Let's just say I did some business with him a few times." She nodded toward the bloody corpse lying face-up on the ground a dozen feet away. "Robbie's working days are done. Shotgun about tore him in half. He was after you and didn't even see me come up. I had to move in close so you didn't take some shot."

Audra helped Darby climb into the saddle. "Hold on to the saddle horn," she directed. "I'll lead the horse back to camp." She retrieved her shotgun and Darby's Winchester and cradled them together under one arm.

Darby's mind was clearing now. Trace. They couldn't go back without Trace. "No. We've got to find Trace."

"Yes, we're headed to camp. You're in no shape to look for anybody. And I've got the reins. We'll get you back to camp and settled in. If Trace doesn't show up, I'll go looking for him. Remember, Jubal said there were two men. There could be another one out there."

Audra had taken charge, and Darby, swaying in the saddle and battling the pain that was turning her nauseous, conceded she was in no position to challenge her new friend. "You're the boss . . . for now."

"The storm's letting up," Audra said, as they worked their way past downed trees and broken limbs toward the campsite. "Wind's dying. Rain's steady but not so bad now. I think we caught the edge of a twister. Probably swept over the top of the canyon. Aren't you glad we were here?"

"Not especially."

When they reached the campsite, Audra helped Darby dismount from Longtree's gelding. Darby tumbled awkwardly out of the saddle, and Audra held tight and virtually caught her. Darby thought that the little varmint must be pure muscle. Audra half dragged and half carried Darby to their shared pup tent, pulled back the flap and eased the detective down at the front, giving her some shelter from the steady rain.

"Keep your poncho on," Audra warned. "I'm surprised these puny tents are still standing."

"Army makes them to stand up to anything."

"Certainly not for comfort. I'll be right back."

Audra returned with Darby's rifle, as well as her own shotgun and shell bag and laid them in the tent next to Darby. "You still got the Wesson under that poncho?"

"Yes, but you might want your shotgun."

"I've got my derringer in the little holster against my butt cheek. I'm riding Robbie's horse, and he's got a rifle in the scabbard. I know what to do with it. You can't take off on the run. Bad guy comes, let him get up close and blast away. Hold that scattergun like it's your baby."

"Yes, ma'am."

"I'll saddle the buckskin and take him along. It's not that far, but just in case . . . ."

Darby didn't allow Audra to finish the thought. She refused to consider the possibility that Trace was down or dead, but the fact he had not shown up yet was ominous. "Just find him. Bring him upright in the saddle."

"I will. I promise. And when I get back, I'll work some more on that face of yours. I'll fix you up like new. Know something?"

"What?"

"I can't remember the last time I had so much fun." She wheeled and jogged toward the horses.

Darby thought Audra sounded and acted like she meant what she said.

Chapter 24

Audra, mounted on the black gelding she had inherited from the dead Robbie Longtree, kept to the canyon's edge as she led Trace's buckskin toward the canyon's mouth. The rain showed no sign of easing up, but the wind had stopped its assault on the canyon, and a relative calmness had settled in. As she neared the entry, her gelding whinnied and received a like response from the woods off to her right. Audra slipped her Winchester from its scabbard, readying the rifle to fire.

She could hear the crunch and crackling of brush and limbs as the horse moved toward her, and her gelding nickered again just as a riderless bay emerged from the trees. The horse ambled up to her mount, and they rubbed noses in evident recognition. Audra took the horse's appearance as a positive sign and nudged her mount forward. The greeter, a mare, fell in beside the trailing buckskin and followed.

When she neared the canyon opening, Audra saw the body lying in the mud, facedown and sprawled out like a ragdoll. She dismounted and gave a sigh of relief as she stepped nearer and saw that the form was that of a small fine-boned man. But where was Trace Crockett? She cast her eyes about and saw him no more than thirty feet distant at the base of the canyon wall, perched on a huge slab of limestone, leaning forward with head resting on his knees. He did not appear to be aware of her presence. But he was alive.

Audra walked across the clearing and tied her mount and the buckskin to a few saplings, deciding the bay mare could go or leave as she pleased, and negotiated a path littered with broken tree branches to Trace. As she moved beside him and placed a tentative hand on his shoulder, he still did not respond.

"Trace, you okay?" Then she saw the blood dripping down the side of his head and intermingling with the rain before it disappeared beneath a blood-soaked shirt collar.

"Will be," Trace replied, seemingly unsurprised at her presence. "Doesn't hurt that much. Just dizzy. Weak as a gutted coyote. I try to stand, and I fall back on my ass. Need some time is all."

She ran her fingers through his thick hair, probing for the injury, which she found several inches above and behind his left ear. A gaping wound, still pumping some blood, but more cut than lump, which she thought was positive. "You need some stitching. You got needles and thread in that medical bag you brought?"

"Yep. Can you stitch?"

"I've done my share of it. I was as near a doctor as they had in Stone Creek, me and Suzanne at The Manor. We even dug out bullets from time to time. A patient or two even lived."

Then, as if it just occurred to him, he said, "There was another man."

"Don't worry. That was Robbie Longtree. He's dead."

"What happened?"

"I gave him a taste of scattergun pie. But not before he beat the hell out of Darby. She still needs some help. I left her at camp. We've got to get back to her."

Trace finally lifted his head. "What did he do to her?"

"Broke her nose, for one thing. And she won't be seeing out of her right eye for a few days."

"But she's going to be okay?"

"Yeah. But she's going to hurt a lot for a while—the nose especially."

"Somehow we've got to get back there. Or you go back and leave me here. I'll hike up there when I can."

"I brought horses."

"You did?"

"I'll go get the buckskin and see if we can get you in the saddle."

Trace, with Audra's help, was able to stand long enough to get a foot in the stirrup and swing into the saddle. He told Audra he could handle the reins if she would lead the way. He leaned forward in the saddle, eyes down, and pretty much gave his horse free rein as they rode through pounding rain that had resumed and showed no indication of calling it quits.

When they reached the campsite, Trace slid out of the saddle and stumbled to the shelter of the wall overhang and awkwardly let himself down to the ground. "Give me a few minutes to clear my head. Then I'll help with the horses. Where's Darby?"

"In our tent." Audra had already staked the buckskin. The other two seemed set on staying, so she left them for the time being while she went to check on Darby, who sat where Audra had left her earlier and seemed alert but obviously in pain.

"Trace," Darby said. "I saw you ride in. Where is he?"

"Right here." Trace had crawled over to the tent. "I'll be fine."

"Thank God."

"And Audra, too," Trace said. "She saved our hides tonight."

"Get under cover," Audra said, pointing to the space next to Darby in the tent. "I've got doctoring to do after I unsaddle the horses. Fire's about doused out, too. Once I get that done, I'll put on some coffee and get biscuits baking. You might hurt like blazes, but I don't think either of you is going to die on me."

"I'm fine. I can help," Trace said.

She didn't need him collapsing out in the rain. She wasn't near to being big and strong enough to move a man his size. "You'll stay put. I'm in charge till morning." She pulled what remained of her kerchief from her pocket and tossed it to him. "Hold that against the hole in your head till I can fix it. Don't want what's left of your brains leaking out."

Nobody challenged her declaration of command, so she left her patients and went about her business. She unsaddled the buckskin and the newcomers. She decided she would wait until morning to check the gunmen's saddlebags and bedrolls to see what might be salvaged.

Audra thought it likely there was money stashed someplace, but she would feel more comfortable having one of the detectives witness or make the search. This was a new feeling for her. Why did she care what Trace and Darby thought when it came to her pursuit of an easy dollar? She was even starting to have remorse about the money she had stolen from Trace the night they first met. She promised herself she would pay him back the instant they returned to Dodge City.

Rain had about drowned out the fire, but, using the short-handled camp shovel, she found some surviving coals, moved them up to the edge of the canyon wall and took some of the dry wood they had stored under the canvas tarp with other supplies and soon had another fire going. While she brewed a pot of coffee, she scraped some coals from the rejuvenated fire to set the Dutch oven on and prepared biscuit dough for baking.

While biscuits baked, she took tin cups of coffee to Darby and Trace, who had apparently helped each other out of their ponchos during her absence. Their clothes were still soaked, and she noticed Darby was trembling uncontrollably. She handed Trace both cups of coffee. "Hold these."

Audra reached down and grasped Darby's hand, pulled her out of the tent and led her to the fireside, sat her down, went back to the tent and retrieved the coffee cup. "Stay put," she instructed Trace. "Drink your coffee."

"Yes, ma'am."

Returning to the fire, she told Darby, "We need to get you into some dry things. Do you have a change?"

"One. Rolled up in the knapsack. It's with the others we put under the tarp along with Trace's med-kit."

Audra took the oven hook and lifted the lid on the Dutch oven. The biscuits were browning nicely, so she took the oven off the hot coals. "Can you eat something?"

"I don't think so."

Audra forked a biscuit out of the oven anyway and placed it on a tin plate and sat it down near Darby. By the time Audra returned with the knapsack and medical kit and her own possible bag, Darby had finished the biscuit and washed it down with coffee. Audra said, "Now get out of the wet stuff and into the dry. I'll get a drying rack set up later. Need help?"

"No, I can do that on my own. Audra, I'm sorry you got stuck with this."

"I'm not," she said and meant it. While Darby changed, Audra rummaged through her possible bag and found the little bottle she always carried and plucked it out. Then she checked on Trace. He still seemed in something of a daze, but he was sitting. "I won't be long," she promised.

"Do what you need. At least I'm not taking on more water here."

When she turned her attention back to Darby, she found that the detective had pulled on a dry shirt and was working britches over her thighs. "Sit down when you've finished. I've got plenty of biscuits, and I can heat up some beans. Can you eat some more?"

"No, really, I can't."

Darby sat down, and Audra knelt in front of her. "Let me look at your face."

The blonde detective's face was almost a monster's mask, Audra thought, swollen and bruised beyond recognition. The eye was sealed by puffy flesh, and the nose bloated and misshapen. She gently traced her fingers over the injuries but stopped when her friend flinched and gasped. "Trace has some adhesive tape and cloth pads in the medical bag, and I'm going to tape some padding across the bridge of your nose. It will help cushion against contact for a few days. It's going to be tender for a long time."

"Do whatever you think's best."

After she finished the patch job, Audra thought she would never envy Darby's button nose again, but it was aligned as much as she could get it. She was afraid she might do more damage if she tried to manipulate the nose. She had seen such injuries many times and concluded that Darby's nose might turn a bit aquiline, but it would heal in time and not impair her beauty—at worst, make it less perfect. She doubted that the Darby she was coming to know would give the minor change in her appearance a thought.

"I've got to go pee," Darby said.

"Go further south along the wall, you can still have cover there. When you come back, I'll give you something to help the pain."

Audra poured a bit of coffee in Darby's empty cup and added a few drops of the clear liquid from her bottle. When Darby returned, she handed her the cup and said, "Drink this. It will ease the pain and help you sleep. That's what you need right now."

Darby drank her spiked coffee. "You're spoiling me."

"Let's go back to the tent. Your bedroll's in there, and I'll lay it out "

Audra took Darby's arm and led her to the tent some ten paces away. She noted that Darby was already starting to relax. Trace watched as they approached, seemingly uncertain about what he should be doing. She resolved his uncertainty. "Can you get up and walk to the fire?"

"I think so. Yeah."

"Your knapsack's over there. Get into some dry clothes. Help yourself to biscuits and coffee. When I get Darby settled in, I'll be back and work on your head."

Silently, he scrambled out of the tent, stumbled to his feet and headed toward the fire. She was pleased to see he seemed steadier on his feet now. She crawled into the tent and rolled out Darby's blankets and took her own bedroll out and tossed it in the vacant tent. After she got Darby bedded down, she returned to the fire, where she caught Trace naked as a jaybird fumbling with his shirt. Her eyes could not ignore his admirable physique, but she did not betray her interest. "Put your boots next to the fire by Darby's. I'll keep an eye on them till they're dry. I'm going to get your bedroll and put it in the tent while you get your ugly ass covered." It wasn't close to ugly, she thought. Still as nice as it was in Kansas City.

She found his bedroll, which consisted of a light blanket and a buffalo robe he had purchased at the Dodge general store. He explained he had used one during the Red River War, and it had made for the best ground sleeping he'd ever experienced, serving as both mattress and cover. With the night's chill, she was seeing some sense to his idea now. She took the robe and blanket and laid them out next to Darby, who was sleeping soundly now and likely would be well after sunrise—if they had a sun tomorrow.

Trace was sitting by the fire, a biscuit in one hand and a coffee cup in the other. "You make good coffee and biscuits," he said.

"Thanks. Do you want some beans and bacon?"

"No, thanks. You didn't put anything in my coffee, did you?"

"What do you mean?"

"Like the chloral hydrate you gave Darby."

"You noticed?"

"She was already fading when you brought her to the tent. I don't want any."

"You won't get chloral hydrate even if you beg for it."

"Good. I had a bad experience with it once," he said, chuckling. "Did you know it's not eight o'clock yet?"

"Your watch is working then?"

"Yep. I'd be lost without it. Of course, I've got a back-up in my possible bag."

"Are you serious?"

"Of course."

"You're insane. Turn the left side of your skull toward the fire so I can see the damage to your head."

She tossed a few more wood chunks on the fire to capture more light and then took a wet rag and wiped about the wound to get a better look. The bleeding had stopped. "You bring a razor?" she asked.

"Yep. I don't like stubble on my face."

"Why am I not surprised?"

"West Point thing, maybe. But I guess I never did. Straight-edge and shaving stick are in my possible bag."

She stepped over to the bag, which was propped against his knapsack, picked it up and tossed it to him. He caught it in his lap, opened the bag and fumbled through the contents, finally producing the razor and a cylinder-shaped tin.

"What's in the tin?"

"Shaving stick. I prefer a mug and brush but got to using these in the Army since we were always on the move. Wet the stick of soap and rub it on your whiskers. Better than nothing."

"I'm going to shave the hair around the cut."

"Now, wait a minute."

"Trace, I won't take much off. Your hat will cover it. I need to clean up the area to see what I'm doing and to apply a bandage."

He sighed. "Let's get it done. Just don't scalp me."

She wet down the hair around the wound and rubbed the soap stick on the hair until it was slick. Her fingers were deft and the razor sharp, and Audra quickly shaved away the hair about the wound, leaving a smooth patch of bare skin about four inches square. The vain idiot would not like this, but she thought he might have trouble picking up the spot with a hand mirror. Of course, he could touch it and comb over a good part of the area. She found thread and a needle in the medical bag.

"It's a nasty gash but not as deep as I feared. Four or five stitches should do it. This is going to hurt. Are you ready?"

"Make it fast."

She pressed the needle into flesh, expecting complaint or flinch. Nothing. She ended up placing six stitches in the scalp before she was satisfied that she had closed it nicely. Then she took some tape and covered it with a cotton compress. "Done," she announced. "You were a good patient." *This guy's tough*, she thought, deciding that from what she had seen the past few days that Trace's sometimes genteel manner was just a quirk.

"You could have been a surgeon."

She laughed. "Late for that."

He helped himself to another biscuit from the Dutch oven. "Did you know I got—shall we say—'disinvited' from West Point? Middle of my last year."

"You mean kicked out? I know you mentioned West Point."

"I was given a chance to resign. I thought Darby might have said something. She knows more about me than I do."

"She hasn't said a word about your background. I just know she likes you and respects you . . . a lot."

"Anyway, after I left the Point, before I enlisted in the cavalry, I went back home to tell my dad—hardest thing I ever did. I worshipped him, me and my brother and sis all did. The idea of disappointing him was almost more than I could take. When I told him about my so-called resignation and why, he hugged me—he'd never done that before. We just weren't a hugging bunch, our family. And he said this: 'Trace, just think of all this as a new beginning, and always remember it's never too late for a man to be what he might have been. Not till he's dead."

"I'm not sure I understand."

"I think about what that means all the time, and I suppose you can look at it a lot of different ways. Audra, I want to thank you for all you've done for Darby and me. I misjudged you. You're a good partner to ride the river with, as the mountain men used to say. And I know what Dad said applies to ladies, too. It's never too late to be what you might have been. I'd be the last guy to preach, but think about it."

Chapter 25

TRACE WOKE UP when he felt something stirring beside him. He turned his head and saw that Darby was snuggled close, shivering but still sleeping. He shifted and tugged his buffalo robe around so it would cover her, and then he pulled her close to give her body heat, hoping she would not awaken and misinterpret his actions.

Her head rested on his shoulder, and he looked down, trying to study her face in the dusky light that signaled sunrise was imminent and that the storm had passed. Her nose and the right side of her cheek nearly blended into a single mass almost swallowing her eye socket, the flesh colored with swirls of purple and black. She would not likely find the comparison flattering, but from his angle, she might have been a one-eyed cyclops. The bastard hadn't held back anything when he struck her last night, but, thanks to Audra, he wouldn't harm anyone again.

Audra. It was quiet outside, so hopefully she had gotten some rest. He remembered her directing him to Darby's tent, where his bedroll was already spread out. She had explained she expected to be up and down most of the night and didn't want a tentmate in her way. He still found it odd, although not the least unpleasant.

He felt fine after the dead sleep he'd had, only some soreness on the side of his head. He supposed he should get up and get the fire going and start some breakfast, but his good intentions were thwarted when he dozed off again.

The sun had arrived by the time Trace's eyes opened. A one-eyed creature was watching him, face mostly covered by the robe. She was still pressed close to him as they continued to provide warmth for each other, but Darby's nearness was starting to awaken his imagination. He wondered what would happen if he tried to kiss her. Best not to test his luck.

She inched away just a bit and her head emerged from the robe like a turtle's from its shell. "How did this happen?" Darby asked.

"Audra's idea. I'm not responsible."

"Not professional. We can't let this happen again."

"Nothing happened. We slept."

"I mean we can't share sleeping quarters. Unprofessional. Allan Pinkerton would not approve."

"We've got bigger problems than Pinkerton right now."

She pushed away and sat up. "I've got to pee bad. I'm getting up."

Darby worked her way out of the robe and twisted blankets and crawled to the tent entry, tossing back a flap before she clambered out and disappeared. Trace took her cue and got up and went to the fire coals where Audra was already feeding tinder and sticks and bent over puffing in bursts to bring life. Soon a flame flickered and started to eat the offering. Trace slipped into his boots and helped gather wood, and soon they had a toasty fire.

"It's not that cold," Trace remarked. "It's the dampness. You get any sleep last night?"

"Some. I got up a few times to keep the fire going in case somebody wanted to warm up. But you and Darby didn't seem to have a problem," she said with a mischievous grin. "And then I couldn't turn my brain off, thinking about what you said."

"What'd I say that did that?"

"It's never too late to be what you might have been."

"Oh, that. I guess I was just sentimental about Dad last night. Sorry if I got philosophical."

"Too late. I'm going to be sorting this out for a spell. You could take it that if you wanted to be a doctor, for instance, you're never too old go back and study for it. But I'm thinking it's more about how we face what's in front of us, how we live our lives. If we don't like what we are or what we've done, it's never too late to change. What do you think?"

"Could be. If that's the case, I've still got some work to do."

"Yeah, I sure do, too. I'm sort of jealous of Darby. I've got a notion she pretty much put whatever was chasing her behind her."

"You think something was chasing her?"

"Yeah. Ghosts. Most folks have ghosts."

"I suppose. Some more than others, maybe." He bent over and lifted the Dutch oven lid. "Six biscuits. I can warm these up and fry some bacon if you wouldn't mind doing the coffee. That was good stuff you brewed last night."

Later, the three sat around the fire, soaking in the warmth and eating breakfast. Trace furtively studied Darby as she ate. Appetite was good, and she was moving around fine, it seemed. The nose and eye still rendered a grotesque appearance, Audra had declared the swelling would start to recede by nightfall and that was consistent with his experience on the battlefield. It would be days before her appearance normalized, though.

"Darby," Trace said, "we need to make a decision. Are you going to be fit to ride today?"

"If I don't sit on my face. I don't know why you'd even ask. We've got to be on our way."

A bit testy. "Just wanted to be sure. I thought, at first, I'd just leave those gunslingers for the vultures, but it seems kind of uncivilized somehow. If you'll tell me where you left Longtree, I'll load him on one of the horses and haul him down the canyon to where we left his friend. There's a low spot there and loose dirt and rock about. I'll dig a shallow grave they can share and at least get them covered up. That doesn't mean varmints won't dig them up, but I'll feel like I tried."

Darby said, "Audra and I will clean up and tear down camp. We may need your help with packing the damn mule. He's carrying a good load, and I think he hates women. It wasn't a love bite he gave me yesterday. The bruise on my shoulder matches my face."

Audra asked, "We've got two more horses. Do we turn them loose or take them with us?"

"They look like sound animals. I especially like the black gelding, and you never know when another horse might come in handy. We have plenty of rope, so I can make rope harnesses and we can lead them along with the mule. I guess we can saddle them. I hate to leave good saddles behind."

"The saddlebags," Audra said. She looked at Trace challengingly. "I didn't open them, but there's got to be some money there. Not much, but likely some."

"Go ahead and check the bags out while I'm on burial detail. We'll account for it when we report to Pinkerton or turn it over to a good cause." He got up. "I've got work to do. Point my way towards the body."

By mid-morning, the riders were back on the trail. Footing was sloppy in places, and some of the gullies and ravines, still swollen from the previous day's rain, presented minor crossing challenges. When they stopped shortly after noon to snack on beef jerky and a mix of pecans, almonds and dried berries, they discussed plans for the next stop.

"Are we near the Cimarron?" Trace asked Audra.

"Another two hours, maybe a little more, I'd guess. And I'm worried."

"Flooding?"

"Yes. The water in the gullies is headed, sooner or later, to the Cimarron. And from the looks of last night's clouds, there's likely even more pouring in from west of here. If the storm didn't wander too far south, I don't think the Beaver will be so bad. Usually the Cimarron catches it first."

Trace said, "Once we cross the Cimarron, the maps show we shouldn't be far from Stone Creek . . . a half day maybe?"

"A fair guess, if the Beaver River isn't flooding."

Darby said, "I've been trying to figure out how we reach Sarah Pierce after we get there. I doubt if we've thinned out the hired guns on the Lazy P all that much."

Audra said, "Cain always talked about ramrodding more than a dozen men, but he tended to be loose with the truth in his favor. I think there were two or three real cowhands around the home place when I was there. The gunfighters stayed in an abandoned house a mile from the place and usually just showed up for meals. They did the rustling for the operation, and, of course, a few split off with Cain to rustle from the boss. I suppose they could have taken on a few more guns by now, but it's not like there would be an army."

Trace said, "If we could take the girl, we could outrun them or fight them off. It's getting to the girl that's the challenge."

"Or if we could cut off the two heads of the snake," Darby said. "The gunfighters would lose interest if the money flow was cut. And they wouldn't have anybody to tell them what to do."

Audra said, "I could draw Max Pierce out. I know a stable boy who would take a message to him for a few dollars. I could tell him I'm pregnant and he's the father and that I will tell Romy if he doesn't meet me. I'll think of a place to meet where we can capture him and hold him. I don't know what we'll do with him."

"We'll think of something. What about the other head?" Darby asked.

"We need to get somebody in the house," Trace said. "How easy would it to be to get in the house after dark?"

"Not easy. They have two huge dogs that Max turned out at night to roam the grounds when I was there. They call them wolfhounds. Max said they were Sarah's dogs, and if anybody came around, they'd make a racket and eat the trespasser alive. They were friendly enough to me, though."

"Could a woman ride up to the house in a carriage in the middle of the day and gain entry?" Darby asked.

"The dogs wouldn't be out, and I suppose Romy would let you in if you gave a good reason. I could try it, but she probably knows who I am. I suppose I could use the same story I'll tell Max. Ask for money to go away. But I don't think she'd pay. She'd figure on having me killed."

"No," Darby said. "Your job ends with the note to Max. Time for me and Trace to earn our pay."

"Your face . . . ."

"I'll tell her Max beat the hell out of me. Can I find a dress in Stone Creek? I'll claim to work for your friend Estelle. I want money or I'm going to have Max arrested and go to Fort Supply to have somebody contact the U. S. Marshal's office to investigate their rustling operation. I might even mention that somebody at the bordello was asking about a kidnapped girl."

"That's dangerous," Audra said.

"I could drive the carriage," Trace said, "and wait outside. I'd come running at the first sign of trouble. We can't leave without the girl, though, and she might put up a fight."

Darby said, "Or we could just ride out to the ranch headquarters and tell the woman the truth about who we are and why we're there."

"I don't see how that would be riskier than anything else we've been kicking around," Trace said.

"I wonder," Audra said, "if you would like me to teach you about the magic of chloral hydrate?"

Chapter 26

THE CIMARRON RIVER was spilling over its banks, its red, murky mass creeping into the bottom-lands, seeking out low spots to fill before claiming higher ground. Trace's father had always bragged that his younger son could "swim like a fish," but Trace respected water. Raised within a mile of the formidable Duck River, which twisted more than 280 miles through Tennessee, he had been a river rat during his youth, swimming and fishing along the Duck with friends. Countless times they had lashed poles and fashioned rafts and ventured downriver until they ran aground on a sandbar, crashed against rocks in rapids or abandoned the craft before tumbling over waterfalls.

Looking back, he wondered how he had survived his childhood. Nearly sucked into bottomless whirlpools twice. Slammed by a tree propelling down the swollen river and knocked senseless before recovering just in time to struggle, half-drowned, close enough to shore for his older brother, Jim, to pull him in. He could probably list a dozen such close calls. He still loved the water, though, but with a healthy wariness.

The riders sat astride their mounts on a grass-shrouded knoll overlooking the river. An hour earlier they had passed the twisted uprooted trees and flattened line shack where a twister had gone to ground, confirming that their decision to seek refuge in the canyon, regardless of the inevitable encounter with the hired guns, had been prudent. Now they faced nature's wrath again but could not run from it. Trace studied the bloated river, casting his eyes downstream, looking for a possible crossing.

"I don't see how we cross," Darby said. "It would be suicide."

Audra said, "I can't swim. River crossings scare me to death even when the water's running low. I've got to tell you this gives me the shivers. I don't know if I can do it."

Trace understood. Heights sent such fears his way. He shuddered as he remembered narrow trails that he had followed horseback along sheer cliffs in pursuit of Comanche warriors. The height had frightened him far more than any thought of confrontation with the enemy.

They needed Audra on the next leg of their journey, and he was glad she had spoken of her fear so he could try to address it some way.

"How deep is the Cimarron when it's not flooding?"

"I've only crossed it a few times. When I came down to Stone Creek with Estelle, the guide she hired found a crossing where we drove the wagon right through. Water didn't come near the wagon box. When Cain and I took off for Dodge, we rode right across. Horses stayed grounded, and we didn't get our feet wet."

"Same crossing?"

"I hadn't thought about it. Cain just led me there, and a lot of years passed between crossings. But, yeah, it was in the same direction, anyway. Now that I think about it, I guess it was on the main trail. It just twists and follows the river east for a ways to the crossing. But we can't see it today. It's under water."

"Is the riverbed at the crossing mostly mud, or rock and sand?"

"Rock. And pebbles. I remember the horses didn't even get their feet muddy. Estelle's wagon was never close to getting stuck in mud—that's what I worried about. Most of the low ground along the river here is rocky with shortgrass grazing more fit for goats, Cain told me."

"We'll stay on high ground and head east along the river and see what we can find. Tell me if you see anything familiar," Trace said.

They had ridden for the better part of a half hour when Audra said, "There. I know that's it. On the far side of the river. That big cottonwood. I'd forgotten. It stood there all by its lonesome, like it was marking the crossing. Maybe years back somebody planted it there for just that reason."

It was a towering tree, ancient, probably a century old, Trace thought, surrounded now by red swirling water that had surely visited many times over the decades. The ground rose not far past the tree, and he could see the ruts where the trail continued. The river was wider here, he guessed half again as broad as the channel coming from the west. That gave some hope for touching bottom on a crossing, but it was hard to say.

Trace said, "I doubt if we'll find anything more promising." He dismounted, and the others followed suit.

Darby said, "You've already decided, and we'll have to bend to your judgment on this. What do you have in mind?"

"The buckskin and I are going to take a swim and see if we can reach that old cottonwood tree. If we make it, we'll turn around and come back and get Dynamite and the gear and supplies. You can decide between you who comes next. I'll ride close by in case there's trouble. Now we're all going to get shucked."

Darby looked at him dubiously. "Just what do you have in mind?"

"Undressed. Keep what you need to cover your private places, but there won't be a dry spot on you after you cross that river. I'll empty my canvas knapsack and find another place for what's in it. Stuff your clothes in my knapsack—your boots, too, if you can squeeze them in. You don't want to be fighting the river with water-filled boots and soaked clothes to drag you down. You can help me strap the knapsack to my back, and I'll carry it across first trip and leave it on high ground so you can get dressed as soon as you're over there."

One hand braced against his horse, Trace bent over and started pulling off his boots. Soon he was stripped to his cotton undershorts. He emptied the knapsack, pressing the contents he wanted to salvage into his saddlebags and packed his own garments and boots snugly in the vacated knapsack. He turned and looked at his partners, who had been watching him. "Well?" He held out the knapsack.

Darby stepped over and took it from his hand, and the two women led their horses a short distance away and began disrobing while he started salvaging as much rope as he could find, anchoring the coils to his saddle. By the time he was finished, Darby and Audra had returned with the knapsack, both stripped to chemises and baggy underpants they had selected for the horseback journey. He slipped an arm into one of the knapsack straps, and Darby helped with the other before cinching it tighter onto his back.

"Here goes. I'll turn back if it looks like it's going to be too much."

"Trace, I don't know if it's worth it. We could wait out the flooding."

"That could be four or five days—if we don't get more rain. We've got to cross if it's possible."

He slipped his bare foot into the stirrup and swung into the saddle, nudging the buckskin down the slope toward the flooding river. The stallion did not hesitate when they reached the overflow and stepped into the water. Trace dismounted and, keeping his eye on the cottonwood on the far side, led the horse, estimating nearness of the channel by the tops of saplings and bushes poking out of the water. The flood water reached his knees when the last of the trees and undergrowth were no longer visible in front of him, and he climbed into the saddle again.

The riverbank sloped gradually at this juncture, and horse and rider eased into the channel. The force of the water increased considerably now, but the riverbed leveled off when the water barely creeped above the buckskin's belly. This is too easy, Trace thought, although Jubal had told him that this segment of the Cimarron was noted more for width than depth. It made sense that the normal crossing would be shallowest of all. He also knew that rivers could change in an instant, the rush of water, especially during floods, digging new holes in the river bottom, even cutting entire new channels. No sooner had the thought passed his mind than the stallion dropped beneath him, and the red water poured over his hips and saddle.

There was no footing for the stallion's hooves now, and he lunged forward. Trace knew his mount's legs would be moving in a trotting motion because that was how horses swam. Nature had endowed them with surprisingly strong inborn swimming skills—so long as the animals could maintain their heads above water. Unfortunately, a horse could not hold its breath, and a wave of water or whirlpool pulling it under could bring the end quickly.

The buckskin was a powerful creature, however, and when the river's flow pushed him, the horse kept pressing forward, and Trace abandoned the reins, grasped the saddle pommel and allowed the river to lift him from the saddle. He held fast, the horse's body blocking the current that would have otherwise swept him downriver. In moments, he felt the stallion raise up, signaling the animal had found footing. Trace held on to the saddle pommel as the horse continued up the grade and out of the roiling waters, the tension in his body fading rapidly when he planted his own feet on a rocky surface and stood upright in shallow water.

He turned back and looked across the river, where Darby was waving with obvious excitement. Audra, on the other hand, seemed frozen in place. He took the buckskin's reins and led him up a gentle incline to dry ground and grass. Trace maneuvered the wet knapsack off his own back and dropped it on the ground and then he removed the wet saddlebags carrying the gold coins from the stallion's back. He rubbed the horse's muzzle, and patted the muscular neck. "You're a mighty one," he said. "I'm calling you 'Atlas' from now on, and I'm going to see if I can do some horse trading with Jubal."

Atlas nickered and nuzzled him like he understood.

Now he had to figure out how to bring the remainder of his procession across. He unhitched one of the ropes from the saddle and waded back into the water to the big cottonwood tree. He anchored the end of the rope around the trunk and then stretched it out. He guessed the ropes would be about forty feet long, and he had three. Allowing for lengths surrendered to knots in hitches, he had a good one hundred feet. That would easily reach the other bank. He tied the ropes together and led Atlas to the water's edge again. He held onto the rope's end as they made the journey back, stretching it out into the river where it twisted and whipped like a giant snake pursuing horse and rider. This time, the stallion and rider knew what to anticipate, and Trace did not need to dismount mid-channel. When they stepped onto the flooded banks and the rope had stretched its limit, Trace tied the end to the stallion's saddle to hold it fast, while he joined Audra and Darby on higher ground where they awaited with the other animals and gear.

He noticed immediately that Audra's eyes were wide and terror-stricken. "Here's what we do," Trace said, adding "in the absence of objection. The mule can't make it with the supply load. We're going to dump everything we don't need here—pots, pans, axes and the like. We wrap the rifles and a few canned foods in the tarp and lash those to Dynamite. Your handguns, ammunition and whatever else you think you can't live without go in the other canvas knapsacks. I'll take one this trip and the other next time."

Darby said, "These shouldn't be so heavy. I can take one. I swim. Learned in the Atlantic."

"Split the guns and ammunition between bags. If it's between you and the knapsack, let the river have the bag."

"You can count on it," Darby said.

Audra spoke softly, her voice hesitant. "Trace, I . . . I can't do this. The thought of going into that river scares me shitless. I'd rather die right now on dry land."

With horse and supplies, Trace was confident Audra could easily make it back to Dodge. With the stalkers dead, she was unlikely to be in danger there, for now anyway. "It's your decision. I understand. You can just head back to Dodge. You're not an agent, and you've met your part of the bargain. If we've still got some dry paper and a pencil—and I'll bet Darby does—we'll sign a letter verifying that you're entitled to the rest of the payment for the information, just in case we don't make it back."

"It doesn't feel right. I don't think I can live with that, either. It sounds silly, but I feel like we're all partners now."

"Just hear me out. I'm going to lead Dynamite across the river now. Darby will follow. That way she can watch me and see when we step into the channel. I'll hitch the end of the rope around Darby. I don't expect any problems, but if she was swept off her horse, the rope would keep her from disappearing downstream and give me time to help."

Darby said, "And what if you get swept off your horse?"

"I won't."

"If you do, I won't have a chance to say I told you so."

"We're all going to be fine. Anyway, after we have you over there, I'll come back for Audra, if she's willing. I'll bring the rope with me again, but Darby will be on the bank to help if needed."

Audra asked, "And how do I get across?"

"You'll ride on Atlas—that's what I'm calling him now—you'll have the rope around you, and I'll be in the water beside you, hanging onto the saddle pommel and ready to catch you and grab the rope if it comes to that. I will be within reach, and you can grab my arm anytime you feel the need. I'll leave your mare this trip. If you don't want to do this when I get back, you take what you want of the supplies we've left behind and head back to Dodge. Just think about it."

Darby asked, "What about the extra mounts?"

"I'll release them now. Like Audra, they'll have a choice."

Chapter 27

THE CROSSING WITH Darby had gone without serious problems. Her gelding had begun to drift away with the water midway through the channel, but the flow had taken horse and rider closer to the bank, where the current's force eased, and the blood bay had gained a foothold and broken free of the raging waters. Dynamite had been a strong swimmer and made the journey with no difficulty.

Now, Atlas scrambled onto the Cimarron's bank, where Audra and three horses waited. Trace dismounted, hitched the rope to Atlas and walked toward where she waited on the higher, dry ground, water splashing about his knees and ankles, oblivious to the stones that gouged the bottoms of his feet, barely aware he was all but naked, his soaked undershorts clinging like a second skin to his flesh.

He was near enough now to see the fear in her dark, teary eyes. He assumed she would be turning back to Dodge City, and he thought it was probably best. "Well, Audra, if you're heading back, I want you to know I'm grateful for all you've done for Darby and me. Our mission would have been over without you. Darby, for sure, would be dead if you hadn't come with us this far. Probably me, too."

"I'm not going back."

"You're not?"

"No. I want to finish this. Somehow, I think it's important we stick together till the job's done. Tell me what you want me to do."

Trace was relieved to hear her words. They needed Audra. She knew people who might be helpful. She was their connection to lure Max Pierce away from the ranch. The plan wouldn't work without her, and they would have been forced to devise an entire new strategy if she went back to Dodge City.

Trace said, "I'll put a lead rope on your mare. You'll ride my buckskin. The rope will be looped under your arms just like I did with Darby. The knot that holds the loop is called a bowline. It won't slip or tighten around you. It's anchored to the mule on the other side now, and Darby's going to lead Dynamite away from the river and reel in the rope as we come across. Just give Atlas free rein, and he'll get you to the other bank."

"Where will you be?"

"Right beside you next to Atlas, holding to the saddle horn with one hand and the mare's lead rope with the other. The first sign of trouble, I release the mare and you get my full attention. I'm not telling you things can't go wrong, but you just hang onto that rope and trust. Don't panic. Hold the rope. That's your lifeline." He paused for a moment. "Think about it. Can you do this?"

She replied in a near whisper. "I can. I will."

Minutes later, Trace tied the loop under Audra's arms, fitting it tightly enough about her upper chest that it would be nearly impossible for her to slip out, yet taking care to allow enough slack she could maneuver some and be freed if she raised her arms above her head.

They moved toward the Cimarron's channel, Audra mounted atop the big buckskin, Trace wading at her side, leading Audra's bay mare, one hand resting on the saddle's pommel. The black gelding entered the water behind the buckskin, and the other mare followed, the horses evidently opting to stay with their adopted family. Trace thought the water did not seem to be rising now. The water flow into the adjacent lands seemed to have slowed, if not ebbed, so he thought the river may have crested, meaning the waters would gradually recede in the days ahead if there were no further storms upstream. But that would not be soon enough to aid this crossing.

As they entered the channel, Audra's hand clutched his, and he adjusted his grip on the saddle's pommel so she could grasp it tightly with one hand and hold the reins loosely in the other. He moved his hand and placed it on top of hers to maintain his anchor to the stallion. Darby and Dynamite slowly pulled up the rope's slack as Audra and the buckskin headed for the opposite bank, and everything was unfolding as Trace had hoped.

Everything changed when the horses neared the middle of the channel and he heard Darby scream, "Trace. Upstream."

He looked northwest, but his view was blocked by a bend in the river. He knew that from her position Darby would be able to see beyond the bend. Then he saw it, sweeping around the bend and charging them like a giant crocodile chasing prey, a splintered and twisted tree, uprooted by flood or twister. The trunk was nearly three feet wide, and the shattered limbs that remained protruded like wooden spikes. The top of the tree had broken away, leaving a missile of perhaps fifteen feet in length.

All they could do was forge ahead, but Trace could see they were not going to evade the strike. "Audra," he yelled, "off the horse. Grab me." He reached up to catch her when the tree stump rammed into the buckskin's flank with a jolt that propelled the stallion sideways, knocking Trace backwards and launching Audra into the air, as it rolled past and continued its journey downstream.

Trace recovered quickly, and, treading but losing the battle with the river's surge, his eyes searched for Audra. Then he saw the rope leading into a churning whirlpool no more than ten feet distant. But no Audra. He swam for the rope, drawing upon all his strength to reach it. His hand closed on the taut rope, which told him that the mule was pulling against the whirlpool's sucking power. Clinging to the rope, he surrendered to the churning force and allowed it to pull him in. Underwater, his eyes were impotent against the red soup, but his hand touched Audra's head, and he grabbed her hair and yanked upward. At first the water resisted, then it suddenly released its hold and Trace shot upwards, Audra in tow.

When their heads broke through the river's surface, Audra started coughing and choking, but she was alive. She threw her arms about Trace's neck, buried her face in his chest, sobbing. They were moving against the current now, slowly, but steadily. He lay back, using his body as a raft for Audra while she clung to him and allowed Dynamite to do the work as they were pulled to the riverbank.

When they reached shore, Trace struggled to his feet and lifted Audra into his arms and carried her to dry ground, where Darby waited with the mule and horses. He was relieved when he saw that Atlas and the other horses had all survived the flooding Cimarron's assault.

When he knelt to let Audra down, she held fast for a few moments before releasing him. "I didn't have time to think about dying," she said. "But it was close, wasn't it?"

"Too damn close."

"But we beat the river, didn't we?"

"I guess you could say we did."

"You didn't give up on me."

"I would never have given up on you, Audra. We're partners, the three of us."

Chapter 28

THE RIDERS REINED their horses to a halt on a hill overlooking the cluster of ramshackle buildings that made up the town of Stone Creek, No Man's Land. Darby thought some of the houses off the fringes, of what Easterners would have called a business district, looked habitable, and she could see a white colonial mansion set off from the community. It seemed an unlikely place for a town, nary a river nor a lake that she could see, and the red hills and ridges allowing only tufts of grass here and there reminded her of desert country.

At least she could see with both eyes now. The swelling of both eye and nose had shrunk away considerably by this morning. Although the flesh was sore to the touch, the pain was tolerable now, and she had been too exhausted the previous night for anything to interfere with sleep. They had all found sleeping spots next to the fire a few miles up the trail from the river, where they had dried out the buffalo robe and a few blankets. The fire. Thank God, Trace had come up with a shard of flint and a little steel bar in his possible bag that he had squirreled away for emergencies. The river's water had not spared the lucifers, but Trace's adeptness with his back-up implements had saved the day. She felt she smelled like a buffalo from the robe Trace had insisted she and Audra share, but she was not unmindful of his kindness.

Darby realized now that there was much more to John Trace Crockett than the fashionably attired dandy who had appeared at their first encounter. She should not have been surprised. She had read his history in the Pinkerton files. Son of a Tennessee cattleman, veteran of the Red River War and West Pointer. He had not lived an aristocrat's life. It was the West Point note that had raised her suspicion, though, and prejudiced her evaluation of him. A young man with an enviable scholastic record did not just resign from the Point during his final year. But who was she to judge? She had skeletons stashed away in her own closet.

She was glad to have the rivers behind them now. The Beaver River, though swollen some, had not challenged them seriously, and she had been surprised to see Audra face the waters without fear. Of course, a rope had kept her anchored to Trace during the crossing astride their mounts.

"How many people in Stone Creek?" Darby asked Audra.

"Depends. Not more than fifty or sixty right now. As many as ten times that some nights when the cattle drives start coming through during the fall. More business folks then, too. They come in and set up tents all up and down Main."

Darby asked, "Whose beautiful home is just outside of town to the south?"

Audra smiled. "That's called 'The Manor.' My friend Estelle owns that. It's where I lived and worked when I wasn't making house calls."

She sounded like a doctor, Audra thought. Maybe she was in a way. "Why Stone Creek? I don't see signs of water anyplace nearby."

"Somebody's sense of humor, I guess. There's a little dry creek bed that cuts in close to town. Full of rocks. When it rains, water's like it's being sucked in with a sponge. Just disappears. Good water wells, though. Underground springs, they say."

Trace broke his pensive silence. "Tell me about the town. What will we find there? Restaurant? It's been a long time since we had a decent meal, and I'm half starved."

"One eating place during off-season. Cramped and dirty, but food's edible. 'The Bean Pot.' Beans are the only thing for certain on the menu. Always has fresh-baked bread or biscuits. Might get beef or venison, if we're lucky. Pie or cobbler depends on whether Pickles has been on a binge or not. Pickles is a good fella, but the demon rum owns him."

"So, we've got a place to eat. Where do we bunk?"

"I'm counting on Estelle. This would be slack time for her. She should only be operating with three girls, so that would leave at least two spare bedrooms. The Manor hires extra girls for the spare rooms and sets up tents out back when the drives are coming through. Labor's not a problem. You'd be surprised how many wagons ferry gals from town to town just ahead of the drives to handle overflow from the regular houses on shares. Of course, prices double during that time, too."

Trace said, "Adam Smith's theory of 'supply and demand' vindicated again."

"I've never heard of Adam Smith, but Estelle would make him welcome at The Manor, if he's a friend of yours."

"An old friend from economics class at West Point. You've already said there's a stable, and you mentioned a hotel."

"Yes, but the hotel tends to be buggy. I never stayed the night unless I was well paid for it. Three saloons, hurting for business right now. Aristotle Papadopoulos—everybody just calls him 'Ari'—has a general store that covers all of one side of a block of Main. It's got everything. Even marriages or funerals if you need them. It looks like a big old barn that's about to cave in, but if you're patient, you'll find whatever you need. Ari's a sweetheart and a . . . a . . . good friend. I can count on Ari."

Trace said, "A bath and a shave. Where do I go?"

"We can get cleaned up at The Manor. Suzanne does barbering on the side. She was talking of giving up her other work when I left. Chester—the boy who works at the stable—helps with the bathhouse late afternoons and evenings. If he's working, I can talk to him about taking a message out to Max tomorrow."

Darby was glad to see Audra had bounced back from her harrowing experience in the river. She was on board with the mission again and was already proving invaluable. The Manor sounded inviting, and she was desperate to get the red clay and slime out of her hair and off her skin. And, poor Trace. She thought the dark, sandpaper-stubble on his face added to his rugged handsomeness, but she knew it would be driving him crazy. A man of such interesting contradictions. The more she came to know him, the more she liked him. Darby reminded herself their relationship was a professional one, and the line could be crossed only at great peril.

Chapter 29

DARBY WAS NOT surprised to learn that everyone they encountered in Stone Creek loved Audra. Of course, other than the ladies at The Manor, all their contacts had been male. She marveled that Audra seemed unfazed by the fact that the businessmen obviously were aware of her profession, and Darby sensed that several had likely been customers or clients, or whatever prostitutes called their patrons.

The horses and mule were stabled, and Audra had negotiated a half price deal based upon the quantity of renters they were bringing in. The Bean Pot had had both steaks and apple pie on the menu tonight, and the owner, who answered to "Pickles," had been grateful for three customers, rag-tag bunch that they were, and been attentive to the only occupants of the seedy place. The food had been excellent and plentiful, for starving folks, anyway. Standards had a way of shifting with one's environment.

Before heading for The Manor, they had stopped at Ari's General Store to pick up a change of clothing, since the knapsacks had not totally escaped invasion by the rancid water. They agreed they would decide what was salvageable later, and Audra assured Darby and Trace she could make laundry arrangements. She seemed to regale in command, and Darby and Trace had gladly ceded authority for the moment.

As predicted by Audra, Estelle, who seemed to claim no surname, had welcomed the visitors with open arms and had been thrilled to welcome Audra back. She was a tall, busty woman with wavy black hair that cascaded over her shoulders. Darby supposed some would say she had "meat on her bones," but the woman, probably in her late forties, had not gone to fat. Their hostess had immediately assigned two ground floor rooms to her guests, one which Trace would occupy and the other to be shared by Darby and Audra. "Of course, if you had different sharing arrangements in mind, that's fine with me," Estelle had said, winking and laughing. Darby had enjoyed seeing Trace blush.

There were separate male and female bathhouses attached to the house that was an isle of opulence in the middle of a vast wasteland, Darby thought. A red-haired, fourteen-year-old boy, Audra's friend, Chester, carried pots of boiling water to the claw-foot tubs, adding to the cold until the bather-to-be approved. Darby was sure his head had popped in the doorway more than once to sneak a peek, but the bath was exquisite, and, even though she had tipped generously, she did not begrudge him the bonus. She pressed the hot washcloth against her bruised nose and face, and the relief was exhilarating.

Audra soaked in an adjacent tub, separated by a curtain, and the women chatted while they bathed. Audra said, "Suzanne will come and help us wash our hair when we're ready. She fixes hair and shaves and trims the men. Estelle doesn't let her girls bed grungy, smelly men. To get in a bedroom door, they've got to bathe and clean up. Exceptions are made for the temporary girls who do tent business outside during busy season. Of course, the bathing and barbering aren't free, so her split with Suzanne turns out more income. She's a good businesswoman. There's a back door for ladies that can be used from noon to five o'clock to come in for baths or to have their hair fixed. Some wouldn't be caught near here, but you'd be surprised how many find their way through that door. Suzy does okay without lying on her back and spreading her legs."

"This is nicer than the best hotel I've ever stayed in. I still can't believe it."

"Yes, you'd be surprised how far men will travel to visit The Manor. Men with money or some who are willing to spend their last penny for a night or two here. A fair number of officers from Fort Supply enjoy a few days' leave at The Manor. Most are bachelors. Estelle has a special deal that includes meals, too. Incidentally, she doesn't want us taking any more meals at The Bean Pot. She'll feed us as long as we're here."

It was only an hour or two before bedtime when the trio assembled in The Manor's dining room, clean and refreshed. Suzanne, a sweet, young woman with hair even blonder than her own had applied a salve, which she claimed as her own concoction, to Darby's bruises, insisting it would shrink the remainder of the swelling away. It seemed to Darby that the formula was working. Certainly, the pain and discomfort were easing. Suzanne had plans beyond Stone Creek and appeared to have solid entrepreneurial instincts. Darby had encouraged her and given her the address of the Denver Pinkerton office, where she might contact Darby when she was ready to move on and might need the help of an investor.

Darby and Audra sat on one side of the table, attired in borrowed dresses, and Trace was seated in a chair facing them on the other. He wore a new buckskin shirt, and it appeared Suzanne had given him a hair trim in addition to the shave. She decided that maybe she liked his clean look slightly better than the rugged one. It was hard to say, but he certainly smelled better tonight. He might be thinking the same thing about his partners.

Trace started the conversation. "Audra, your friend, Estelle, has been too kind. I spoke with her about payment for our accommodations, but she won't accept a nickel, except for what we pay for Suzanne's services."

Audra teased, "Upstairs services aren't free, either, but I know you're here on a different kind of business. Got to act professional when we're on the job. I've heard Darby say that more than once. No playtime."

Trace tossed her an annoyed look. "Tomorrow's make or break day. Time to get things sorted out. You've made arrangements with Chester?"

"Yes. I've written the note, and he's got it. I've promised him a five-dollar gold piece when he reports here that it's been delivered personally to Max. That'll be more money than he's ever had at one time in his life."

"And Max is to come here?"

"To the back door. Estelle knows roughly what we're up to. She'll back us. She's not worried about Lazy P business. It's not like she sells grain and farm supplies. And The Manor's the only game in town for horny cowhands."

Trace said, "If Max doesn't take the bait tomorrow, we'll have to put off the trip to the ranch a day and take our chances with him there."

"He'll show up before the day's out. He won't want to risk my going to Romy. He's scared of her for some reason. I think she controls the money and calls the shots. He's more of a hired hand or a kept man."

Darby asked, "Okay. He comes to town. What do we do with him?"

"I'll offer him a drink, and maybe more. But all he will get is the drink."

"And it will be spiked with chloral hydrate?" Darby asked.

"Enough to last till you return with the girl. If not, I'll keep him locked up or tied up, if you don't need me at the Lazy P. Otherwise, I'll see if Estelle and a few of the girls can help."

"No," Darby said, "Estelle's already sticking her neck out too far. You should stay here and keep an eye on our captive and be ready to ride when we show up, with or without the girl. If we can't bring Miranda Wheaton with us, we need to report our findings to the Pinkerton headquarters and the law and head out back to Dodge."

"In the morning I'll give you a chloral hydrate bottle and give instructions on how to use it, just in case you get a chance. Is there anything else I can do?"

Trace said, "No, you just take care of our friend, Max. Darby and I will decide how we're going to approach the Lazy P place. Darby, I think we should both go to the telegraph office in the morning. We need to let Allan Pinkerton and Myles Locke know where we're at, and it's time for a chat with the telegraph agent."

Darby agreed. Trace had taken the words from her mouth. They were singing harmony, it seemed.

Chapter 30

THE TELEGRAPH AGENT'S single room office was a barren abode with no wall hangings, a rolltop desk, chair, and equipment behind a warped, scarred counter separating the work area from customers, who were accommodated with rickety, straight-back chairs. No sign of a file cabinet, but Darby suspected there were drawers accessible from the business side of the counter. Always interested in the economics of an enterprise, she doubted a dozen telegrams monthly made the trip in or out of Stone Creek. Western Union was supporting the local concession based upon either speculation or mismanagement. The operation could not pencil out.

The agent, a middle-aged man with thinning hair and pear-shaped body, put the dime novel he had been reading on the desk and got up, the frown on his round face signaling he did not appreciate the interruption in his busy day. Darby and Trace had agreed Darby would do the talking until Trace judged it was time to intervene. The agent looked up at Trace, who towered over him from the other side of the counter.

"You want something?" the man asked.

She supposed that, despite the fresh-pressed dress borrowed from one of The Manor ladies, she did not look very respectable with her black eye and bruised nose and cheek. Darby, pushing her spectacles down to the end her nose, part for effect but mostly to ease the pressure on her sore nose, peered over the wire rim and said, "If you are Tobias Thomas, the telegraph operator."

"Who's asking?"

Darby ignored his rudeness for the moment. "My name is Darby Maguire. This is my friend, Trace Crockett."

The telegrapher studied Trace, who was dressed like a cowhand this morning and had his Army Colt holstered on his hip. He apparently decided that Darby was, indeed, the spokeswoman.

"Yeah, I'm Tobias Thomas. What do you want?"

"First, a bit of courtesy. I doubt Western Union earns enough from your little station to pay your salary. A letter to the right person from an unhappy customer might cause management to reconsider the investment in Stone Creek."

This got the man's attention. "Didn't mean for you to take offense, lady. I'm here to help."

"I'm pleased to hear that. If you will give me paper and pencil. I will write out a message that should be sent to two different locations."

Thomas retrieved a pencil and several sheets of paper and placed them on the counter. Darby entered addresses for the Locke firm in Manhattan and Allan Pinkerton at the Chicago office and then wrote: *Agents in Stone Creek, No Man's Land. Subject believed at Lazy P Ranch. Darby and Trace.*

She handed the message to the telegrapher, who read it and looked up, obviously wanting to ask questions, but thinking better of it. "I'll send these later," he said.

"We're going to wait until they are sent," Darby informed him, "and I will want you to sign this sheet and enter the date sent. We need to be able to document that this message was sent." Darby did not trust the agent and thought it best to remove any deniability on his part. "Then we have a few questions."

"That'll be two dollars, a dollar for each, since it's under twenty words."

Darby extracted two one dollar bills from her bag and placed them on the counter. He picked up the money and walked to his desk and sat down. Soon, they heard the tapping of his keyboard. When he was finished, the telegrapher returned, signed and dated the message sheet and pushed it across the counter to Darby.

"Now, we have a few questions." She displayed her Pinkerton badge, and the man's lips tightened.

"You're not the law."

"No, we're not. But we often work with law enforcement and certainly notify authorities of any suspicious or illegal activity. I don't know why you wouldn't wish to cooperate." She placed a five-dollar gold piece on the counter.

"What do you want to know?"

"We would like to know about any messages sent to or from the Lazy P or the Pierce family within the past several weeks."

"I don't keep copies of messages after they're sent or delivered. I keep a logbook--Western Union says I got to do that. Write down who and where and the date and such. Don't have much to or from the Lazy P folks. Kind of strange for ranch outfits. Don't have all that many cow people here—half dozen or so. But others are sending telegrams to other cattlemen about breeding stock or to bankers in Dodge or Denver or wherever from time to time. Messages to Fort Supply complaining about things the Army ought to be doing and such."

Thomas pulled the logbook out from under the counter and placed it on top, opening it and sliding it to Darby. It was a book with simple columnar pages and handwritten column titles for marking the message date and whether it was received or sent and names of recipient or sender. Darby figured the book would last for some years, since a single page was adequate to handle a month's business. She quickly perused the dozen or so June transactions and passed the book to Trace.

Darby said, "Message from Manhattan to Romy Pierce our second day there. Same day, a message from Romy to our late friend, Robert Longtree, in Dodge City. The Manhattan sender is just identified as 'Flint Hills Friend.' Not much help."

Trace asked Thomas, "You didn't have the actual name of the sender?"

"Nope. Sometimes, there's a name at the top, but not always. Telegraph operator on the other end probably has it in his log."

Darby said, "This was less than a week ago. Do you remember at all what the messages said?"

"The one from Manhattan said something about 'Pinkertons snooping.' Very short. No more than five or six words. I thought it was strange. The one sent to Long-tree—I know Robbie, talk in the saloon sometimes—said 'take care of problems immediately. Add Pinkertons to problems' or words to that effect. I don't recall there was anything else."

Chapter 31

TRACE AND DARBY stopped by the stable to confirm that Atlas and Darby's blood bay would be ready to ride on short notice. They also planned to take the black gelding on their mission to the Lazy P. Originally, they had planned on taking a buckboard for a possibly unconscious passenger but decided it would hinder their escape. Better to hitch Miranda Wheaton to the horse, if necessary. After speaking to the telegrapher, the detectives had agreed they were not likely to fool Romy Pierce, since she was obviously aware Pinkertons might be coming her way. They had decided to appear at the residence and tell her why they were there and play it by ear.

The livery owner, a stooped, old-timer with a scraggly, white beard, whose moniker was "Windy," assured them that the horses had been fed and watered and would be ready to ride at a moment's notice. Chester would be on duty in an hour's time, and he would help with saddling and anything else they needed. Earlier, they had collected supplies and gear from Ari's General Store and hauled it to the stable in case they were required to make a quick exit from town after returning from the Lazy P, which appeared likely.

After stopping at the stable, they went to The Bean Pot and found that roast beef sandwiches and, of course, beans, were the day's offerings. No dessert, but coffee came with the meal. It was only a few minutes past eleven o'clock so they had the place to themselves.

After they sat down at their table and ordered, Trace looked at the blonde woman sitting opposite him. He liked her hair down and flowing over her shoulders, especially after Suzanne's styling the previous night. Her wire-rimmed spectacles did not conceal the chocolate-brown eyes that so often spoke her thoughts without the necessity of words. Smart as a whip. He said, "I was prepared not to like working with you, Darby. I was wrong. I think we make a good team."

She surrendered a sheepish smile. "I agree. We are a good team. And I was guilty of prejudging you as well, so I guess we're even. But you still keep me guessing."

"How's that?"

"Well, when I first met you, I thought you were kind of a 'swivel dude.' You know, one of those guys who dresses fancy and is afraid to get his hands dirty. Expects the common folks to clean up after him. Boy, was I off target. Forgive me."

"Nothing to forgive. I have some swivel dude in me sometimes, I admit. But I was raised on a Tennessee ranch and Dad saw to it I got my hands dirty plenty. Love cattle and horses. That's all I wanted to do—ranch."

"I'm surprised you're not in the ranching business."

"War took care of that. Dad went off to war as a confederate cavalry officer. Left my grandpa—his father—and my mom in charge of things. I was only six when it all started, so I wasn't a lot of help till the war got closer to the end. My brother was three years older than me, and my little sister was just two when Dad left. Grandpa could still put in a good day's work and we had a hired hand too old for fighting—no slaves. Dad said people don't own people—white, black or any other color. I took most things he said to heart."

"I've heard that most Southerners didn't own slaves."

"No. Slaves were rare in our hill country. We didn't raise cotton or tobacco. A little corn for feed, maybe. Anyway, I didn't see Dad more than three or four times during the war years, but we held things together well enough till the Yankees came. It was three months from the end of the war. A whole damned company, a hundred or more, like a swarm of locusts, going from ranch to ranch and burning folks out. They came to our place and started shooting cattle in the pasture, way more than they could ever haul off to butcher and eat. Gramps got the crazy notion he could chase the soldiers off and took his shotgun out in the farmyard. He took so many bullets you couldn't count them."

"It must have been terrible."

"Ma held us kids in the house to keep my brother and me from going Gramps's way. Then six or seven soldiers barged in. One grabbed Ma—she was a pretty thing—and started to drag her off to the bedroom. She screamed at me and brother Jim to pick up my sister, Allie, and go. I did, and I took her to a cave down by the river. I thought Jim was coming with us till I turned around and saw he'd stayed back. Well, we hid out till the gunfire ended and I could smell smoke. We headed back toward the house, and I saw my brother staggering around in the yard with blood pouring down the side of his face. He'd taken a Yankee's rifle butt on the side of his head and didn't even know where he was at. The house and all the outbuildings were in flames."

"And your mother?"

"She was in the house, and there was no getting to her. Later, Jim said some of the men took turns raping her. He didn't know if they killed her first or just left her there while they set the fires."

The waiter brought the food and the two ate silently for a bit before Darby spoke. "What did you do after you lost your mother?"

"Ma had a sister that lived nearby with her family. They were small farmers that lived off the beaten trails, and their house was spared. She took us in till Dad got back. My brother and I walked over to the ranch to do chores every day to care for what critters were left, but twenty-odd horses were now three, and a cow herd of over a hundred had dwindled to less than twenty. Hired man just disappeared, but, of course, we had no way to pay him."

"And your father?"

"He came home after the surrender, less one arm. Then the carpetbaggers from the north came, bought up mortgages from the banks for ten cents on the dollar. Of course, with the stock gone, we couldn't raise enough money to make payments. By the time I was fifteen, we'd lost the place and moved to Arkansas. Dad had a friend in the banking business there, and Dad was an educated man who understood money matters, so he took a job in the bank and soon became vice-president—same bank Jim's with now."

"And you ended up in West Point?"

"Seems strange, with my war experience. But Dad said the atrocities went both ways. War, he told me, brings out the worst and best in folks. I wanted the best education I could get, so Dad encouraged me to check into the possibility of West Point. My tests qualified me, and I'd worked on our United States Senator's farm whenever I wasn't in school, and he helped get me an appointment. I felt I let both him and Dad down when I resigned from the Point."

"And your father's not living?"

"Killed by the James gang during a bank robbery five years ago when he refused to open the bank vault or provide the combination. He was the only one in the bank who had it at the time, and he'd closed the vault when he saw the robbers coming in the door. That was Dad. He saw his job as a trust for all the folks that had money at the bank. Ironic, though, that he lived through a war to die like that."

Darby said, "I'm sorry. He sounds like a remarkable man."

"He was. I loved my mother dearly, but I was so young when she was killed. Dad was a man who never let adversity change his core character. He lived what he preached and forgave all but himself for human flaws. He always blamed John Crockett for not being there to protect his wife and family when the Yankees came."

"Then the Red River War. You've dealt with your own share of adversity."

"Some of my own making." He didn't know why, but he had to tell her. "It's not on my official record, so you probably didn't pick it up—the reason I resigned from the academy."

"It's none of my business."

"I was romantically involved with a professor's wife. He was a colonel, no less. When he discovered our . . . uh . . . relationship, he demanded my dismissal. His wife said I took advantage of her kind nature. I won't speak ill of her. I loved the woman. I take full responsibility for my life and my shortcomings. I wasn't a victim of anything but my own poor judgment. I was lucky the superintendent permitted me to resign."

"I don't know what to say. But you sound as if you haven't forgiven yourself. Like your father?"

Trace shrugged. "I told Dad about the circumstances of my resignation. You're the only other person I've ever told. Somehow, it's a relief, yet very strange at the same time."

"Another time, perhaps you'd be willing to hear about my ghosts. I've taken a twisted trail myself to the place I am today."

Chester, the stable boy, entered the restaurant and came directly to their table. "Miss Suzanne told me to get word to you that Max Pierce has showed up at The Manor."

"Time to go," Trace said. "You've got riding clothes stashed at the stable?"

"It won't take me ten minutes to change."

Chapter 32

AUDRA HAD NOT heard Max Pierce enter The Manor and started when the voice came from behind her. "I got your message, Audra. Where is everybody?"

She turned and saw Max standing not more than ten feet behind the stuffed settee she had settled in to await his appearance. Suzanne had been watching the manor from outside with instructions to get word to Trace and Darby when Max appeared. She would wait at the stable until she received word it was safe to return. Estelle and the others had vacated the parlor and moved upstairs to the client lounge to afford Audra privacy, although Estelle was within hearing distance, double-barreled shotgun in hand in case Audra hollered.

"Upstairs," Audra said. "Estelle is having a meeting."

"A meeting of whores. Now that's something I'd like to sit in on," Pierce said, stepping around the settee and taking a matching chair on the other side of the large, oak tea table that separated them.

Max, a wiry man of medium height, looked tired, she thought, eyes bloodshot, face unshaven for several days. The odor of stale sweat and cow shit invaded the perfumed room. She supposed he was about forty years old, but today he looked fifty. Things must not be going well at the Lazy P. She noted his Colt was holstered at his hip. He did not remove his wide-brimmed plainsman hat.

"Thank you for coming. This is important," Audra said.

"I don't get it. You're knocked up. You're a whore. I'm guessing these things happen all the time. You know how to get rid of 'em. Drink something or see a doctor. Besides, it could be anybody's kid. You've spread your legs for dozens of men."

What he said was mostly true, and she had mostly come to terms with that until recently. But she no longer thought of herself as a prostitute, and no matter what lay ahead, those days were done. "I was at your ranch a month ago, and there hasn't been anyone else since," she lied. "And I can count."

"Don't matter. You can't prove nothing. Who'd believe a whore?"

"Your wife might. Especially if I tell her about your party time while she was gone."

"Blackmail, huh? Is that a step up or a step down from whoring?" He laughed. "She knows about you anyhow. I had to come clean on it a week or so ago. Don't think she'd even have given a shit, but somehow you got into her lockbox and took something when you were there. She accused me, but why would I take it? I was in on the game."

"You're talking about the pendant, aren't you?"

"Damn right, I'm talking about the pendant. And that's when some things started to make sense. We sent a crew to Dodge, figuring Cain Abel had headed there—closest place to make railroad connections out of these parts. We was going to bring him back to hang for cattle rustling. No law here in No Man's Land, so we'd do it quick. It didn't take long for us to find out you lit out of Stone Creek with him. He was my connection to you before you come out to the house. Then Romy got the telegraph from Manhattan about Pinkertons, and we knew you and Cain was up to something. That's when Romy sent a message to Robbie to take care of things in Dodge. Never heard back, but you're here, so he messed up."

"He was ordered to kill me?"

"Not in so many words. But he knew what he had to do. You and Cain wasn't to leave Dodge."

"Cain didn't. And I came back. Robbie Longtree's rotting in a shallow grave north of the Cimarron, along with some other hired gun of yours. Two more of your hired guns are planted in Boot Hill."

Pierce's eyes could not hide his surprise. "Who did it?"

"I killed Robbie. Tore him in half with a shotgun blast. Pinkerton agents took out the others." He started to fidget nervously in his chair now.

"So we were right. You and Abel snitched to Wheaton. Romy said you'd be trying to make your own deal. You brought Pinkertons here." He began tossing his head about, as if he expected agents to emerge from the walls. "How many?"

"Seven. They should be on their way to the Lazy P by now. Why don't I get us something to drink, and we can discuss this calmly? I may be able to keep you from spending the rest of your life in prison." She started to rise, but Pierce was on his feet, Colt drawn and aimed at her chest. She could see Max was frightened, and scared people were dangerous.

"You bitch. You started this trouble when you stole that pendant. You went through everything in the box, didn't you?"

"I read the newspapers, saw the clothes and, of course, the pendant. And I didn't start this 'trouble' as you call it. You did, Max, when you kidnapped Miranda Wheaton."

"I didn't do it. Romy did. She still had a key to the house. She went in while Robbie kept a lookout. He was a stableman there. She took Sarah—that's her name now. I met her outside the gate, and we took the kid to a deserted shack outside of town. I was one of the sheriff's deputies, so I would be on duty to keep an eye on things. But the sheriff ordered us out to intercept the kidnapper. The other deputy—his name was Ray somebody—was a sharpshooter and tough hombre. There wasn't no way I could get him out of the way, so I signaled Romy off. She was going to make the exchange herself, dressed like a man and a flour sack over her head. Kid wouldn'tve been much over a year old when Romy got booted out of the house, so she wouldn't know her from anybody."

Audra said, "And you didn't have the nerve to try the exchange again."

"U. S. Marshals come in from Topeka and took over. She got the hell out with the idea of trying again after time had passed, and I stayed on with the sheriff for a time so as not to raise suspicions. Then we joined up for a spell in Kansas City and decided to come out here where nobody'd be looking for a missing girl."

Max kept the Colt leveled at her while he spoke, and she knew he wouldn't be spilling the beans this way with any intention of allowing her to repeat his story. Her derringer was holstered on a strap about her thigh, but there was no way she could lift her skirt, draw the weapon and fire before he squeezed the trigger. She decided her best bet was to keep him talking and hope for an opportunity.

"So, you've raised the girl out here in No Man's Land. Where'd she go to school?"

"Didn't. Little filly can't read or write. Romy wanted to keep her ignorant so she didn't learn nothing dangerous. Thought to cash in on her a long way back. Had pictures taken to prove a birthmark on her ass. Things kept coming up and we was doing good in the business out here, but we got word old man Wheaton was failing bad, so we thought we'd better move fast. That's why Romy got in the box to get the pictures and pendant and found out some thief had been snooping. How'd you get the key? I don't even got one."

"Let's say I have certain locksmith skills."

"Guess that don't surprise me none."

"What does the girl you call Sarah know?"

"Nothing. Thinks Romy's her ma, and I'm her step-dad—thinks her real dad's name was Smith and he died in the war. Guess the last part's true." He grinned, "She's a real beauty, though. A real beauty. Worships her old stepdad."

"How long have you been messing with that girl, Max?"

"What makes you think I've been messing with her? Besides, we ain't related."

"I know things like that, Max. I can read your mind. You've been taking advantage of her."

"Maybe she's been taking advantage of me."

"She's a child. And you're sick and despicable."

"Those words coming from a whore."

"Romy runs things, doesn't she? She's the real boss at the Lazy P."

"It was her money that set things up. Her divorce set-tlement from Wheaton. Hell, we ain't even married. Just took my name because the Wheaton name might make a trail. I didn't give a damn. At first, I got privileges with it, but that didn't last. We did what suited us that way. I stayed on because she gave me a cut of the money and a good place to live. I took care of a lot of nasty business for her. Of course, she couldn't boot me out. I knew too much."

"I suppose she would have had you killed sooner or later—probably after she got her ransom money. There's something I don't understand, though. Let's assume you finally made the exchange for ransom money. Sarah would have eventually identified you, and the law would be on your tails."

"Yep. There's the problem. That's why Romy lost her nerve every time we talked of making a move."

"And then you'd have to get Sarah to go along with it."

"Yeah, we were getting that worked out. Told her she was going to pretend to be somebody else for a few days, and then we'd meet someplace in Manhattan and pick her up. Of course, we couldn't do that. But we'd have enough money to disappear."

Fool, Audra thought. Romy would disappear. If Max was lucky, he would be abandoned some place. If not so lucky, he would be dead. "Max, sit back down. We need to talk about this. I know two of the Pinkertons. I know I can persuade them to help you with the law. They're going to recover Miranda Wheaton—Sarah Pierce, as you have come to know her. They may take Romy into custody for the authorities. Who do you think Romy's going to blame? She'll sell you out in a minute. You know it. She'll end up with a slap on the wrist, and you'll spend the rest of your life in prison. Unless Kansas hangs kidnappers."

Pierce said, "She wouldn't do that to me."

His words were spoken like he was trying to convince himself. Audra thought Pierce had the brains of a grasshopper and was a coward at his core, a sad combination. But a creature cornered could be unpredictable and dangerous. "She would, and you know it," Audra persisted in planting seeds of doubt.

"Enough. Get off your ass. You're comin' with me. I got an extra horse saddled out back for you. I ain't no fool. I showed Romy your note. She said to do what needed to be done. She didn't have to spell it out."

She had underestimated Romy's hold on him. He had planned to kill her from the moment he left the ranch. Certainly, he had not run off at the mouth the way he did with any notion she was going to be around to repeat his words. If she stayed put, he would kill her here. That would bring Estelle and some of the girls out, and others who had not volunteered for this fight might die. Without a word, she slowly stood, turned toward the rear of The Manor and started walking.

She pushed the heavy oak door open and stepped outside, then wheeled and slammed it shut, crashing the door into Max Pierce's shoulder. He grunted and stumbled backward for an instant, giving her time to lift her skirt and slip the derringer from its holster. She stepped back just before he charged through the doorway enraged as a wounded grizzly. His eyes fastened on her, and he aimed his Colt and squeezed the trigger in the same instant she fired her derringer.

Audra had no chance to see if her aim was true, as the echoing crack of his gun and the sledge-like blow to her chest obliterated conscious thought. She was driven backward and landed face-up on the ground. Her eyes opened for a moment, and she looked at the slick, bloody hand that she lifted from her chest, unable to recall how this had come to be. The pain had jerked her awake, but it was not so bad now as her body began to numb. Strangely, she was not afraid when she lay her head back and waited for death to come. She was more consumed by sadness that she would never be what she might have been. That was her final thought when a black cloud dropped over her, swallowed her up and carried her away.

Chapter 33

DARBY HAD CHANGED into her riding boots and britches and, mounted on her blood bay gelding, rode next to Trace, who was astride the buckskin stallion and leading the black gelding that had adopted them after the canyon gunfight. From Audra's directions, she figured they should not be far from Lazy P headquarters.

The rugged terrain was pocked with mounds of red clay and sliced with ravines and gullies. Buttes and spiny ridges erupted randomly from the earth outlined on the horizon by a blistering early afternoon sun, and at first glance, Darby thought hell might look like this. But Trace, ever the cattleman, had pointed out swaths of prairie grasses that carpeted some of the slopes and richer soil along bottomlands adjoining several spring-fed streams that snaked through the landscape. "There's worse cow country," he had remarked. "It would take fifteen or twenty acres to support a cow and calf here. Some places south in Texas might take fifty acres or more. Compare that to six or seven acres, some spots probably less, in the Flint Hills near Manhattan."

They reined in the horses when they came over a knoll and saw the hazy outline of the ranch headquarters in the distance. Darby could make out a two-story house and a big barn and assorted other outbuildings scattered about the premises.

"No cover," Trace said. "I don't think we're going to surprise anybody."

"It doesn't matter if we're going right up to the door to introduce ourselves."

"I suppose not, but I'd feel better if I had a few trees to head for if somebody started shooting before we get there."

"I'm more worried about those wolfhounds Audra mentioned."

"You brought the beef strips and chloral hydrate?"

"Yes. She said to put two drops on each strip. But you don't really think if they're coming after us they're going to stop and devour a chunk of meat I throw at them?"

His silence answered the question.

Darby said, "I don't want to kill them. If they are attack dogs, they're just doing what they're trained to do."

"Maybe they've got them locked up someplace during the day."

"And maybe my butt isn't sore from all these hours on horseback."

"Darb, I don't want to hurt those creatures any more than you do, but if they're going to take us down, I'll pull the trigger if I've got to. Anyway, be ready to treat the meat. Can't hurt to try." He had started calling her "Darb" sometime, just seemed to slip into it. Nobody else had ever called her by a shortened version of her name, but she rather liked the sound of it coming from Trace.

"It's in my saddlebags. Just warn me if you see anything."

They rode at an easy lope toward the house. She noticed three men watching something in the corral near what she guessed was a stable. As they neared, she could see several horses in the corral, and the men turned and directed their eyes toward the riders more with curiosity than anything. While they wore guns at their hips, they made no hostile moves. When Trace and Darby reached a hitching rail in front of the veranda of the big, stone house, they dismounted and tied their horses. No wolfhounds. One of the men from the corral separated from the others and started walking their way at a hurried pace.

"Well," Trace said. "Let's see who's home."

No sooner had the words escaped his lips than two enormous, shaggy dogs tore around the corner of the house nearest Darby. She reached for the beef strips in her saddlebags and plucked them out, but one of the dogs was on her before she could open the little bottle of chloral hydrate. She dropped the meat, and the slower dog stopped to gulp it down. But the first dog had her down, huge mouth open within a few inches of her face. She raised her arm to thwart the attack just before a wet tongue splashed drool across her lips.

"Trace," she yelled. "Don't shoot, don't shoot. It's not hurting me. I'm okay."

Then a female voice yelled. "Colene, Tara. No. Come."

Darby patted the dog's head and received a last kiss before the animal retreated in the direction of the voice. She sat up and grabbed the hand Trace extended, noting he held his lowered Colt in the other. When he pulled her up, he holstered the gun and wrapped an arm about her back to steady her while she collected herself.

"I couldn't shoot without hitting you. Turns out that was a good thing."

She stepped away. "It was just glad to meet me, I guess."

Then she saw Miranda Wheaton, standing not fifteen feet away, dressed in faded denims and cowboy boots and one wolfhound sitting on each side of her, tails wagging excitedly. It had to be Miranda. Red hair, freckles sprinkled across her nose, sapphire-blue eyes. Not quite blossomed into full womanhood. Several inches taller than her own five and one-half feet. Stunning. She had a nervous smile fixed on her lips.

"I'm Sarah," she said. "Sorry about the girls. They love company. Supposed to be guard dogs, but they wouldn't hurt anybody. Not on purpose anyhow. Well, unless somebody tried to harm me. They're Irish wolfhounds. Sisters."

Darby walked over to the girl and extended her hand. "I'm Darby Maguire." She nodded toward Trace. "This is my partner, Trace Crockett. We're with the Pinkerton Detective Agency. We're here to visit Romy Pierce."

Sarah returned a surprisingly firm handshake. "Detective Agency. Don't know what that is, but it sounds important."

"Sounds more important than it is."

"Romy Pierce. She's my mother. She's in the house. I'll get her." She started for the veranda when the front door opened and an attractive black-haired woman with a severe face stepped out. Early forties, Darby guessed. Trim, but showing a little wear from life in this hard country. She wore a blue gingham dress that did not come out of a local general store.

"Sarah," the woman snapped. "Get up to your room and take those curs with you. Stay put till I tell you otherwise."

Sarah looked at Darby, rolled her eyes and shrugged. "Sorry again, ma'am—about the girls." She walked up to the veranda and disappeared through the door, the dogs following obediently.

"It's quite all right," Darby said. "I love dogs. I hope I can get better acquainted with them."

The man from the corral stood just off the veranda now, feathering his fingers on his pistol grip, signaling he had not been hired to punch cows. A tall, beefy man, whose face had not been touched by a razor for more than a week, he wore a dust-caked black hat pulled low on this forehead, not quite shading menacing dark eyes.

"What's your business here?" the woman asked.

"We wish to speak with Romy Pierce," Darby said. "Is that you?"

"It might be. Who's asking?"

"I'm Darby Maguire, and this is my partner, Trace Crockett, we're operatives for the Pinkerton National Detective Agency."

Trace nodded and touched his hat brim, "Ma'am," choosing to let Darby continue to take the lead.

"You've got a spare saddled horse. Where's your other rider?"

Darby said, "That's what we're here to talk about. Could we come in?"

Romy turned to her hired gun. "Morg, get Curly and Red up here. Then, you come in the house." Speaking to Darby and Trace, "Come in the house. Leave your weapons outside."

"We can't do that, Missus Pierce. If you prefer to talk out here in the presence of your men, we're willing to do that."

"Oh, hell, come in."

She led Trace and Darby into an elegantly furnished parlor that belied the ordinary appearance of the residence's exterior. Darby could see into an adjacent dining room that was no less dazzling. Without invitation, she and Trace claimed seats on a leather-covered settee. Ignoring nearer stuffed chairs, Romy seated herself in a straight back chair more distant from the settee.

The big man called Morg came in and remained standing in the foyer just outside the parlor. "Curly and Red are on the veranda just outside the door. I told them nobody leaves without my say-so and to come running if they hear trouble."

Darby took the statement as more warning for the visitors than information for Romy.

"Okay, state your business," Romy said. "We've got things to do."

"I can't imagine what that would be," Darby said. "There aren't any cattle drives coming through right now, so your rustling operation should be quiet."

The woman blanched. The rustling accusation obviously caught her off guard. "You've got no proof we're rustling cattle."

She wasn't denying it, just probing to see what Darby had on her. "Cain Abel's testimony would be solid evidence."

"Cain's a damned liar. He's the rustler. Cain's trying to save his own hide."

She evidently had not received confirmation of Cain's death. Darby decided Romy was not going to get it from her. "Then why did four of your men try to kill him . . . and us."

"I don't know what the hell you're talking about, lady."

"Well, those men can't testify against you. They're all dead, including a longtime friend of yours, Robbie Long-tree. You know, the one who helped you kidnap Miranda Wheaton fifteen years ago."

Dead silence. The woman refused to meet Darby's gaze.

Chapter 34

TRACE FINALLY SPOKE. "We're not interested in your rustling business, although we're obligated to report it to the United States Marshal's office in Fort Smith, Arkansas. The Pinkerton Agency was employed by your former husband to reopen the case involving the abduction of his granddaughter, Miranda Wheaton. Our investigation has turned up evidence that Miranda Wheaton is alive and now known as Sarah Pierce."

She stood up. "You lying son-of-a-bitch. Sarah's my blood daughter. I want you out of here. Now."

"The issue could be resolved very quickly. Miranda had two distinguishing marks on her body. An unusually prominent scar on her upper left arm and a birthmark on her left hip, roughly the shape of a half moon. If you will allow my partner to examine Sarah, we will leave immediately if the marks aren't present."

"I'm not going to let you put her through that indignity."

"It's all right, Mother. I don't mind. Miss Maguire seems like a nice lady. I do have the marks, you know. I don't understand this at all, but I think I should know what this is about." Sarah stepped into the parlor through the dining room entry. She had apparently been in that room listening to the conversation.

Romy turned on her. "You stay out of this, you whiny brat. I told you to stay in your room. Get your ass upstairs."

Darby stood now. "No. Sarah stays here. Sarah, could we go in the dining room a moment?"

Her eyes fearful, Sarah looked at her mother, who was glaring back at her. "Yes. It's time for me to know some things." She turned away and walked with Darby toward the dining room.

Romy darted for the foyer. "Kill them, Morg," she screamed

Trace was on his feet, Army Colt in his hand and got off two gut shots before Morg raised his pistol. Morg looked down in disbelief at the blood soaking his shirt, and then he dropped his weapon and toppled forward to the hardwood floor. Romy disappeared through the open door, and another gunman appeared in her place. He saw Morg on the floor and Trace coming his way with Colt ready. He ducked back out, closing the door behind him. When Trace stepped cautiously out onto the veranda, he caught sight of Romy and the two gunmen heading toward the stable. He considered a chase but then thought better of it. Miranda Wheaton, also known as Sarah Pierce was their only mission, and they had not extricated her from hell yet.

When Trace turned to go back into the house, he almost stumbled into Darby, who had been just a few feet behind him with her .38 short-barreled Smith & Wesson poised to fire. She had moved quickly and quietly to back him up.

"You're not going after them?" she asked.

"No point. Our job's in the house. The girl."

Darby said, "She's shaken and confused, but considering everything that's suddenly come down on her, she's amazingly calm. Some girls would be hysterical right now."

They went back into the house, and Darby joined the young woman in the parlor while Trace drug the gunman's body from the foyer and deposited it on the veranda. When he re-entered the house, he noticed he had left a trail of blood on the floor. Darby and Miranda—that was her name in his mind—were seated on the settee now, Darby with one arm wrapped about the girl's shoulder as they leaned forward and spoke softly. Tears rolled down Miranda's cheeks faster than she could swipe them away, but she seemed rational enough. Trace decided that dealing with the young woman was best left to Darby.

"I'm going to take a look around the house," Trace said, "and you ladies can talk."

Miranda looked up. "Colene and Tara. They're shut up in my bedroom. Would you let them out? They won't attack you or anything. Well, they might want some attention."

"Sure. I can do that. They don't seem very ferocious."

He climbed a winding staircase to the second floor, and at the top of the stairs discovered there was a hallway with two sleeping wings. He heard the wolfhounds whining at the far end of the shorter wing, which appeared to access two rooms. He walked down the hall and opened the door, and the monster dogs rushed out and began dancing about him excitedly, licking his hands, standing on hind legs and resting paws on his chest. He surrendered and let them have their way with him for a spell, as he rubbed ears, stroked heads and backs and wiped away their drool from his face.

He had read about wolfhounds before and knew they were big creatures, but he had not imagined anything this large. He guessed they would weigh over a hundred fifty pounds each and would be formidable foes if trained to attack. These were obviously Miranda's pets, however, and could not be counted on as watchdogs. He wondered how they would respond to an attack on their mistress.

He finally shooed the hounds downstairs. He had only one thing he wanted from the place: the lockbox containing the artifacts pertaining to Miranda's abduction.

Chapter 35

DARBY DID NOT know how long it would be safe to stay at the Lazy P ranch house, but they could not leave without Miranda Wheaton. If she could not be persuaded to leave voluntarily, Darby would find an excuse to retrieve the chloral hydrate from the saddlebags and induce the young woman to take a drink of water. They were prepared to bind her and take her forcefully if it came to that.

She could not waste time consoling the girl any longer. Darby removed her arm from Sarah's shoulder and scooted away from her. "Sarah, you were listening to our conversation. You must have some idea what our visit is about."

"Yes. You don't think I'm Sarah Pierce. You think I'm somebody named Miranda. You're saying Mother is not my real mother."

"You were going to show me the marks we were talking about. Are you still comfortable doing that?"

"Yes." She commenced unbuttoning her shirt and slipped the garment down her left shoulder enough to expose the scar high on her upper arm.

Darby examined the raised tissue. It was not an unsightly thing, just white flesh raised where vaccination had occurred and perhaps twice the diameter of the typical residue. Alone, it would have no real significance. Sara pulled her shirt back on, fastened it, and stood up without asking. She unbuckled her belt, lowered her britches to her thighs, and tugged up the right leg of her underpants. There it was, the half-moon birthmark. Darby nodded, and Sarah re-positioned her britches and fastened the belt.

Sarah sat back down and looked expectantly at Darby. "Well?"

"You were born Miranda Wheaton. The woman you call 'mother' was once married to your grandfather, Congrave Wheaton, who was a very wealthy businessman in Manhattan, Kansas." Darby gave Sarah a quick rundown on the kidnapping and told her why the investigation had been reopened with the Pinkerton Agency.

"I can't believe this," Sarah said. "And still, I can. I don't know how other people live, but our way has not been normal. Well, I guess I don't know what normal is. But I've never had a day of schooling, and I know Mother is an educated woman. She always insisted I speak properly and scolded Max when he said 'ain't' and didn't talk the way she did. He claimed to be my stepfather, but I came to hate him. Mother read books but wouldn't teach me letters or numbers or anything. I begged her, but she said I was too dumb. Never knew a kid my age. She gave in and let me have dogs, and Max did teach me to ride when I was little, before he started doing things to me. I love horses but couldn't have one of my own."

"Before he started doing things to you? What do you mean?"

"He started coming to my room at night and touching me places, and later he made me touch his . . . his, you know."

"I know." *The bastard.* Darby wished she had told Audra to overdose Max with the chloral hydrate.

Sarah continued, "Now he comes to my room naked at night and takes off my clothes and crawls in my bed. That started over three years ago. I fought him at first, but he said he would kill me and that since we weren't the same blood, it was okay."

"Did your mother know about this?"

"Yes. I went to her a long time ago. She laughed and said, 'Better you than me.' She fights with Max all the time. I don't think they even like each other."

"Sarah, your grandfather died recently, but you will be a very wealthy woman someday. There is a home for you in the Kansas Flint Hills. You can afford tutors to teach you to read and write. You are an intelligent young woman. I can see that. Come with Trace and me. I don't know how to deal with the life you've had, how to fix everything that needs fixing, but I will be your friend, and you will find many friends who will help."

"But Mother—she's the only family I've ever known. I know she hates me, but she's been my mother."

"She's not your mother, and she always planned to sell you back to your grandfather for a fortune. I know it hurts terribly when I say this, but you have always been disposable property to her. If I allow you to stay here and she doesn't come back, what will you do? And I fear that if she does return, your life is in danger. You've become a witness to her evil acts now."

Sarah held her head in her hands, obviously overwhelmed by decisions to be made. She said, "I wondered when Mother told Morg to 'kill them' if that included me. But I'm afraid to go."

"You don't have a choice."

"What do you mean?"

"You're coming with us, even if we have to tie you to a horse. Don't try to make up your mind. The decision has been made. You just have to tell us if you're going to come on your own."

Darby could see that Sarah was visibly relieved. The two monster dogs bounced into the room and raced for their mistress, and Sarah wrapped her arms around their necks and hugged them. "Can Colene and Tara come with me?" she asked.

"Of course. We wouldn't think of leaving them behind."

"I'm scared, but I will go with you."

"That's called courage, Sarah. Gather a few things that are special to you, maybe a change of clothes. Forget your dresses because we're going to be riding too far to carry much."

"We'd better hurry. Mother has scary-looking men who bunk on another place a few miles away. I think that's where she headed, and she'll probably come back with help."

Darby stood just as Trace walked into the room, carrying a metal box. "This is the only box I could find. This has got to be the one. I couldn't find the key, but I'm sure Audra can pick the lock. If not, I can always use my Colt."

"Sarah," Darby said, "grab your things. Stuff them in a cloth or canvas bag, if you have one—something we can tie to a horse's saddle."

Sarah leaped to her feet and raced for the stairs, the two wolfhounds trailing after her. Darby turned to Trace. "Sarah's reluctant. But she knows it's best she go with us. I just had to tell her she had no choice. But she thinks Romy will return with gunfighters from the old farmstead Audra mentioned. I don't think they'd come into Stone Creek—too many witnesses. But we'd better move."

Trace said, "I'll get this box hitched to my saddle and keep an eye out for trouble. I'll leave it to you to help the girl—I guess we're calling her Sarah for now."

"I suggest that. But I've confirmed it. This is long lost Miranda Wheaton."

Chapter 36

TRACE KEPT AN eye to the south as he readied the horses to ride. Sarah had brought nothing with her except a few items of clothing stuffed in a cloth bag, which he quickly tied to the back of her saddle. It occurred to him that the girl, having resided most of her life in this remote hill country, might never have owned a piece of jewelry or other keepsake. She had been excited when she came out of the house to learn they were headed for Stone Creek. She had viewed the town from horseback on occasion but had been forbidden by Max and Romy to enter the village, which was located no more than six or seven miles west of the ranch headquarters.

When they were all mounted, he saw a cloud of red dust in the southeast, where Sarah had said the old farmstead was located. "Darby," he said, "why don't you take the lead, and, Sarah, you fall in behind her. I'll hang back a bit to see if we're being followed."

Darby reined the horse west, easing the blood bay into a lope, and Sarah followed with the wolfhounds, finding it all great fun, racing beside their mistress's black gelding.

Trace waited in the yard to confirm that the dust cloud was, indeed, headed for the Lazy P headquarters. Any doubt was soon removed, and he gave the buckskin a nudge with his heels and moved out after the others. He figured they had enough head start to easily outrun any pursuit to Stone Creek. Winding through draws and between the buttes and hills, he worried some that the hired guns knew the territory better than he and Darby and might be aware of shortcuts that would shave the distance between them. They were forced, however, to stick to the well-used trail taken on their journey to the ranch.

The comfort granted by their lead disappeared when he saw Darby and Sarah dismounted in front of him. Darby was steadying the black gelding while Sarah was leaning over the horse's right foreleg with the leg bent back at the knee joint, her fingers probing the fetlock and hoof. The young lady knew something about horses. Trace dismounted and joined them. Sarah said, "Blackie threw a shoe. I warned Robbie about getting the poor thing to a blacksmith. He never took care of his horses."

"You recognize the gelding?"

"Sure. Blackie's sweet. I'd have owned him if I had any money of my own." She continued to study the horse's foot. "Might be a little muscle strain from being off balance. Can't ride him. We can lead him."

"Wait here."

Trace sprung onto the buckskin's saddle and nudged the horse to high ground. He looked back in the direction of the ranch buildings. Riders coming on fast. He pulled his Henry from its scabbard and grabbed a box of cartridges from his saddlebags before leading his mount back down the slope.

"Sarah," Trace said, "you take my horse. Leave the gelding with me and you two keep riding for Stone Creek. I'll discourage the bad guys."

"Like hell you will. You're not in charge, Trace," Darby snapped. "We're partners, and this is no time to play hero. Where were you going to position yourself?"

He sighed. "Back up the slope. We've got about five minutes."

"Sarah," Darby said. "Wait here, but if something goes bad, take the buckskin and ride for Stone Creek. Ask how to get to a place called The Manor and go there. You'll be safe. Ask for Audra. Understand?" She did not wait for an answer and turned away and ran up the slope with Trace on her heels.

They dropped on their bellies when they hit the hilltop. Trace could make out the riders now. Five of them. He said, "When they get a little closer, I think we should fire a few shots above their heads. They might lose interest and turn back."

"Do you really believe that?"

"No. But I'd feel better about it. Killing isn't really supposed to be our job. And we've done enough of that."

"Okay. If it will make you feel better. I don't see Romy with them."

"No. She'd be back at the house packing. She likely knows she's got some time, but she'll be gone in a day or two. She probably held back a few men to help with preparations. Whatever happens, she knows her game's over. She'd have money stashed in a bank someplace, probably under another name. She'll go there, draw her funds out and try to disappear. Or maybe it's in a city where she'll move right in to a new life. She went back east not long ago, remember?"

"Trace, they're getting close."

His eyes searched the horizon. Yes, they were moving within range, and he didn't want to risk anybody breaking through and reaching Sarah. "Ladies first."

"Such a gentleman." She pressed the rifle against her shoulder, aimed and squeezed the trigger. The rifle cracked, and a hat flew off one of the riders.

"Show off." Trace fired a shot well above their heads, and they now had the pursuers' full attention. They reined in their horses and looked around frantically, trying to pick up the source of the gunfire.

Darby said, "We've got the sun at our backs. That's as good as an extra gun."

Return fire came now, but the aims were random, the shooters trying to get the ambushers to respond and reveal their locations. Trace hoped to see the riders turning back, but they regrouped and pushed their mounts forward again. He took aim at the lanky front rider. His first shot missed but the second drove home, and the man slumped forward in his saddle and reined the horse around to retreat before slipping out of the saddle and falling face down in the dust.

Darby's rifle was firing now, and another man tumbled off his horse. Wisdom came to their friends, and, after firing a few token shots toward the hill where Trace and Darby were dug in, they wheeled their mounts and headed back up trail in hasty retreat.

"Cover me just in case somebody comes back. I'll go down and check on the men we took out. I wouldn't walk away from the wounded."

"I'm sure you wouldn't," she said with a hint of sarcasm. "Go ahead. I'll cover. But mine was a kill shot."

Trace had taken only a few steps when he heard Sarah's screams and the wolfhounds' ferocious growling and barking downslope. He changed course and started racing toward the racket, Darby at his side, matching him step for step. He heard a man's voice yelling now. "No. No. Please. Call them off." He was sobbing now.

When they reached Sarah and the horses, they found the dogs atop a man who was struggling hopelessly to escape the clamping jaws, crawling to grasp the pistol lying on the ground beyond his reach. Sarah saw Darby and Trace and yelled at the dogs, "Yield. Colene. Tara. Yield." The dogs released their holds on the man and raced toward Sarah.

Darby hurried to Sarah's side, and Trace walked over to the hapless man stretched out on the ground. He was a young man with curly blond hair, face and arms bloodied and ripped where the hounds' teeth had dug in, but he would live to carry the scars through life.

"That's Curly," Sarah said. "He was at the house when you came, and I think he left with mother. I hate him. He cornered me in the stable once. He was going to . . . I can't say it. But Tara was with me. I didn't tell her to attack that time, but I threatened. This time I didn't threaten."

"What were you up to, Curly?" Trace asked.

He groaned. "Help."

"I asked you a question."

Still lying on the ground, he replied, "Missus Pierce said I should cut past the hogback ridge and try to set up an ambush if I got ahead of you. I did and then heard gunshots and headed up this way. I didn't do nothing. Just pointed my Colt. Would never have shot Sarah. But she said 'sic' and those monsters took me down. Please help me."

"I'll help you with advice, young man. Look for another line of work. Come up the trail with me to check on your friends. Pray that we can find an extra horse roaming there. If we don't, we're borrowing yours. You can pick it up at the stable in Stone Creek."

Curly turned out lucky. One of the two dead hired guns' horses had lingered and recognized the injured man and came to him. Before the would-be gunfighter departed, Trace mentioned that the capture of his employer by authorities with his help could bring a one thousand-dollar reward. "Just contact me—Trace Crockett—through the Pinkerton Agency." Curly rode away hunched over on his own mount. Trace suggested he could procure medical assistance from the surgeon at Fort Supply.

Chapter 37

SUNDOWN WAS NO more than an hour away when Darby and Sarah dismounted in front of The Manor. After removing their personal items from the mounts, they hurried to the front entrance. Trace led the collection of horses to the livery. They had been slowed by the limping black gelding, but the party had been spared further pursuit by the Lazy P hired guns.

Darby rapped on the thick oak door with the brass, horseshoe-shaped knocker. The door opened a crack, and a young, dusky-skinned woman peeked out. "Sorry," she said, "The Manor's closed this evening." Then her dark eyes widened. "Oh, I know who you are. You're Audra's friend. I'm Nanette. Come in." She pulled the door back so Darby and Sarah could enter.

Darby said, "This is my friend, Sarah. Is Audra here?"

Nanette pushed the door shut, and Darby could see tears in the young woman's eyes. "She's here on the main floor in the bedroom where you stayed last night. But you should know that she's not doing good."

"What do you mean? What happened?"

"I'm not sure exactly. Estelle knows more. She was there first. She and Suzanne are with Audra now. You can go on and see for yourself."

"We'll leave our things here," Darby told Sarah, dropping her saddlebags in the foyer. "Follow me." She rushed through the parlor and turned down the hallway that led to the bedroom.

When she stepped inside, she saw Suzanne bent over the bed and Estelle standing a few steps back, her face grim and eyes teary. As she inched nearer, she caught a glimpse of Audra in the bed, her serene face framed by sable hair and eyes closed, like a corpse in a coffin. Was she dead? Dear God.

"Estelle," she whispered. "What happened? Is Audra alive?"

The older woman started, evidently unaware Darby had entered the room. She turned and spoke softly, "Alive? Yes, for the moment. Bullet wound. Suzanne has staunched most of the bleeding and has been nursing her ever since it happened, but Audra won't wake up, and it looks awful. Suzanne can do stitches and the like, help with a birthing even, but when it comes to something like this, she doesn't have a clue."

Immediately Darby thought of Trace. "We need to get Trace over here. Now. He's at the stable. He's not a surgeon, but he's dealt with battlefield wounds."

"Let's step out," Estelle suggested.

In the hallway outside Audra's room, Darby quickly introduced Sarah to Estelle.

Estelle seemed taken aback and nearly speechless when she heard Sarah's name.

"What is it?" Darby asked.

"The man who shot Audra was this young lady's father, Max Pierce."

"Stepfather," Sarah corrected. "I guess not even that."

Estelle said, "Oh, God. Why do I have to be the one to tell you this? Max is dead. Audra shot him. It was just outside the back door of The Manor. We heard gunshots, and I ran out and found them both down. Max was already gone."

There was no outburst from Sarah. She was silent, evidently trying to process the information. Darby knew that Max was the only father Sarah had ever known, but she had come to despise him. Yet, she knew many who grieved those they had spent a lifetime hating, and the girl likely had some good memories of times before the abuse started, perhaps even intervals during the bad years. But Darby was impotent to help Sarah now. Audra came first.

"Can Sarah stay with you, Estelle? I have to get Trace at the stable."

"Chester's out back. He's finishing some cleanup and then he was going to take Max's body over to the stable to hold till it's claimed. Windy's all we got for undertaking hereabouts, and we don't have a sheriff or marshal to tell us how to handle this mess." She looked sympathetically at Sarah. "Sorry, sweetheart, I know it's hard to hear these things."

Sarah said, "I'm okay. I've heard Mother say this about some men. 'He's flirting with death.' That's what Max was doing where I was concerned."

Estelle's brow furrowed. "I'll go tell Chester to hightail it to the stable."

Chapter 38

DARBY WATCHED AS Trace examined Audra's wound. She had retrieved the medical kit from his room, pleased to find that the floodwaters had not invaded the contents. She doubted there was much in the kit that would be of value for treating a gunshot wound, but Trace had a way of surprising her about such things. When he saw Audra's condition, Trace immediately took charge but asked Suzanne to stay near and assist. Darby was pleased that he had shown respect for Suzanne's earlier efforts. The young woman was a diamond in the rough working out of a bordello in No Man's Land. She promised herself she would find a way to open a door to a more promising future to this young woman when the Wheaton case was closed.

Sarah was with Estelle in the dining room where the two were having supper with two of The Manor prostitutes who had been granted a night off because of the commotion at the establishment. When Darby had passed by earlier, the young woman appeared to be enjoying the company of the other women, and it occurred to Darby that Sarah's contact with others of her gender, except Romy, had likely been rare.

Audra was still unconscious, but she moaned and rolled her head when Trace probed the wound with a darning needle he had commandeered. "Darb, would you fetch the chloral hydrate bottle you had in your saddle bag? We may need it if she wakes up. Hope you remember the instructions she gave you."

Darby ran to the foyer where she had deposited the saddlebags, plucked out the bottle and hurried back to the bedroom. She placed the container on a lamp table next to a bottle of carbolic acid Trace had produced from his medical kit.

"Darb, could you take the lantern from the table and hold it over my shoulder? I need more light on the wound. Suzanne, I'd like you to take your fingers and spread the opening as wide as you can so I can get a better look. The bleeding's a trickle right now, and that's good."

He positioned his eyes a few inches above the wound and eased the darning needle into the cavity a few inches above her right breast. "I can't see far enough to tell where the slug's at, but it's got to be buried deep, and I'm afraid to probe any deeper with this thing. Damn, she needs a surgeon."

Suzanne said, "The wagon trail to Fort Supply's fifteen or sixteen hours by buckboard. It's rutted and got two creek crossings. The smoothest part is like a washboard."

"I don't know if we've got a choice."

Audra commenced moaning again and tossing and twisting on the bed, so Trace had to back away for a moment. "She can't drink anything right now. Darb, did she say how to give that chloral hydrate directly."

"On the tongue, she told me. Two drops for this concentration. I gather it's pretty strong. She thought we might have to hold Sarah down and give it to her that way if we couldn't drop it in a drink."

"Not going, you sumbitch. Go away," Audra mumbled. "Get out."

"Delirious," Trace said. "Put the lamp down. Suzanne and I will hold her steady while you try to get two drops on her tongue."

"She won't just stick her tongue out for me."

"Put some on your finger twice and try to wipe it on her tongue. I've seen Army surgeons go damned heavy with the stuff without killing anybody. If that doesn't work, we'll try more."

Darby found her hand shaking when she picked up the bottle and had to take a deep breath before tipping the bottle and collecting a drop on her finger. "This is a huge drop." She slipped it in Audra's mouth, touched the tongue, but teeth clamped down on her finger before she removed it. Pulling it free with no small effort, she repeated the procedure, this time evading a bite.

"It takes a while, but I don't know how big a dose she gave me," Trace said.

"You've taken this stuff?" Darby asked. "You were wounded?"

"Uh, no. Just talking to myself."

He didn't want to tell her. For a moment, she wondered if Audra was "she." No. That was a silly notion. It was none of her concern if he didn't want to talk about it, but she couldn't help being curious.

A half hour later, Audra calmed and slept again. Trace said, "I don't know if it's the drug or if she just blacked out again, but we've bought some time to decide what to do. It was positive she was at least semi-conscious for a bit. She seemed to be coming out of the deep coma." He looked down at the sleeping Audra. "I wonder . . . ."

"Wonder what?" His unfinished thoughts were starting to annoy her.

"Give me some gauze to staunch any new bleeding. Then we're going to turn her over on her belly."

That seemed an odd approach, but she held her tongue and counseled patience to herself. She found a roll of gauze in the medical kit and passed it to Suzanne, who picked up scissors from the table and began rolling out the gauze and cutting, passing strips to Trace. Not for the first time, Darby found herself awed by the young woman's efficiency.

They rolled Audra over, and Trace pulled the sheet down to expose her upper back and shoulders. He ran his fingers gently over the right side. "Light."

Darby turned the lantern flame up to the maximum and held it above Audra's back. Trace nodded and pressed his fingers several inches left of the right shoulder blade and nodded.

"I'll be damned," he said. "Touch that, Suzanne."

Suzanne placed her fingers tentatively where he had indicated. "A lump."

"Yep. And in the light, you can see some bruising coming on. I think there's a chunk of lead buried just under the skin. Just about punched through. This was a close-range shot. My straightedge is folded up in the kit.

Can you find that for me, Darb? Maybe Suzanne can cut a slice of the gauze and wet it with the carbolic acid and wipe the blade."

A few minutes later, Trace made a tiny slice near Audra's shoulder blade. Then he squeezed the flesh as rivulets of blood ran between his fingers. Suddenly, a tiny object popped out, rolled across her back and landed on the mattress bedsheet. "Eureka," he said, sighing heavily. "We need to douse this with carbolic acid, get out my needles and the catgut and take a few stitches. Then we'll get her back over and do the carbolic as deep as we can go at the front entry and do some more sewing. Can you stitch, Suzanne?"

"I've done stitches. Never had the luxury of catgut and people sewing needles."

"Why don't you do the back?"

Audra was still sleeping soundly when the makeshift doctors finished patching, but Darby noticed her breathing seemed strong and normal. She assumed that would not have been the case if she had ingested excessive chloral hydrate.

"Darb," Trace said. "There's nothing we can do but wait and pray. Why don't you round up Sarah, and the two of you can take my room tonight? I'll be staying here."

Several hours later, Darby returned, walking stocking-footed into the room, where she found Trace sitting on the floor at the foot of the bed, leaning against the wall. She went to the closet, found a folded blanket and removed it. She walked over to Trace and sat down beside him, tugging the blanket around them.

"She's still sleeping," he said. "But she was fighting a war tonight, and I think she was planning on winning."

Chapter 39

WHEN TRACE OPENED his eyes and saw soft rays of sunshine seeping through the curtained window, he realized he had dropped off on his watch and slept most of the night. And now he was stretched out on the floor with a pillow under his head and a soft blanket covering his shoulders. He got a glimpse of Suzanne hovering over Audra's bed and remembered now that she had appeared with pillows for him and Darby sometime during the night and that Darby had appeared earlier with the blanket. She was nestled beside him now, and he had to admit it was a nice feeling, something a man could get used to.

"I need to pee . . . bad." It was Audra's voice. It seemed to him the women around him were always needing to relieve bladders. Trace heard the clanging of lid against pot as Suzanne worked the chamber pot out from under the bed.

Darby rolled away and clambered to her feet. "I'll help."

Trace followed and went to Audra's bedside. Her eyes were open and alert, but the pain was reflected there, and she would have to handle it for some days yet. That didn't worry him. The potential onset of an infection did. A man could die from a splinter. The risks of infection setting in from a gunshot were incalculable, and it was mostly up to the body to fight it off. There were no medicines to help, beyond those that might ease the journey to inevitable death.

"You're looking better this morning."

"Hurt like hell, but I'm going to beat the bastard." Her voice was raspy and hesitant.

"What bastard?"

"I don't know who it was. He had hold of my wrist and kept pulling. Said it was over and I was to go with him. But I wouldn't. I told him what you said once."

"I don't know what you mean."

"I haven't been what I might have been yet. I wasn't leaving until I had a go at that. But I've still got to pee first."

He smiled. He was placing his bets on Audra Scott against anything that might try to take her down. "Listen. I'm going to lean over, and you see if you can wrap your arms around my neck. Then I'm going to slip my arms under you and carry you around to the chamber pot. Maybe Darby and Suzanne can take over from there."

"I don't think I can raise my right arm."

"Just do what you can."

"I'm naked as a jaybird, you know."

"I won't look."

"Yeah, I know. Doesn't matter. In the time we've known each other, I guess you've seen about all there is of me to see."

He worked his arms beneath her back and thighs, noting the hot flesh that signaled possible fever. He felt an arm clasp about his neck and another rest on his shoulder. An easy lift, and he carried her around the bed to where Suzanne and Darby waited. He helped Audra plant her feet on the floor before the ladies took over and then exited into the hallway. Considering Audra's lack of modesty, he probably could have remained without objections, but the observation of a woman carrying out her bodily functions was an experience he was glad to forego.

As he waited, he heard Audra's groans while her friends helped her negotiate the chamber pot. Darby called for him when the chore was finished, and when he returned, he found Audra in a droopy nightgown that had obviously been donated by a larger woman. He helped ease her into bed again, amazed at her improvement from the previous evening.

"Can you eat something?" he asked.

"A bear or two."

Suzanne said, "Estelle and Nanette do breakfast today. I'll see what we can put together."

"I want her to have a glass of water first. She needs lots of it with the blood she lost. And would you see if Estelle has any laudanum? The worst of the pain is around the corner. I don't think the nap drops have worn off yet."

"I know she's got laudanum. I'll get some and bring it with a glass and pitcher of water."

Audra said, "Max. I know the son-of-a-bitch shot me. I thought he killed me. I think maybe he did, but I wouldn't go. But I'm sure I got off a shot. Did he get away?"

Darby said, "He's dead. Your bullet struck him in the neck, according to Estelle. You must have hit an artery because she said there was a bucket of blood where he fell."

Audra nodded. "I've killed a few men now. Not much pleasure in it. But I guess some deserve it. And what about Romy and the Lazy P bunch? And Sarah or Miranda, or whatever her name is? Should you be on your way? Is somebody coming after you?"

"There's nothing to worry about. They'll be doing the running. And Sarah's with us. She was in the room last night, but you were unconscious. You'll meet her soon. Know this, Audra. Trace and I have talked. We're not leaving Stone Creek without you."

She looked up with tear-filled eyes. "You're not? But you don't need me anymore."

"We always need our friends and partners, Audra. You're family now. We have a lot to talk about, but for now, you eat a good breakfast and get some sleep. We're here until you can go with us."

When Suzanne returned with water, coffee and breakfast, Trace gave her instructions about the laudanum. "We've got to parcel it out carefully. You can give her half a teaspoon if she's got more pain than she can take but keep track of what you give her and talk to me after she's had two doses. People can get addicted to the stuff, and then you've got a new problem that can't be dug out like a piece of lead. One of us will spell you in a few hours so you can get some rest."

"Estelle wants to take a shift and so does Nanette. I know Carla would help, too."

After Darby and Trace stepped into the hallway, Darby said, "I hope you're not angry."

"Why would I be angry?"

"I told Audra we'd talked about not leaving without her. I fibbed."

"We didn't talk about it? You had me convinced. I guess you just read what was in my head. It never even occurred to me we'd leave without her."

Chapter 40

TWO DAYS LATER, Audra was back on her feet, walking about the main floor of The Manor with someone at her side in case she was overtaken by the dizziness that still struck her unexpectedly at moments. After breakfast at the dining table, she protested going to bed, and Suzanne walked with her into the parlor, where Darby was seated on the settee with her spectacles perched on her nose and a collection of water-stained papers spread out on the tea table. "Can I sit with you a spell?" Audra asked.

Darby removed her eyeglasses. "Of course." She looked up at Suzanne. "I'll help her back to bed, Suzanne."

"Thanks. I need to do some sorting and packing."

Audra sat down, and when Suzanne left, she asked, "Is Suzanne going someplace?"

"She's going to Manhattan with us. She's ambitious, and I promised to help her find a position or get set up in her own business. We have friends there now who will help. Estelle's going to sell the place here after the next cattle drive passes through. With the railroads, the drives won't be coming this way much longer. She's thinking of moving on to Denver with the girls who want to go. She was glad for Suzanne. She says she's proud when her girls graduate to better things."

"I believe that. She's a teacher in a way. She helped prepare me for something else. I just don't know what."

"You'll have a fair amount of money when you get the remainder of the Wheaton payment, and you said you've been saving. You would seem to have a lot of choices."

"I suppose. I'm done with whoring. And I've been a thief of sorts. Trace might've told you that."

"He never said a word."

Audra was silent a moment. "No, I suppose not. He's a good man, isn't he?"

"He is."

"Is your case done now, when you take Sarah to Manhattan?"

"A few loose ends. Somebody there was involved with this trouble and identifying the person could be critical to Sarah's future. We've got some work to do yet."

"Then you've got some time to see how things work out for you."

"Work out?"

"You're crazy about him."

"It shows?"

"Not to most. You're so easy with each other, know what the other's thinking, so you don't need to talk. It's like you've been together for years."

"Do you think he knows about my feelings?"

"No. And you don't have a clue he's crazy about you. That's where you both get deaf and blind."

"But we've only known each other a few weeks. This makes something he's proposed even scarier."

"Not marriage?"

Darby laughed, "Of course not. But he's suggested a business deal that involves you."

"Me. How do I fit in?"

"Well, he's dead set on investing in ranch property in the Flint Hills near Manhattan. He wants me to partner in it, and he asked me to see if you'd be interested in putting money in the business."

"Me? A cowgirl?"

"He said we could call it 'Three Winds Ranch' and see if a triangle brand is registered. We wouldn't necessarily be doing the direct operating, but I know that's his dream someday. He thinks we could buy land for fifteen dollars an acre, so we could get as much as a thousand acres for fifteen thousand dollars. He says they're not going to make any more land, and in the long run, the value can't go anywhere but up. He said that if you put your money in a bank, you always risk a run on it. The land is always there. It does make some sense. We'd need five thousand each to put in. I could do it, but I'd be cash broke."

"I'll have a few hundred more than that, but I'd need to find other work soon."

"How about being a Pinkerton operative?"

Audra brightened. "That would be my dream. But with my past, they'd never hire me."

"Your background would be perfect for a lot of their assignments. You have instincts about people. You've got imagination, and you're smart. Trace has that all figured out, too. He wants us to set up our own detective group. Manhattan would be home base. We'd still mostly work for Pinkerton, but we'd do it on a contract basis, where the agency wouldn't have total control to assign us someplace. We'd negotiate terms and keep the right to accept or reject a job. He thinks that after the Wheaton assignment, we'd have the leverage to push such an arrangement. If Allan Pinkerton won't go for it, he's got a new competitor. We're playing poker a little bit here."

"He really thinks he can do this?"

"Well, one catch is he wants me to negotiate the deal. He thinks I'm a better negotiator. He's right."

"You sound like you've almost bought into this."

"Not yet. I've got to think about it. The truth is I'm worried about these feelings for Trace I haven't sorted out. We'd be working together all the time. What if personal feelings got in the way?"

"I can only say this. I've come to love Trace—but it's like a brother, one of mine who never lived to grow up, maybe. If I ever come to love a man in another way, he'll be a little more on the wild side. But tell Trace to count me in on his proposal. We can talk later about the details after you've made up your mind. For what it's worth, I think it's time for you and Trace to have a good, long talk about the two of you. Tell him what you're worried about. He won't laugh, I promise. I'm betting this is on his mind, too."

"When he gets back, I'll tell him we need to set aside time tonight to talk."

"Where is he?"

"He and Sarah—and the wolfhounds, of course—are at the stable, spending time with the horses. It turns out that old Windy's a fair blacksmith and farrier, so Blackie got new shoes this morning. Sarah's determined to take that horse with us. Trace thinks the horse should be in shape to make the trip without a rider by the time you're ready."

"And when does he think that will be?"

"If your fever's gone for good, he's thinking three or four days. We'd have to take it slow and easy, maybe allow three days to Dodge."

"I'll be ready, but you've given me a lot to chew on. I'm ready to sleep a while. But get me out for noon dinner."

Chapter 41

RACE FELT REFRESHED after enjoying an after-supper bath and shave and was in his upstairs bedroom putting on clean clothes. He was ready for suit and tie again, but that would have to wait till Dodge City. On second thought, his suits were being stored in a stable and would likely require cleaning before he wore them. He wouldn't mind purchasing a new suit, he decided. He would prefer a tailored garment but supposed he would not have time to wait for tailoring.

Hot water had been boiling for baths most of the afternoon at The Manor, and to make himself useful, Trace had pumped and hauled water and drained tubs. Darby had helped Audra with a tub bath, which had seemed to improve the patient's morale considerably. Her recovery progress was nothing short of amazing.

The bath parade had been necessitated by The Manor's reopening for business. The three active-duty prostitutes were required to be clean for the few visitors that were expected, but all the residents, including the wolfhounds, Colene and Tara, had participated in the cleansing. After the first night, Suzanne had insisted upon moving a mattress into Audra's room to look after the woman she considered her patient. She had insisted Trace move into her room since he had been displaced by Sarah, Darby, and the dogs.

He heard laughter in the adjacent room, which was Nanette's crib. Audra had explained that the prostitutes had nice bedrooms in another wing of the building, and the crib rooms were where they entertained clients. Suzanne's room was not a crib but happened to be located adjacent to the crib wing. Since The Manor had been temporarily closed following the shootings, there had been no activity in the cribs since his occupancy of the room. It felt a bit strange now, though, knowing what was happening in the adjacent room. He hoped they would do their business quietly. Nanette was a stunning creature, and the image of her performing in the adjacent room would not be conducive to a good night's rest.

He sat down in the side chair and started tugging on his freshly shined boots. He was to meet Darby in the kitchen so they would not see, or be seen by, patrons entering or leaving through the parlor. Estelle protected visitors' privacy as much as possible, according to Suzanne, when she had insisted on treating him to a shave earlier. Darby had been uncharacteristically edgy ever since he and Sarah had returned from the stable, and she had announced that they needed to have a private conversation that evening. He had no objection. He was happy to grab any private time he could with the woman who had become more than a friend and partner to him.

He had presented his business proposition to Darby only in part because he needed other investors in the ranch and partners in the detective business. He had been struggling with the thought of separation from this woman. Selfishly, he wanted to maintain their connection until he could pursue something more, but he felt he must tread carefully. Darby tended to be ruled by her head, and if he pressed her, she would point out they had only known each other several weeks, fret about professionalism and find excuses for why their relationship must not extend beyond business. His history was flawed when it came to love, he admitted, but he wanted Darby Kathleen Maguire in his life forever. The question was how to convince her of that.

The bed in the adjacent room was creaking with tell-tale rhythm. It was only nine o'clock, and he didn't know if Darby would be in the kitchen yet, but he decided to head downstairs and wait.

When he entered the kitchen, he was surprised to find her there, papers spread out on the table as usual. He sat down opposite her at the small table. "You can't stay away from pencil and paper, can you?"

"I'm writing my report. Have you started yours?"

"I thought I'd just sign off on whatever you wrote up—unless it was critical of me. Besides, our job's not done yet."

"The boss loves detailed reports. He's a bit obsessed on that topic."

"I know. I've received scoldings about my skimpy reports. Speaking of Allan, I'm surprised the home office hasn't replied to your telegram."

"Allan may be out of the office on a mission. At least Chicago knows we've recovered Miranda Wheaton. I'll check in the morning at the telegraph office for replies. I'm expecting to hear from Myles Locke, too. I was informed by our friend Tobias at the telegraph office that he doesn't deliver to The Manor. Chester stops by a few times a week to see if there's anything. He didn't say why. I suppose it's some moral principle. I never thought about it until Estelle mentioned it, but since No Man's Land isn't a part of any state, there's no mail pickup or delivery here. Mail's got to be posted or received at Fort Supply in the Indian Territory."

"Well, I'm not writing to anybody anyhow, and I'm content to let you deal with the obnoxious guy at the telegraph office." Time to quit talking about telegrams. Trace was sure that wasn't the purpose of their meeting. "Sarah in bed already?"

"She and the wolfhounds. She's studying."

"The dogs are in bed with her? Where do you sleep?"

"The first night, I tried to sleep with all four of us in the bed. After an hour, I took to the buffalo hide rug on the floor, and I've made that my nest."

Trace shook his head in disbelief. "You're spoiling the whole bunch."

"The dogs were the one concession Romy made to the girl. And I think she could use a little spoiling."

"You said she's studying. What's she studying?"

"I printed out the letters of the alphabet in both capitals and small letters. Then I printed the name 'Miranda Wheaton.' She's mesmerized by this. She's learning the alphabet and trying to print out the letters and her name. It's so strange. When I was teaching school, I would sometimes have a ten or eleven-year-old child enrolled who couldn't read or write yet, but never a seventeen-year-old. But she's smart as a whip, Trace, and excited to learn. I told her about the unbelievable library that was waiting for her in the house where she'll be living. She's been having me read stories from the old newspapers we found in Romy's box to her. She's fascinated that they are about her."

"And she's learning to print her birth name?"

"She wants us to start calling her 'Miranda' now. 'New life, new name,' she says. I was afraid we'd have to drag her back to Manhattan screaming and hogtied, but she doesn't seem to have any usual parent bonds with the people who held her all these years. She was a piece of property, a nuisance. And, of course, she suffered Max's abuse without a soul to go to for help. She's nervous about what's ahead, but excited, too. I'm not too worried about her. My only concern is Elisabeth Denney. Does she take over Miranda's care, or does she go to prison?"

"I think we can solve that quickly when we get to Manhattan. Is that what you wanted to talk about tonight?"

"No, I would like to discuss your business proposition and us. Reverse that. 'Us' comes first."

"You don't think we'd make good partners?"

"That's not it. I think we're perfect partners in the detective business. And the land I see as just a place to invest my money. I'd leave the ranching to you, but I don't think you'd object to my handling the bookkeeping."

"I was counting on that. I figured you'd be wary of turning me loose with a full book of check blanks."

Darby said, "Well, you've got one ranch investor. Audra's in. And she's chomping at the bit to be a Pinkerton agent."

"But we don't have enough leverage to form our own agency without you. Audra will be a great agent, but Pinkerton won't go with a contract deal if you're not in on it, too."

"Trace, the idea's exciting. And it would be nice to have a place to call home without being transferred to another office every six months, but I worry about the feelings I have for you. There. I've said it."

He hoped he was reading her right, because he had decided to take a chance. "I'll be honest, Darb. My motive for the business proposition isn't just the money. I'm trying to hold you as close as I can. I'm crazy in love with you and can't stand the notion of you taking off to Denver or God knows where Pink sends you after this job's done." He thought, well, for once she's speechless anyway.

She removed her eyeglasses and placed them on the table, her coffee-brown eyes locking on his own.

Darby finally spoke, "You caught me by surprise. I don't know what to say."

He stood up and stepped around the table, reaching out and gently lifting her from her chair to face him. He lowered his head, and his lips found hers. It was a soft kiss, but she did not resist, and when she responded, it was with fervor, and then they were clinging to each other, and he could not ignore the surging in his loins. He knew she had to be aware of his hardness pressing against her, but she did not step back.

"Come up to my room," Trace whispered.

She looked up at him and nodded.

He took her hand and led her silently up the stairway.

Chapter 42

DARBY WAS CERTAIN of her insanity, following this man to his bedroom. Her mind told her she was a fool. Her conscience screamed that this was wrong. But her body ignored the warnings. When Trace opened the door and led her into the bedroom and she saw the empty bed, she remembered her last intimacy with a male, one that had followed many prior intimacies between an eighteen-year-old boy and a girl just shy of sixteen.

Trace must have sensed her uncertainty. "We don't have to do this," he said softly. "Just say, 'not now.' It won't change what I feel for you."

She pulled him close and kissed him again, hungrily and insistently with parted lips. She began unbuttoning his shirt and then one hand reached the buckle of his belt, and she could feel his hand tugging her shirt up and his fingers brushing against her flesh and raising goose-bumps.

When they landed naked on the bed, they merged frantically, and it was over all too quickly. But the next time was slow and easy like floating on a lazy river, and she was surprised when the explosion came that left her shuddering and moaning in a way she had never experienced.

He pulled the covers up and lay spooned against her, his arm wrapped around her midsection, fingers straying occasionally to the nipples on her breasts, which she had always felt deficient. Trace had wiped out any thought of inferiority this night. My God, the things he had done to her. If she had her way, their coupling was not over this night.

Then she heard the racket in the adjacent room, the creaking of a bed frame and hammering of a headboard against the wall. "Is that what I think it is?" she asked, her voice barely above a whisper.

"Nanette's room. I guess she has an enthusiastic customer."

"Do you think anybody heard us?"

"Could have. But it's not like we're in a church."

"I didn't expect to end up in your room, you know?"

"I didn't expect you to, either, but I'm glad you did. I hope you'll stay. I'd like to get better acquainted."

"You mean until we leave Stone Creek?"

"I mean forever."

"Is that a proposal?"

"Yeah, I guess it is. Will you marry me, Darby Kathleen Maguire?"

"This is very weird. A proposal in a bordello."

"I don't think there's a law about such things."

"No. I'm sure not. I'm just a bit overwhelmed. There was someone else once I thought would marry me."

"Someone you still love?"

"No, nothing like that. I was barely sixteen, and I was pregnant."

"You have a child?"

"No. I had a miscarriage at three or four months. Of course, Ryan never knew that. He left Boston the morning after I told him he was going to be a father."

"I'm sorry."

"I'm not. Well, I'm sorry I lost the baby. But Ryan was no loss. He was a life's lesson. It did make me wary of men, though—cautious, distrustful, until tonight. Ryan was my first and ended up being my last until you. It's funny. We met at an amateur theatre production of Romeo and Juliet. I played Juliet. Guess who played Romeo?"

"Ryan?"

"Yep. One of the Boston newspaper reporters wrote that Ryan and I were outstanding together. If only he knew. After tonight, I don't think we were so good."

"I take that's a favorable review of our performance."

She giggled. "Yep. But there's more. I disgraced my family. I had four older brothers, but I was the only daughter. My mother is a devout Catholic. Someone told her I aborted the baby—I didn't. But she wouldn't believe me. She disowned me. My father, Sergeant Patrick Maguire of the Boston Police, who is your height and a hundred pounds heavier, couldn't stand up to the hundred twenty pounds of Maggie Maguire. I worshipped him, but he let me down, caved in when she sent me to a convent school in Connecticut, where I lived for the next two years. I hated it there at first and was homesick, but I had the last laugh. I received a wonderful education at Saint Mike's."

"Did you go back home after that?"

"No. I worked in the kitchen at Saint Michael's during my stay there. It didn't pay much, but I saved every penny and taught my way west till Dodge when I read about Pinkerton."

"Are you in contact with your parents now?"

"I write to tell them where I'm at and vaguely what I'm doing. No replies."

"I thought you were going to confess some terrible crime you'd committed in your past life. Is that it?"

"Well, yes."

"You come from a Catholic family. Do you need forgiveness or something?"

"I don't think so."

"Well, if you do, I forgive you."

She sat up and pushed him over. "You are crazy." She slipped on top of him and kissed him. "Yeah, I'll marry you. When?"

"Dodge City?"

"That would be good. This is terribly irresponsible. I'm sure it's unprofessional."

"I'm sure."

"Shall we consummate our marriage-to-be now?"

"Consummate me."

Chapter 43

JUBAL HOBBLED OUT of the stable, shielding his eyes against the midmorning sun with his hand, when Trace rode in with his party. "Howdy, Pinkertons. Welcome back to Dodge City. I thought maybe I'd lost you and my horses out in No Man's Land."

Trace dismounted. "A few close calls." He shook the old sergeant's hand. "It's good to see you, Jubal."

"Quite a caravan you showed up with. Four women, two of the biggest dogs I ever seen and three more horses than I rented to you. You kind of a Pied Piper or somethin'?"

Trace continued to talk while the others dismounted, glancing at Audra to confirm she didn't require help. "It's a long story, and we're going to have a very busy day and very short stay here in Dodge. If there's a train headed east, we want to be on it tomorrow. I'm going to have to call on you for a lot of help."

"Tell me what you need."

"I want to deal for horses, but that's later."

"You want the buckskin don't you?"

"His name's Atlas."

Jubal roared with laughter. "You'd better get Darby over to do your horse trading. A man names a horse and that tells me there ain't no limit on the price I can get."

Trace grinned sheepishly. "But you wouldn't screw me over, would you?"

"We'll see. What else?"

"We'd like to have a wedding here at the stable tonight. Make it seven o'clock. Do you know a preacher or a judge who'd come in here to do the job and take care of the paperwork to make it legal?"

Jubal squinted one eye. "You getting hitched?"

"Yeah."

"That's a nice lookin' remuda of fillies you got here. You picked a bride out of that bunch?"

"Well, it's Darby. We picked each other."

Jubal laughed again. "Just joshing. A little sooner than I'd have guessed, but I could see it coming. I'll find Judge Clinton and be sure he shows up sober. He's county judge here. He'll tie the knot for a dollar."

"I'm good for twice that, but don't tell Darby we could have got him for a buck. Do you need some help putting up the mule and horses?"

"Nope. Just hitch 'em in the stable, and I'll see to the critters before I look up the judge. You'll want to pick up the things you left here. We'll settle up on your deposit when we do our horse trading later."

Trace gathered the group after Jubal took over the horses. "Wedding here at seven o'clock. A lot to get done. Just come as you are. Darb, do you want to lodge in a little more class tonight?"

"We need to hang on to our money with all the plans you've conjured up. I think we should all bunk at the Dodge House. You'll need the money for the new suit your itching to buy."

He grinned sheepishly. On to him again. He hadn't said a word about buying a new suit, but it had been on his list. "We need to see about train schedules. If you'd do that, Darb, I'll go to Western Union and send word to Chicago and Myles Locke that we're in Dodge."

Darby said, "Let's get our stuff and see about checking in at the Dodge House. Then we can take care of baths and clean up and join up to eat before we do our errands. Audra needs a long nap, but we'll slip in some time to take care of banking business."

The day passed quickly. Darby negotiated a special rate for three rooms at the Dodge House but had to slip a dollar under the table to gain occupancy of the wolfhounds in Miranda's room. Suzanne and Audra shared a room, so Suzanne could help with wound dressings and keep an eye on her patient. A room for Mr. and Mrs. Trace Crockett was secured at the end of a hallway.

After lunch in the Dodge House dining room, Suzanne took Audra up to their room, agreeing that after Audra's nap, Darby and Audra would go to the bank to take care of business, before all the ladies gathered to do a bit of shopping on the Pinkerton expense account.

The young lady, now known as Miranda Wheaton, acquired scraps from the kitchen to take to her room for Colene and Tara. After the wolfhounds had their fill, she planned to walk the dogs on an exploratory trip around Dodge. Trace did not fear for her safety.

When the others had left, Darby asked, "When do you want to see the jeweler?"

"Jeweler?"

"That's where you buy rings. I don't want a diamond. Let's see if we can make it five years. Then we'll talk diamonds—a big one paid for out of your account. I do think it would be nice if we both had gold wedding bands to exchange at the ceremony. You don't have to wear yours all the time, so long as you behave married. If you don't, it goes in your nose."

"I hadn't thought about rings. I'm not off to a very good start, I guess."

"I'll give you a pass. You can make up for it on our honeymoon."

"We're having a honeymoon?"

"Absolutely—one night at the most luxurious hotel in Manhattan, Kansas. One night. Short honeymoon, then back with the common folk."

"Somehow, I feel like I've already got that ring in my nose." He leaned over and kissed her cheek, which was nearer pink than blue now. "That's all right. I told you my dad taught me a lot of things. He passed on his knowledge about getting along with a woman. A man's just got to remember two words: 'selective hearing.'"

She gave him an exasperated look. "I've got my eyes open. I already figured out that you had that mastered. We're in for some interesting times, I'm thinking."

They purchased their rings, and Trace felt a bit guilty for leaving the elderly jeweler disappointed with the profit the spectacled blonde woman had allowed. He did not begrudge a businessman a decent income and hated to dicker over purchases.

They went their separate ways after departing the jewelry store, and Trace headed for the tailor's where he found a blue suit with thin silvery stripes in stock. The tailor agreed to make the few alterations required in a few hours' time. He thought about a new pair of boots but remembered the pair he had left in Dodge with his other belongings when they rode out for Stone Creek. There was a shoeshine boy at the Dodge House who could polish them up. This would be Trace's tribute to frugality.

His dealings with Jubal suited him. Darby was going to purchase box car space for three horses. They had already agreed that Miranda should take the inherited gelding, Blackie, since the horse's origin was Lazy P and she was in love with the mount. She had difficulty passing up any animal she encountered, and he supposed that was understandable, given her treatment by the people in her life. Trace would take the buckskin stallion and Darby's blood bay and leave the other horses and the mule with Jubal. He walked away with a third of his deposit money and was satisfied with that.

When he met Darby back at their room, she handed him eight gold eagles, which Darby said Audra had sent along for him after their banking business.

"She said it was for a loan," Darby said, waiting expectantly for an explanation and receiving none. Trace changed the subject to his horse trade and was pleased that Darby didn't second-guess.

When he opened the closet door to hang his suit, he saw a robin's-egg blue dress hanging there, confirming his intended had done some shopping of her own that afternoon. "I love the dress," he said. "It will match my new suit."

She smiled, "I don't qualify for white. Besides, it matches my nose."

"I love your nose. The swelling's gone, and the blue's fading fast."

She was as giddy as he'd ever seen her. A bit nervous maybe, but happy. She didn't seem to be having second thoughts, and he certainly wasn't. He was determined that this lovely woman would never regret her impulsive decision to cast her lot with him.

At the stable, they found Jubal wearing a suit. Trace had earlier recruited him as best man, and he had evidently taken the post more seriously than Trace had anticipated. The photographer, Smiley Smith, was also there to record the proceedings.

Jubal said, "I took the liberty. Darby will be happy. Wait and see. And I want you to take the credit. Let me know where to send the photographs."

As predicted, when Darby appeared with Audra, her maid of honor, she was thrilled and gave him a lingering kiss and thanked him for his thoughtfulness. His conscience wouldn't allow him to take the credit, so he fessed up, and Jubal was awarded his hug and kiss.

The judge appeared—a white-haired, portly man, who carried himself with great dignity. Prior to the ceremony he noted the humble surroundings where they had assembled. He said, "Remember, not two thousand years back, there was a baby born in a place like this, and he changed the world."

After those words, he conducted the ceremony quickly in the last of the day's sunlight that filtered through the stable's entryway. The stabled horses looked on, with two wolfhounds and new friends, Suzanne and Miranda.

The judge was effusive in his appreciation when Trace slipped him a gold eagle for his services and didn't hesitate to accept the invitation to join the group at the Long Branch to celebrate the occasion.

Chapter 44

WHEN THEY STEPPED off the train at the Manhattan depot, Myles Locke and Elisabeth Denney were waiting to greet them. It was late morning, and a warming sun lingered overhead. Elisabeth approached Miranda tentatively, and Darby noticed the girl was trembling and appeared frightened and unnerved. The tension eased immediately when Elisabeth put her arms around the girl, hugged her gently and said, "Call me 'Beth.' Welcome home, Miranda. Everything's going to be fine now. I'm so happy and excited to have you back."

Two men appeared to help with the baggage, and Elisabeth pointed to a pair of two-horse carriages. "You're all going to the house, where cooks are preparing a luncheon as we speak. You will take rooms there for as long as you like."

Darby said, "That's too much. We can't impose on you like that."

"It's not an imposition. And I'm being selfish. Miranda doesn't know me. Think of how it would feel to be uprooted like she has and to move in with a total stranger. She's obviously comfortable with all of you. It will make it easier for her if she has a chance to get acquainted with me with friends close by. We can help each other."

Darby nodded. It made perfect sense, of course. "We'll accept your invitation. We have people here who need a bit of breathing room to make choices about their lives. I'll explain later. My husband and I will join you for lunch, but then we have some work to attend to and have reservations at the Wheaton Inn for one night." She would not disappoint Trace, but she would have gladly saved the expense of the hotel room.

Elisabeth said, "Husband? I wasn't aware you were married."

"Since two days ago. I'm now Darby Maguire Crockett."

"Oh, I see. Well, I'm a bit confused, but my congratulations to both of you. I'd love to hear that story later." She turned away and greeted Suzanne and Audra before she began directing the loading of the carriages.

Myles Locke had been standing apart from the gathering and now moved up, extending his hand, "Congratulations, Darby, on a job well done. I overheard the conversation with Elisabeth. I must say, after your first encounter in my office, I had no notion that a romance was in the offing."

She laughed. "I assure you everyone who was in the room that day is surprised. We just decided the partnership turned out to be too good to break up. We do have a case loose end to discuss with you privately after lunch, as well as a few legal matters of our own."

Trace had been checking on the horses and joined them. "They'll be unloading the horses in about ten minutes, Darb. I'll have to lead them down the street to the stable."

He turned to Locke. "Good to see you again, Myles."

Locke smiled and said, "I was just congratulating Darby on the success of your mission. And I heard other congratulations are in order."

"Thanks. I've had more luck than one man's entitled to the last few weeks. But our mission's not quite finished."

"So I've been told. You weren't here when the announcement was made that there will be a luncheon at the Wheaton mansion. We can talk there. I'll catch a ride on one of the carriages." He pointed to the side of the depot building. "That's my horse and buggy over there. You can bring that to the Wheaton house after you've got the horses settled in." He hurried away to claim a place on one of the carriages.

"I'll help with the horses. I'm not dressed for walking horses down the street, but we could hitch one or two to the carriage, and I can drive it over."

After lunch at the Wheaton mansion, Elisabeth showed the visitors to their rooms. Darby was surprised that Elisabeth didn't even flinch at the prospect of the wolfhounds sharing Miranda's room. Of course, it was large enough to house another bed and ten more wolfhounds. Miranda's eyes widened with disbelief when she saw the room and was told it was hers to furnish and decorate as she chose. She saw framed daguerreotypes of her mother and father together, one a wedding picture of the couple with Henry Wheaton attired in his officer's dress uniform. There was another with her mother holding her as a baby and one of a proud grandfather propping a tiny girl on his lap. Miranda looked at each photo, studying the subjects carefully with tears running down her cheeks. "I want to know everything about them," she said.

Elisabeth placed a hand on her shoulder. "You shall. I promise."

Chapter 45

RACE AND DARBY slipped into the library with Myles Locke. They took seats at the long table and gave the lawyer a quick summary of the Pinkerton investigation and Romy's involvement in the abduction and plans to cash in yet for a long-deferred ransom.

Trace said, "We've reported her to the U. S. Marshal's office by telegram, and I will follow up with a letter. She's on the run, but she'll be caught and eventually returned here for trial. We'll be available as witnesses, but, as far as Romy is concerned, we've done our job."

Darby handed Locke the handwritten report she had completed for Allan Pinkerton during the train journey. "If you would like to have someone at your office type this, you may keep the handwritten copy for your file. It's much more detailed than what we've told you just now. There will be a bit to add."

"A fair bargain. I'll take it back to the office with me and get somebody on it."

Trace said, "We wanted to have this chat for several reasons. We couldn't communicate this in the telegraph messages, but we confirmed in Stone Creek that somebody in Manhattan warned Romy we were investigating. That apparently triggered the killing of Cain Abel and attempts on our lives. Whoever did this had to know that Romy was holding Miranda."

"They also had to be aware of your investigation. That would include me and a few members of my staff."

"You were never on the list of suspects," Trace said. "Besides, no motive. If anything, you stand to gain by Miranda's return. Years of legal services for trust administration, sorting out organization of the Wheaton companies."

"I won't deny it."

Trace said, "Elisabeth might have motive. She would have received most of the estate if Miranda hadn't shown up. She had incentive to stop the investigation, but her contact with Romy makes no sense, unless she somehow found Romy, learned Miranda was alive and planned to make a deal for her disappearance."

"Farfetched, I'd say. And I've known Elisabeth for years. I think Miranda is very, very lucky to have this woman here for her. She will be mother, teacher and friend to that young lady. She will try to do all that Con would have ever wanted for Miranda."

"That's a hefty character reference," Trace said, "but I'm encouraged to hear your words. Darby and I need to register and leave a few things at the Wheaton Inn before we continue our investigation, but I want you to be thinking about how you might help us with some personal business. We're going to be in town a spell, so we'll make an appointment." He told Locke about the plan to purchase land for the Three Winds Ranch and to set up an independent detective agency in Riley County that would contract with Pinkerton for services, if a deal could be negotiated.

"I'd be honored to work with you," Locke said. "And I know of several ranchers who are putting their places on the market after this pasture season."

That settled, Darby and Trace went to their room and stuffed the few things they would be needing for a one-night honeymoon at the Wheaton Inn in Darby's carpet-bag. Locke was departing as they headed out the door, and they accepted his offer and squeezed into his buggy for a ride to the Wheaton Inn.

After they dropped their bag at the honeymoon room Darby had reserved by telegram from Dodge City, they strolled the two blocks to Western Union.

"Trace, we didn't need a room that expensive for a one-night stay. There's nothing we're going to do there we couldn't do in a room half that size." She nudged his ribs playfully.

"You've got to think big sometimes, Darb."

She smiled, "I'm thinking big right now. Let's go back to the room."

"You've got a naughty streak I never would have suspected."

"We haven't known each other very long. I may have a lot of surprises."

"I may have a few myself," he countered.

"I don't see boredom as a problem in our marriage."

"I'm sure of that much."

When they entered the telegraph office, they were greeted by a friendly, young man with peach-fuzzed cheeks. Trace said, "We'd like to see the manager of your office, if we could."

"You're seeing him, sir. Manager, telegrapher, janitor. I'm Western Union in Manhattan. Henry Richards, at your service."

"We need your help, Mister Richards. We're Pinkerton agents. I'm Trace Crockett, and this is my partner and wife, Darby." He pulled his badge from his coat pocket and placed it on the counter. The young man seemed impressed, and Trace suspected he credited the badge with more authority than it represented.

"Glad to help if I can. But first, I should tell you I have a telegram that just came in from A. Pinkerton to somebody named Darby. Not a common name, but the last name wasn't Crockett." He turned back to his desk and picked up a telegram. "Darby Maguire."

"That's me," Darby said. "We're newlyweds."

Richards handed her the telegram.

Darby adjusted her spectacles on her nose and laid the message on the counter and read aloud, "Romy Pierce a/k/a Romy Wheaton held at Fort Supply. Marshal en route to arrest and escort to Manhattan sheriff. Confirm arrival with MW in Manhattan. A. Pinkerton."

Trace said, "Looks like our messages to Supply and the U. S. Marshal's office at Fort Smith paid off. I know that country from the Comanche wars, and I couldn't see how Romy could head anywhere without stopping at the Fort Supply trading post. I'm betting the word to her hired gun about the reward played a part, too."

"At least she's going to account for what she did."

Trace spoke to the telegraph agent. "We need to find out the name of the person who sent a telegram to a place called Stone Creek on this date." He passed Richards the note Darby had made in the Stone Creek telegraph office over a week previous.

"Oh, I remember that message. I'd never heard of the place." He went to one of the filing cabinets that lined the wall, opened a drawer, plucked out a sheet of paper and brought it to the counter. "Here it is. Names of sender and recipient. Text of message. Sheriff Rudy Tisdale sent it."

Darby was not surprised, and she knew Trace wasn't either. "We need to notify the U. S. Marshal's office in Topeka," she said. "Mister Richards, do you have a safe?"

"Yes. In the back office."

"You should keep this record in the safe until a United States Marshal requests it, probably tomorrow. And not a word to anybody, or you could be considered an accessory to a crime, or worse. Understand?"

"Yes, ma'am."

"And now I want to send a message to Topeka."

"Yes, ma'am."

She wrote out the message on a sheet of paper the young man furnished. She also quickly wrote a confirmation note to Allan Pinkerton. She paid the fees and tipped the young man generously and went outside where Trace was waiting and staring in the direction of the sheriff's office a block down the street. He held Pinkerton's message about Romy's arrest in his hand.

"You want to confront him, don't you?" she asked.

"Damn right. And then pound him into the dirt. Nothing worse than a corrupt law officer."

Darby said, "We've done our job. We're not law officers. A marshal or deputy from Topeka will be here tomorrow to take over. How long do you think Tisdale was involved?"

"Max, of course, was there from the beginning. Tisdale wasn't in on it before the exchange, or he wouldn't have messed it up the way he did, stupid as he is. I think Tisdale was contacted a few years later by Max to keep them informed about any developments in Manhattan and to help with a future exchange. He likely knew that the sheriff was open to money on the side. Tisdale probably got an annual payment to keep tabs on things with the promise of a cut of the big haul someday. Help from the law would have been critical to make that happen."

"I can see that. It was the presence of the honest deputy who blew up the exchange. And he died later. I'd like to know more about that. I wonder if he figured out what happened?"

Trace said, "More will come out when Romy arrives. They'll turn on each other. We should inform the sheriff that a U. S. Marshal will be bringing a prisoner for lockup in a week or two."

"You aren't going to let go of this, are you?"

"I want to be the one to let him know he'll be spending the rest of his life in the Lansing penitentiary."

She sighed, "The honeymoon doesn't start until you do this, does it?"

"It won't take long."

"If you confront him before the marshal arrives, he'll be out of town before tomorrow morning."

"We'll make a citizens' arrest and lock him up and find one of his deputies and explain the need for Tisdale's incarceration."

"I've heard of Pinkertons doing that, but I don't know what the procedure is."

"I've done several. The procedure is to draw your gun first and get the bad guy locked up someplace."

Trace had already stepped off the sidewalk and was crossing the dirt street, angling in the direction of the sheriff's office. Darby shook her head doubtfully and fell in behind, worried that she was not armed. She decided that she must follow Audra's suit and purchase a derringer or other small gun for her bag or to strap to her thigh when wearing a dress.

Chapter 46

WHEN TRACE AND Darby entered the sheriff's office, they found Sheriff Rudy Tisdale seated in his usual feet-on-desk position. Trace was glad to see a young deputy hunched over a roll-top desk in the corner of the room, evidently tending to the paperwork that the sheriff had expressed such contempt for. He wanted the deputy to hear the conversation that was about to take place.

Trace pulled back the chair in front of the sheriff's desk and nodded for Darby to be seated there. While the scowling sheriff watched him warily, he picked up another chair that was sitting adjacent to the deputy's desk and set it down beside Darby.

When Trace sat down, the sheriff said with icy sarcasm, "Why don't you folks be seated and make yourselves at home."

"I hope this isn't an inconvenient time, Sheriff," Trace said.

"As a matter of fact, it is. But go ahead and spit out what you got to say. Make it quick." He swung his feet off the desk.

"First, I don't think you've met my wife, Darby. She's also a Pinkerton agent."

Tisdale nodded. "Okay. Hello, Missus Crockett."

Darby responded, "Good afternoon, Sheriff. I've been eager to meet you. I've heard so much about you."

The sheriff obviously was not certain how to take her remark, so he turned to Trace. "Okay, Crockett. State your business."

"I assume you've heard that we located Miranda Wheaton and have returned her to her home."

"Heard rumors of it. Is this an official notice? I ain't clear on why you'd report it to me."

"Well, Sheriff, I'm really here to notify you that you that a U. S. Marshal will be bringing in one of Miranda's abductors in a week or two for housing in your jail pending formal charges and trial."

He had captured the sheriff's attention now, and Trace observed the fingers of the man's left hand tapping nervously on the desk, tobacco-stained teeth biting his lower lip. "Anybody I know?" he asked.

"Yes, as a matter of fact, a good friend of yours—Romy Pierce, formerly known as Romy Wheaton."

"I hardly knew the woman."

"Oh, come now, Sheriff. You telegraphed her at Stone Creek recently, warning her that we were investigating the abduction. You've been on her payroll for a good number of years. I'd guess you and Romy are longtime friends. You'll have an opportunity to reunite soon, for a short time anyway, before you depart for Lansing."

The sheriff's face turned scarlet, and Trace would have sworn the sixty-something sheriff had aged ten years in ten minutes. "You ain't got proof of nothing."

"By the way, your former deputy, Max, recently met a violent death, so you and Romy are the only witnesses left. I'm betting Romy testifies this was all your idea and that you were in on it from the beginning."

"She'd be a lying bitch. Max came to me about—"

"Go on."

"Got nothing more to say."

"Deputy," Trace said, "have you heard this conversation?"

The deputy stood and stepped away from the desk. He was a tall gangly young man with a patchy blond moustache drooping a bit over his upper lip. "I heard it. Yes, sir. I heard it." His eyes darted from Trace to Tisdale, filled with uncertainty about what he should do next.

"What's your name, Deputy?" Trace asked.

"Gerhardt. Gerhardt Kling."

"Gerhardt. You've got two choices here. You can place the sheriff under arrest and lock him up until a U. S. Marshal arrives tomorrow to assume responsibility, in which case we will step back, and you can take full credit for his arrest. Or Darby and I will make a citizens' arrest. Either way the sheriff is locked away for safekeeping." Trace felt fingers dancing across his lower back beneath his coat and the Colt slipping from its holster. "What'll it be?"

"I guess I'll take care of it. Rudy, it hurts me to have to do this, but—"

Tisdale pushed back from the desk, reaching for his gun.

"The gun comes up, I squeeze the trigger, Sheriff. No way I miss at this distance. Between the eyes," Darby said, her fingers gripped on Trace's Army Colt, which was pointed at Tisdale's head.

The sheriff's hands went up, and he lowered his head in resignation. Trace and Darby remained until the sheriff was disarmed and locked in a cell.

"Do you have another deputy?" Trace asked the nervous young man.

"Yes, sir. He comes on duty soon."

"Then I'll leave it to the two of you to work out your guard shifts. I'd be sure he doesn't have anything within reach he could use to harm himself. Nothing sharp. Nothing he could hang from. Keep a close watch. When he thinks about this, he might try to do himself in." The young man's eyes widened, but he was nodding with understanding.

Trace turned to Darby and said, "Darb, we probably ought to go over to the Locke office and tell Myles what's happened."

"Tomorrow. We paid a fortune for that room at your insistence, and we're damned well going to use it. Are you coming with me, or are you staying here?" She headed for the door. "Now, I'm going on a honeymoon."

He said, "You won't have much of a honeymoon without a husband, Missus Crockett." He offered her his arm and together they stepped out the door and walked toward the Wheaton Inn.

www.ingramcontent.com/pod-product-compliance
Lightning Source LLC
Chambersburg PA
CBHW030550180626
46816CB00005B/1491